Gangsta Shyt 3

Lock Down Publications
& Ca$h Presents
Gangsta Shyt 3
A Novel by *CATO*

Lock Down Publications
P.O. Box 870494
Mesquite, Tx 75187

Visit our website at **www.lockdownpublications.com**

Cover design and layout by: Dynasty's Cover Me
Book interior design by: Shawn Walker
Edited by: Tumika Cain

Stay Connected with Us!

Text **LOCKDOWN** to 22828 to stay up-to-date with new releases, sneak peaks, contests and more…

Submission Guideline.

Submit the first three chapters of your completed manuscript to ldpsubmissions@gmail.com, subject line: Your book's title. The manuscript must be in a .doc file and sent as an attachment. Document should be in Times New Roman, double spaced and in size 12 font. Also, provide your synopsis and full contact information. If sending multiple submissions, they must each be in a separate email.

Have a story but no way to send it electronically? You can still submit to LDP/Ca$h Presents. Send in the first three chapters, written or typed, of your completed manuscript to:

LDP: Submissions Dept
Po Box 1482
Pine Lake, Ga 30072

DO NOT send original manuscript. Must be a duplicate.

Provide your synopsis and a cover letter containing your full contact information.

Thanks for considering LDP and Ca$h Presents.

Acknowledgements

Most men, past and present, are motivated by riches. Affluence. Fame. Women. To be honored and revered by other men. My son, grandson, nephews, cousins, and my baby sister are my motivation and inspiration to reach for the stars. I do this so they might become stars in their own universe.

I would like to give thanks to my editor, Tumika Cain, who I refer to as a "Godsend."

I would like to thank CA$H PRESENTS and LOCK-DOWN PUBLICATIONS for believing in my talents and giving me the opportunity to display them to the world.

Last and least, I would also like to thank one of my detractors, my ex or let's just say, "someone I used to know," who I won't name as not to make her famous. Thank you for the added motivation. Without your negative words of discouragement, perhaps I wouldn't have felt a renewed sense of mission and urgency to complete the three books in less than one year's time.

In LOVING MEMORY of my dear mother and father who gave me life, taught me how to cook and feed myself, how to survive and more importantly how to be a man. I love you and miss you more than words can describe.

To my childhood friend and partner in dirt, Daryl Perez Wilson aka Heavy D, who I hustled with. Laughed with. Argued with and fought with. I ride by your crib almost every day wishing I could see you sitting on that wall trying to make a dollar.

To my other partner in crime, my sister, Gwendolyn who protected me on more than one occasion. I wish I can have a do-over in our last conversation and tell you how much I love you and appreciated you.

And to my big bruh, Eddie aka Bay Bruh, who never got the chance to reach his full potential. I have often used your tragic example as a warning to your nephews and for myself to keep going and NEVER stop. Rest well and hope to see you all one day but much later. For I have much work left to do here.

CATO

Chapter 1
The Blood Exchange and the Reckoning

After the first black Suburban pulled into the parking lot across from the park, just as the sun was making its morning introduction, the driver cut the vehicle's engine, fired up a Black and Mild, and sat there with a resigned look on his face. The Suburban's other five occupants, however, seemed to be more on edge than the driver. Their heads rotated from east to west as if they were on the lookout for something or someone. The only other people out on this early Sunday morning was a man wearing shades and a ball cap pulled down over his eyes, walking his two prized Japanese Akitas, another who had the look of a prize fighter, punching the air while jogging with a steady pace, and an elderly lady who strolled aimlessly as if she was trying to clear her mind or reflect on the days gone by.

A few minutes later another Suburban pulled in with the same number of men, and like the occupants of the first vehicle, their heads moved back and forth scanning the area like rotating security cameras. One by one, other SUVs filled with goons and gangsters pulled up and parked, some on the same side of the street and others on the opposite sides. The obvious implication to the discerning eye was that these were factions meeting to settle some dispute, or perhaps a score, amid an ominous cloud of hostilities hovering over the overcast skies.

When the last vehicle, a black Hummer, arrived, Lavrov and his widows, dressed in pink leather jackets, led Sugar and her brother in the direction towards the pier. Other than the look of anger and resolve on their faces from being taken captive and having their grandmother's sanctuary violated in the most disrespectful way, they showed no signs of injury. Soon afterwards, the opening and shutting of doors could be heard almost simultaneously echoing across the area. Two of the occupants from a white Escalade were given the cue to escort Lavrov's brother, Vladimir, and his broad, who were taken captive in Africa and held as extended stay guests of the man Lavrov referred to as the "Black Gangster of New York." Tired, frightened, and weak, they were both ushered to the exchange point. The grim looks on their faces spoke to a future uncertain. The tension in the air that surrounded them from all directions was so thick you could cut it with a knife.

Leaning over the pier's rail, peering at the subtle early morning ocean waves forming, wearing a wool trench coat and dark shades, Tony waited patiently for the exchange to begin. His steely eyes were so focused that at times he didn't blink for an entire minute. His resolve on this day was just as absolute and set into stone as one of those old contracts he was commissioned to carry out on people when he was a killer for scriller. With the absence of his Queen, the last couple of days had been the longest in his entire life, even more so than the last 48 hours that ended his tour in that hellish little nation, Afghanistan. With Sugar being gone in just that short amount of time, he felt as if a part of himself was missing and in limbo. Little did he know that his sense of loss was shared by her. And this is how it is with people whose souls are intertwined.

A couple of feet away, Genie paced about back and forth with his a hand in his pocket as he puffed on a Black and Mild. He, too, worried about how this thing was going to play out. Besides that, he also had his own stake in this matter. Revenge! Revenge for the murder of the first woman who made him feel that there was more to life than just the gangsta shyt. Since her death, he had slept seldom and drank often. If it meant his own life, her death was not going to go unpunished. At every corner and pocket of the park there were men in suits wearing long trench coats and dark shades standing by as if to either ensure the safety of the exchange that was about to take place or to deal with any and all drama, if things went awry. The only noises that interrupted the eerie silence, other than the slamming vehicle doors, were the crooning of the seagulls and the crashing waves.

When Tony answered his phone, a voice said, "Let's finish this, Mr. Stallworth." Tony hung up and placed his phone back into his trench coat pocket. He then took one last long look at the subtle waves crashing into the docks before he and Genie, followed by some of the muscle, headed to the exchange point.

As both sides met up in the middle of the park, Lavrov sneered at Tony as he carefully inspected his Queen to make sure she was all right.

"Well, I finally get to meet the black gangster and king of New York," Lavrov said sarcastically. Angel and Blaze, the Widows, who wore dark shades, stood there behind Sugar and her brother Horace looking straight ahead at Tony and Genie. Their eyes not once moved away from them. The look on Sugar's face said what she did not verbalize. *The first chance I get, I'm going to make them wish they never violated me and my family.*

"Mr. Lavrov, the Russian Mafioso cat," Tony replied with equal sarcasm. "The man who is a guest in this country, who thinks he can come here and just take some shit. A man who don't respect rules and boundaries."

"Yes, I take shit from people. I just can't help it. What can I say?" Lavrov said waving his hands in the air, as if to say no big deal. "I've been that way since I was a child and I actually grew fond of it." He looked over at Sugar. "But since we are on the subject of taking shit, aren't you being a little hypocritical here? I mean, you took my brother and his woman. Not to mention my brother's ear. So who's not respecting rules and boundaries here?"

"You alright, baby girl?" Tony asked, still monitoring her intently and totally ignoring Lavrov's protest.

"Yes, bae. I'm good. Just a little pissed right now. But I will be okay soon." Sugar cut her eyes at Lavrov.

"Of course she's good. What? You thought I would harm her like you did my brother?"

"No, muthafucka! Like you did my girl," Genie angrily injected. Lavrov smiled.

"Oh. Are you talking about the thing in front of the mall? I ask you to excuse me for that one," he said looking at the Widows. "Sometimes Angel and Blaze are a little too eager to please me. If it's any consolation to you, Mr. Smalls, we actually thought it was you in that Bentley. But these things happen in this life we chose, right? I mean, Mr. Stallworth here, the black gangster, he violated me by taking my brother, and worst yet, mutilating him." Lavrov's thunderous voice echoed throughout the park. Known as a man who you couldn't gauge, due to his cool and calm veneer, today's mood belied that. His facial expression, tone and his body language displayed a man on fire.

"Your brother isn't a civilian," Tony shot back. "He's with the man who is trying to muscle in on my shit and so he's fair game. But never mind all that shit! I didn't come here to watch some self-righteous display from you. I came here to give you back your blood and to get mine back. And I don't wanna be here no longer than that takes. So let's do what we came here to do."

The two bosses stared at each other in the eyes momentarily, like two male lions sizing one another up before battle. Lavrov smiled while Tony wore that unmistakable trademark cold look on his face. His menacing eyes had turned a dark green, which signaled hostility, spoke both vengeance and resolve. Russian mafia or not, there was no way this muthafucka was going to walk away from this as if nothing ever happened. There was going to be a price paid for taking his Queen.

"Blaze! Bring forth Stallworth's bitch," Lavrov said while keeping his eyes on Tony, who along with Genie, kept theirs glued on him as well, as did the soldiers. The tension in the air had just increased twofold as the first exchange of prisoners was now underway as Blaze and Angel ushered Sugar forward, while two of Genie's men followed suit by walking an ill Vladimir forward. The huge bandage that replaced where his ear once was appeared to have lost its adhesion and was barely hanging on. After a week of having junky fits and being out of his medication, he now looked casket ready.

While the two prisoners were cautiously led to the opposite side, which seemed to be going in super slow motion, everyone's hands eased on their guns inside their coats. Not once did their eyes deviate from each other as the tense stare down had now begun. All eyes present made statements that their lips did not. This shit was ending today. While Tony and Sugar's eyes were fixated on each other with both elation and vengeance, Lavrov's eyes conversely said the same as they were trained on his brother. For what seemed like an eternity, the first exchange was now completed. Sugar was back in the presence and safety of her King, and Vladimir was back with his brother. Now it was time for the second exchange as Horace and Vladimir's woman, Velma, were ushered forward. And it was not without its misgivings on Lavrov's part, because in his mind he questioned over and over if she was even worth the trouble. If she wasn't involved in the exchanged, or if she was dispensable, he would have greater leverage with Stallworth or could even end this shit right here and now. Years ago, Lavrov made his feelings known about Velma, who Vladimir had found in a strip club in Holland. For that reason and others, he totally objected to his brother having her around. He even tried to pay her off to leave him on a couple of occasions, but she refused. Since that time, even to this day as this prisoner exchange was taking place, she meant nothing to him. His whole attitude was like fuck her. This was the perfect time to get rid of the bitch. However, he knew that his brother, the only person in the world he actually had love for, would never forgive him for not securing her release.

"Are you okay, Vladi?" Vladimir seemed like he was mustering the strength to respond.

"Yes. I'm okay now," an emaciated Vladimir said in a strained voice as he leaned against his brother whose arms were wrapped around him to hold him up. "Now for my Velma." Velma's fright-filled eyes were trained on her man as if to say, "What about me?"

"Okay. Now for my brother's woman," Lavrov said. Genie nodded to the muscle to make the exchange. Lavrov then reciprocated by giving the okay for Angel and Blaze to fork over Horace. Before they began pushing him towards his people Lavrov stopped them. "Hold on a second. I almost forgot something." He walked up to Horace and looked him in his eyes momentarily before quickly grabbing his hand and severing his index finger with a knife.

"Ah muthafucka!" Horace yelled to the top of his lungs. The soldiers reacted by pulling their guns. Tony and Genie stepped in front of them and waved them off.

"Muthafucka!" Sugar yelled as it took all Tony could to restrain her. "You touched my fucking family?! You touch my fucking family?!" she said angrily. Lavrov grinned wickedly.

"I think this is a fair exchange for my brother's ear," Lavrov said as he held the bloody finger in his hand. "Just be glad it wasn't his fucking head." The Widows smiled at the site of the blood while they held a grimacing Horace by his arms. The mutilation seemed to excite them. When they released Horace, Sugar grabbed him and immediately began to tourniquet off his severed finger to stop the blood flow with a string from one of her boots.

"Muthafucka!" Horace again yelled in anguish and with a strained look on his face. Tony's eyes had narrowed to small slits that you could slide a razor blade through. The two Japanese Akitas, perhaps driven by the instinct to protect, suddenly broke away from their master and ran towards the two factions of gangsters. Their owner ran behind them yelling for them to come back. This seemed to distract everyone who took their eyes off one another and began training them on the two approaching dogs who looked poised for an attack. While the master ran up to retrieve his dogs, Lavrov re-trained his eyes back on Tony.

"I guess this concludes our little meet and greet, for now," Lavrov said smiling. Just as the dogs reached them, Angel and Blaze stood in front of Lavrov to shield him from the canines. Staring at the dogs without even blinking, and not budging one inch, the Widows clutched their pistols inside their jackets. The two dogs who were used to humans being intimidated by them, seemed to be intimidated and confused by the sister's coldblooded stares....so much so they stopped dead in their tracks short of Lavrov, who appeared to have been their target. Rather than move any closer towards him, the dogs stood there growling and whining. By this time their master who wore a hat pulled down over his head and dark shades, yelled at them and grabbed their collars.

"Trey and Trek!" he yelled. The wayward dogs and their master, seemingly appearing out of nowhere to interrupt a meeting of the minds, caused a small diversion as Lavrov's men momentarily took their eyes off Tony's side, which is why Lavrov nor his people noticed that Sugar had reached down in her boot to retrieve the .380 she stashed there prior to the gun battle at her granny's crib, where she and Horace were taken captive. When the Widows were supposed to have been giving her a thorough body search, they seemed more interested in groping her and getting their cheap thrills. Delighted they missed the pistol that could fit into the palm of a small hand, Sugar waited for the right moment to pull strap.

"Trey and Trek! Didn't I tell y'all to stop?" The owner continued to admonish them. "I'm so sorry about this," he said. "I don't know what got into them." The two sides ignored him and his apology and retrained their focus back on each other.

"Yes, I guess this does conclude things, for now," Tony said to Lavrov just as the man once again apologized and looked as if he was about to walk away with the dogs. "But there is one more order of business." Tony added as he and Lavrov stared each other in the eyes.

"And what's that?" Lavrov turned around and said just as he and the Widows were about to walk away. The explosion from the dog owner's hand ripped through his newspaper and into the side of Lavrov's face. It was Yancey, Sugar's main bodyguard. Lavrov yelled in pain as another quick shot from Sugar's .380 hit him in the shoulder sending him to the ground, as all hell broke loose in the park. Everyone, including the little old lady who had been walking aimlessly in the park, one of Genie's female soldiers in disguise, rushed up to the fight spraying an HK assault rifle, while the others exchanged fire and took cover behind anything they could find in a place where there wasn't much of any other than small patches of bushes and small trees.

As the Widows quickly began dragging their man out of the line of fire, who bled profusely from his face, Angel hit the two charging dogs off with a burst from her Mac 11, killing them instantly. Lavrov's muscle fired from behind the small trees just as Genie's muscle rushed to the scene in three more SUVs to join the fight. Using their vehicles as cover from the deadly flying projectiles, they laid down cover fire for the men who darted inside the park with their automatics out in front of them blazing. Realizing they were cornered, Lavrov's men were now looking to escape the death trap rather than fight. A weak Vladimir, who trailed behind his wounded brother and the Widows, perhaps operating on pure adrenaline, managed to garner up enough strength to grab his woman. When he realized his attempt to make it to the waiting vehicles about 200 hundred yards away was futile, he elected to try and pull her to the safety of the park's restroom. Just as they were about to make it inside, they were both cut down by a hail of gunfire from Genie's fully automatic Glock that was meant for the fleeing Lavrov, who he had dead in his sights. Desperate to take their wounded man to safety, Angel and Blaze fired behind them wildly with their machine gun pistols as they made their way to the Hummer.

"Baby girl, you stay put," Tony said. Sugar objected.

"No! Bae! I'm going!" she insisted, brandishing her pistol.

"No! Take your brother to the hospital to get that finger treated," he said to her in a stern voice. Sugar looked over at Horace who was writhing in pain.

"Okay," she said as her concerned was shifted to the wellbeing of her brother. Tony then kissed her on the cheek before he tore out towards the vehicle to give chase to Lavrov.

"You okay, Bug?" Sugar asked, using Horace's childhood nickname as she began walking him to the vehicle.

"Yeah, I'm good, sis," he said, holding his injured hand. Sugar knelt down and picked up Horace's severed finger and wrapped it up in a napkin before they continued on to the vehicle.

Totally outgunned and out gorillaed, the rest of Lavrov's men had either escaped along with him or surrendered to Genie's soldiers. Just as Sugar and Horace stepped inside the white Range Rover, driven by Yancey, the sirens could be heard quickly approaching the area.

While Blaze drove fast and furious to take Lavrov to safety, Angel kept pressure on the gaping wound to his jaw, while Lavrov held his bloody shoulder. The entrance wound to his jaw was the size of a quarter and exposing his jawbone and teeth. The shoulder wound wasn't nearly as bad, but nonetheless painful. As he continued to writhe in pain he gave instructions.

"Head home, Blaze!"

"We're going to have to get you to the hospital," Angel said.

"No!" he yelled. "Call the doctor and have him to meet us at the safe house." Lavrov continued to wince in pain. The bullet from Yancey's gun hit a nerve in his face that caused a burning sensation that was nearly unbearable. It felt like his entire face was on fire. Angel followed his instructions by placing a call to Lavrov's own private doctor he used on these occasions for he and his men whenever he didn't want to raise any suspicions by going to the hospital. Lavrov had many safe houses all over the city, but this particular house served as a mini hospital to treat him or his people.

"Where is my brother?" Lavrov asked as he lay back in the seat on the verge of drifting in and out of consciousness. They didn't dare answer him. They saw when Vladimir and his broad got the business from Genie's Glock in the park. From that point there was silence in the truck as Lavrov briefly passed out from blood loss and pain.

In hot pursuit of Lavrov and his remaining men, Tony's plan worked like a charm. The rat was fleeing to his hole to hide and take cover where there was a trap waiting on him.

"Hey, Genie, let up, bruh," Tony said as Genie drove madly around the slow moving Sunday morning traffic.

"Huh?" The order confused Genie.

"Let'em go, bruh."

"What? Let'em go?" Genie looked over at Tony with a confused look.

"Yeah. Let'em go. We got Sugar and Horace back. Trust me on this one. We will catch up with them later."

"For real, bruh? Are you fucking serious?" Genie looked back and forth at the road and Tony.

"Yes. I'm serious. Let them go. Let's head home, bruh." Genie's face showed both frustration and disbelief. In his mind, there was no way they should be letting this muthafucka get away. This shit should be ending today.

"Alright, T," Genie said in a dejected voice before radioing the soldiers. "Okay. Y'all stand down." Although he totally objected to letting this man breath air one more day, Genie knew that this thing was best left up to Tony to deal with.

"Sir?" Shawn, the temporary head of the muscle, asked.

"You heard me!" Genie said sharply. "Stand the fuck down! Back off! Peel off and go back to the crib!"

After dropping Genie off, Tony thought about his partner's silence the entire trip to his crib, but elected not to address at that time. Eventually he would see the wisdom in being asked to stand down against the man who murdered his woman. When Tony walked onto the surgical floor of New York Methodist Hospital, Sugar was sitting outside in a waiting room. Her face displayed an obvious concern for her brother, although his wound wasn't life threatening. As they were leaving the park, Horace had found his own severed index finger in the hopes that it could reattached.

"Baby girl, you alright?" Tony asked as he embraced her tightly and kissed her.

"Yeah, bae, I'm good."

"Are you sure you're alright? He didn't hurt you, did he?" Tony began inspecting her.

"Yeah, bae, I'm fine. And no he didn't hurt me."

"How is your brother?" he asked as he again kissed her.

"The doctor said they would be able to reattach his finger. We found it on the ground as we were leaving. But, Tony, how is my grandmother?"

"She's fine, baby girl. Your uncle Roy is with her now at the hospital."

"At the hospital? Is she really alright, Tony?" Sugar monitored his facial expressions for deceit.

"Yes, baby girl, real talk. She had some chest pains, but it wasn't a heart attack. They decided to keep her overnight for observation. I think she just got a little excited and with good reason. Her crib was turned into a war zone. When I saw it, I feared the worst, as did she, when you and Horace didn't show back up." Sugar closed her eyes and let out a deep sigh of relief as she embraced Tony again, glad to be back in the arms of the man she loved. She wouldn't know what she would do if something happened to her granny, especially behind some drama that she brought to her home.

"As soon as Horace is out of surgery, I'm going back to Florida."

"No, baby girl, *we* are going back to Florida together," Tony said, placing a kiss on her forehead. "I'm never letting you out of my sight again."

Not long after the doctor came out and assured Sugar that Horace's finger was successfully reattached and that he would make a full recovery. Sugar, Tony, Horace, and Yancey left the hospital and headed back to the mansion.

Gangsta Shyt

Chapter 2
Sending A Message

When Blaze and Angel pulled into Lavrov's safe house in Manhattan, his soldiers grabbed him and gently led him inside. Due to the blood loss and pain he was experiencing, which he typically had a high tolerance for, he was in a near total state of unconsciousness produced by shock. He was basically out on his feet as his pulse and heart rate had dropped significantly. If it weren't for Angel applying the right amount of pressure to his jaw and shoulder, he probably would have died from blood loss by now. Fortunately for him also, the bullet didn't hit a major artery. But nonetheless, he was by no means out of danger.

"Bring him inside and place him on a table," the doctor said. The men rushed Lavrov into the room where they gently laid him down on an examination table. The inside of the safe house looked exactly like a medical clinic. There were huge medicine cabinets with damn near everything you would find in a clinic or hospital. There were vitals monitors, an EKG machine, several IVs, defibrillators, multiple cases of saline bags, potassium bags, antibiotics, and even a refrigerator with every human blood type, just for occasions like this when Lavrov or his men needed blood.

After the doctor cut away Lavrov's blood soaked shirt, he started an I.V. of potassium and a blood transfusion. The blood pressure monitor showed Lavrov's pressure had dropped to a dangerous level. It was 70 over 55. The Widows and Lavrov's soldiers stood around with an almost helpless look on their faces. These coldblooded killers could not help exposing their worry and concern for their boss as it began to look pretty grim for him. His skin began to turn blue and black from the severe blood loss and his breathing became labored.

"Is he going to be okay?" Angel asked. The doctor continued to work on his jaw, which was the most severe wound.

"I'm not sure yet," he replied. "Can I get some privacy here? I'm going to do all I can. I can't work with you all standing and hovering over me." The doctor was already nervous. He knew exactly who Angel and Blaze were and their reputation. His fear was if their man died on his watch, he too would die right along with him. Angel and Blaze kissed Lavrov on his cheek before walking out of the room followed by the soldiers.

Later that evening, the gaunt doctor emerged from the makeshift operating room.

"He's going to be alright," he said with his medical bag in hand and an exhausted look on his face. "I got him all patched up and cleaned those wounds. I'm not sure how sanitary that room is since the last time I worked in it. So what we worry about now is infection. But the antibiotics I prescribed him should prevent that. Just in case, I would advise he be taken to the hospital for a follow up." Before the doctor could leave, without saying a word, the Widows rushed inside the room to see their man. Though weakened, he was now awake and sitting up on the side of the table.

"Where is my brother?" he asked as he winced. Though groggy, the Demerol was doing its job as he felt very little pain at this point. The Widows did not answer and instead looked away. "Well? Where is Vladi?" He had now begun to make his way off the table as he noticed the looks on their faces that gave him his answer.

"Yuri, you must rest," Blaze said as she and her sister grabbed his arms.

"No!" he said in an exasperated tone, shrugging them off. "I need to see my brother."

The Widows helped him to his feet before walking him to the Hummer, followed by the soldiers. After getting Lavrov inside, the Hummer pulled away from the clinic with the two SUV loads of soldiers following.

After Lavrov's Hummer pulled through the long, winding, white granite driveway and into the parking garage of his colossal 4-story mansion, Angel and Blaze helped him from the vehicle and began walking him into the crib. He was almost like dead weight since he was knocked nearly out on his feet from the medication and a weakened state. Angel and Blaze barely noticed that the soldiers who normally guarded the home were missing, as were the four German Rottweilers who patrolled the yard. But their main concern at this time, however, was to get Lavrov to his bed, where he could get some much-needed rest and begin his recovery process. As they ushered him to his bedroom, the remaining soldiers stood outside smoking nervously and reliving their near death experience earlier at the park.

In all their years with Lavrov, they had never known anyone to challenge him in the manner that Stallworth did. What was so astonishing to them, this was a black gangster that gave their boss this type of grief. This new reality was such a concern to them, they had now begun to wonder if their boss, Lavrov, was in over his head. Perhaps he should request some assistance from the Russian Mafia council back in the Fatherland. But little did they know, the council had a meeting concerning Lavrov after the attacks on his business interests, in which they received a portion of his earnings. It was at this meeting the council had decided to cut him off and the only reason why he wasn't marked to be whacked was because of his uncle being the *Krestniy Otets*, The Godfather, or Boss of Bosses. The logic behind their decision was just to allow nature to take its course. Without their protection and resources, sooner or later, Lavrov would become a victim of his own greed and treachery. Either way, for his men, there was an air of nervousness and anxiety now about their future prospects for not only employment, but for survival. Every other single enemy in the past they rolled over with relative ease, which gave them an arrogant air of invincibility that they couldn't be touched. But this time was different. This new formidable nemesis, a black gangster, was here to stay.

When one of the soldiers went behind the guard's quarters and began taking a leak, an arrow cut through the air and into his brain. His death was quick. A gloved hand grabbed his feet and dragged him into the bushes out of sight. After a couple of minutes, his comrade went to check on him and headed into the kill zone calling his name.

"Vishni! Vishni! What is taking you so long back here?" When the soldier looked down to see a trace of blood on the ground, a steel throwing ball crashed into the back of his head crushing his skull and smashing into his brain. He fell face first into the dirt and began a death spasm. Again, the gloved hand pulled him to the same place alongside his partner.

Up front, the last four remaining soldiers met with similar fates. The carotid artery of one exploded when the sharp combat knife raked through his neck like softened butter. The others were hit directly in the heart with arrows. Other than a couple of kicks and involuntary movement, they didn't move ever again.

Inside the mansion's elevator, the Widows stood on each side of Lavrov, who was now beginning to wake up as the drugs started to wear off.

"Where are we?" he asked.

"We're home, baby," Blaze replied.

"Where is Vladi? Where is my brother?"

"He's okay," Angel looked over at Blaze and replied. "You must rest now."

After the elevator door opened, the Widows began leading Lavrov to his room. Finally reaching the dark room that was dimly lit by the flashing alarm clock someone forgot to turn off, they gently laid him across his bed. As Blaze began taking off his black combat boots and undressing his long frame, Angel walked over and laid her jacket and her HK assault rifle on top of the dresser before turning on the light switch. The powerful flash of light momentarily blinded Lavrov who had been asleep for the entire ride. When Angel turned around she saw a baby-faced black man sitting in a chair with a relaxed look on his face as if he lived there. Clutching the machine gun pistol he had trained on them, he had a smug look on his face.

After noticing him also, Blaze stared as if she awaited the next move. Without saying a word, Angel was the first to go into attack mode and lunged at him with her knives in hand. Before she could get within 3 feet of him, the short burst from the tip of the machine gun's barrel stopped her dead in her tracks, knocking her back into the mirror and smashing it. As she sank to the floor, she wore an anguished look on her face, leaving a blood smear on what was left of the shattered mirror. Her sister, still frozen in place, seemed stunned with a look of disbelief.

Looking down at her sister and last surviving relative laying there on the floor with her eyes wide open, Blaze gently rubbed her face as she stared at her affectionately. This was the first time in her young life that she felt any emotions for another human being. But this wasn't just any human being. This was her blood kin with whom she'd shared a spot in their mother's womb. After quickly gathering herself to become the vicious savage she'd been since she was a young teenager, she then trained her attention on her sister's killer like a Cobra poised to strike. Resigned to her fate, and having nothing else left to lose or live for, Blaze let out a death yell before launching herself in a full charge. And just like her sibling, she was cut down by another short burst from the machine gun, killing her instantly. Her lifeless, limp body fell on top of her sister and they both lay there with their eyes trained on one another. The identical sisters who were the products of incest, which some theorized was responsible for their psychosis and penchant for blood lust, their days of murder and mayhem were now over. Though they did not meet the same fate as their parents, brother and sister who died in California's gas chamber for serial murders, they nonetheless died by the very violence they seemed to thrive in.

After slowly standing up from the Gator skin recliner chair and walking over to their bodies, a stoic Macky looked down at the two murderers of Genie's girl, Sissy, and his homie Cassadine who died in the most gruesome fashion. As he stared at the bloody, bullet riddled bodies he couldn't help but to take some satisfaction in avenging their deaths. For years things were never personal to him, but this time was the exception to his self-imposed rule.

After making sure the sisters were dead and kicking their guns away, Macky looked up to see Tony and Ike standing at the door dressed in all black with their assault rifles in hand. Lavrov was a mutual enemy of Tony and Ike due to his attempts to strong-arm the diamond mines they owned. Ike now had his diamond trade back. A trade that Tony gladly relinquished back to its rightful owner who considered the diamonds much more than some precious stones men fought, killed, and died over and women drooled over and coveted. These stones were a gift to his people by the Creator. Although this venture was a lucrative one for Tony, he never envisioned it as a permanent hustle. So not long after taking over the diamond business, he had already concluded that after the Lavrov threat was over, there would be a right of return. This thing was Ike's and Ike's alone.

Tony smiled and gave his young killer a nod of respect before. He and Ike then turned their attention to their nearly incapacitated avowed enemy and nemesis, Yuri Lavrov who looked up at them, but was either too weak to move or just resigned to his fate. With his two female attack dogs now dead, his brother dead, his men decimated, his criminal enterprise and organization in shambles, body perhaps damaged beyond repair and his enemies standing inside his house with no one to help or save him, he knew for him, this was the end game.

As for his enemies, a plethora of thoughts and emotions surged through Ike and Tony as they continued to look down at the man who caused them so much grief. They knew that this chapter was now at an end. *But now what of this villain, Lavrov?* They both thought. Ike came all the way from Africa to make sure this shit was finished. So a simple death like a quick bullet to the head or a knife rake across the throat was too good for him. As far as Tony was concerned, Lavrov's death must be legendary and one that would send a message to his people here in the states and in Russia in the event they had reprisal on their minds, and to anyone else who dared to get in their way. A death that would make a lasting statement that would endure for all times, like the one made when Tony fed the OG Natty Boy Ward to the Polar Bears. Seeming to have their minds made up on what to do, Ike and Tony shook hands as they gave one final look at Lavrov.

The next morning when the three Ukrainian maids showed up for a six-day a week job of cleaning Lavrov's huge mansion, they noticed the usual vehicles were there parked at the guard house, but no warm customary greeting at the front gate by the guards who were from their homeland. Vishni was the young wild one who always flirted with the young blond maid who actually looked forward to the attention, against her mother's and fellow maid's objections. Her mother admonished her that it was improper to be cavorting with such men. But as young people typically do, the daughter gave her supervisor mother the invisible hand and rebelled against those wishes and admonitions. As the three women drove through the winding driveway, the driver noticed something peculiar hanging in the huge tree in the yard they couldn't quite make out because of the blanket of fog that enveloped the area. As the work van got closer to the mansion and the tree that sat in front of it, the driver slammed on breaks and grabbed the Russian Orthodox crucifix necklace around her neck.

"Shcho ye tse?" *What is it?* the elder maid asked.

Looking all wide-eyed and turning a shade whiter, she pointed up at the huge tree. The other two women's heads slowly turned upward to see Lavrov's disemboweled body hanging from the tree in a Christ pose. The mother passed out as the two women's high-pitched screams echoed across the property.

When the news traveled back to Russia and throughout the states of Yuri Lavrov and his brother Vladimir's demise, there were mixed reactions. Some wanted to make further inquiries, while some didn't give a shit, like his uncle Konstantine who was the boss of bosses. Others wanted to avenge their deaths on principle. But the latter reaction would prove to be problematic for a couple of reasons. One, the black gangsters who ultimately brought Lavrov's Russian mafia days to an end, were dangerous people and who could give back whatever violence came at them with equal measure. And two, these black gangsters were obviously powerful, and perhaps powerful enough to go hard in a full-scale war, which the Russians didn't need.

But nonetheless, Yuri's uncle went through the motions of acting like he was going to get to the bottom of what happened to please his sister and to save face with his Russian mafia associates and family members. His real sentiments, however, was fuck'em. His two renegade nephews had been a problem for years and whoever took them out, actually did him a favor by saving him the dilemma of one day having to give the order himself to have his own blood clipped. So for Tony and his people there wasn't going to be any reprisals. At least at this time that chapter was now closed.

Gangsta Shyt

Chapter 3
Safe and Sound In Your Arms Again

At home Tony and Sugar lay in their bed hugged up as if they hadn't seen one another in a lifetime, while soft music played in the background. Both had doubts they would lay in each other's arms ever again. This time, they promised themselves to never let each other go. But there were some things that Tony knew he had to resolve for them to pick up their lives where they left off before the Lavrov debacle.

"Baby girl, I wanna apologize to you for a couple of things and explain a couple others. First of all, I should have fully disclosed this thing with Lavrov. I also should have got your input on Ike's offer before I accepted. You and I are a team and that was wrong for me to make a decision without first consulting with you. I guess that is something I have to get used to. Before, I made moves on my own, because there was no one there to consider."

"Not even Angela?" she said laying on her side waiting on her answer, referring to Tony's ex-girlfriend. Tony smiled.

"I can assure you I was going to get to that part. But I guess I need to do that now, huh?" Sugar smirked and quickly nodded her head up and down. Tony laughed.

"Okay. I didn't explain anything to Angela about what I did, because first of all, she didn't know what I did for a living."

"Oh really?" Sugar raised up off her elbow and sat up in the bed. "So you're telling me that she didn't know you was a gangster?"

"No."

"Well, what did she think you did to make money?" Tony paused momentarily, smiled and looked away. Sugar gently turned his head back to her. "Well?" she asked again. She wasn't taking silence for an answer.

"Okay. She thought I was a salesman."

"A what?" Sugar's right eyebrow raised.

"You heard me," he said laughing. "A salesman."

"A salesman? What kind of salesman?"

"Imported goods."

"Really? Imported goods? How long were you and this female together now? Because it seems like to me y'all were either not together that long, she was lame or you put on one helluva acting performance worthy of an Oscar." Tony chuckled.

"We were together for a l'il over 5 years, off and on."

"Five years?" Sugar sat back up in the bed again. "So y'all were together for five years and she bought that line that you were a salesman? She's lame." Tony cracked up laughing. Sugar however, wore a serious look on her face. She knew where she was going with this line of questioning and to her, wasn't a damn thing funny. "I ain't playing, Tony. That broad was lame to believe some pissy weak shit like that."

"Well, she wasn't really lame. She just wasn't from the streets and didn't know what to look for."

"Awww come on. Street or no street, no one is that fucking lame, bae. There must be more. Is there?"

"Okay. I think what made her believe that I was what I said I was because there was this mark I had business on who worked at the same office she worked in, which was actually how I met her. I came through with some imported oils, soaps and other toiletries acting as a salesman. The whole thing was a ruse to get the info I needed on the mark. She ended up buying those things from me, and took my card. I killed the mark, we started dating shortly thereafter, and the rest is history."

"Wow. Touching love story," Sugar said sarcastically. Again, Tony laughed out loud. He was somewhat amused by her antics. "Okay. So when did y'all meet? I mean what year was this?"

"Baby girl, listen. I know where you're going with this."

"You should. I mean, inquiring minds would like to know."

"Okay. I'm going to be straight with you. When you and I were in the dating stages, Angela had not long left the country." Sugar monitored him closely.

"Sooooo, was y'all seeing each other after you and I took things to the next level and became intimate?"

"No, sweetie. By the time that happened, Angela was already gone to Europe." Again, she monitored him closely for deception.

"Okay. So you and her were pretty much history before you and I did the thing?" Tony grinned.

"Yes. We were history before we did the thing." Sugar tried to maintain her game face, but she couldn't help smiling at him repeating her comment.

"Okay. That's fair. You and I weren't an item. Just in the dating stages. So why did y'all break it off?"

"She told me she was given a job offer overseas. I told her that I wouldn't stand in her way and that was that." Sugar continued to monitor him and thinking what her next question would be.

"So it ended just like that?" Tony nodded his head. "You didn't object?"

"No."

"But you two were in a relationship. It's one thing to take a job in another city or even another state. That is something that could be maintained. But moving out of the country is something entirely different. Something that most men would have objected to."

"Well, I just couldn't stand in her way. Besides all that shit, I'm not most men, am I?"

"Wow. Sounds like somebody is feeling himself right now," Sugar said with a raised eyebrow. Tony laughed again.

"Hey, I'm not being boastful. I'm telling the truth here."

"Okay. Okay. I already know you're not like most men. But you were in love with her, were you not?"

"Well…let's just say I loved her."

"Wait a minute! So are you saying you weren't in love with her?"

"You know, after Angela broke the news to me about the job offer, I began to really ask myself that question of whether or not I was really in love with her."

"And what did you conclude?"

"I concluded two things shortly after she left and since that time. If I was in fact in love with her, there was no way I would have even considered letting her take that job."

"Okay. And what was the other thing you concluded?" Sugar raised up again to anticipate his answer.

"I concluded since that time that the only woman I have ever been in love with is the one I'm laying next to right now." He then kissed her on her lips. "The one who is grilling me like a prosecutor," he said before kissing her again. Sugar smiled. "And the woman who I swore a vow to that says 'til death do us part." He then pulled Sugar down to him and started kissing her passionately. For a few seconds she seemed receptive to his smooth ass move. Then she stopped him by placing her hands on his chest and pulling away.

"Hold on. All that you just said, I loved it. It was hot. In fact, it made my heart skip a beat and my pussy wet and throbbing. But I haven't finished my line of questioning yet." Tony's laugh echoed off the walls. "You laughing. But I have a couple more things that I need to know." Sugar's face showed a seriousness that Tony was all too familiar with, but nothing ever along these lines, being that they never had any of these type of issues to be having a conversation like this one. But nonetheless, Tony made it up in his mind that he would not only be patient, but he would keep it real with her and be forthcoming.

"Okay. I'm an open book, baby girl. Shoot."

"Alright. So I get that whole part about you not being in love with ole girl, but was she in love with you?"

"Yes. She said she was."

"Okay. Did you tell her that you weren't in love with her?" Tony looked up at the ceiling as if to search his memory banks. He never recalled telling her that.

"I would say, no. And it was because it never came up."

"Okay. Here is where I'm going with this, Tony. You guys never truly ended your relationship. It's as if you two just put it on hold." Tony had a bewildered look on his face. Although he knew his woman was right, he felt that as far as he was concerned, she ended it when she left the country.

"Which brings me to my next two and final questions." Tony nodded. He was ready to come all the way clean after getting past the most difficult part. "Did you ever tell her about me? And why is she trying to contact you so hard for now?"

"No. I never told her about you and I."

"And why not?"

"Because it never came up. Since the time she's been gone, I only communicated with her a couple times. And the extent of our communication was like hello how are you, type of stuff." Sugar thought about it for a second. She knew her man damn near better than he knew himself. He wasn't lying to her and as far as she was concerned, he never has. "You wanna see our texts?" Tony reached for his phone.

"No. That isn't necessary. I believe you. So why has she been trying to contact you?"

"Her mother is dying. She contacted me to tell me that." Sugar looked down at the bed as her mind immediately drifted back to what her granny said, *Maybe she had a good reason to contact him.* "Wow. I'm sorry to hear that. So were you close to her mother?"

"Yes. I went to see her a few times after Angela left. Other times I would call to check on her. I promised Angela I would do that. According to Angela, her mother concealed her illness and didn't let anyone know about it."

"So this is why she was trying to contact you?"

"Yes, baby girl. She told me that she would be here this week to be at her bedside. The doctors only gave her a few weeks." Again, Sugar looked down at the floor. She felt like shit for going in on Angela like she did. She couldn't help but to think how she would take if her own granny were given the same grim prognosis.

"I want to personally apologize to her," Sugar said. Tony smiled.

"That's fine, baby girl. When that time comes, I'm sure Angela would appreciate that. But I also have an apology to make to her. I also have to bring closure between us. I need to let her know that I am now with the woman who I plan on spending the rest of my life with." Upon hearing those words from the only man she truly loved, Sugar's eyes slightly welled up with tears. She never doubted Tony. She just doubted herself. But now, however, she knew to never doubt or question herself again.

"I love you, Tony." The two pairs of eyes in the dimly lit room moved closer to each other as their lips met. Tony's tongue then charted slightly off course onto her neck, which was received with low subtle moans. Almost instantly, Sugar felt the sweet nectar had begun to drip and soaking her panties as her nipples hardened full and firm. As he began removing her last article of clothing, Tony slowly kissed nearly every inch of her body from her feet to her inner thigh all the way up to her soft lips. Sitting there naked on the bed with their legs and arms wrapped around one another, they stared and kissed for nearly a half hour before they started their legendary lovemaking ritual, but this time without the extra foreplay. Getting right down to the business at hand, Sugar mounted Tony and began bearing all her weight down on him, simultaneously kissing gently as inch by inch went inside of her. When she went as far as she could go, her almond-shaped eyes narrowed, her breathing became deep and her head slowly flung back in position to ride the shit out of him to prove just how much she missed him. Staring up at her with glazed eyes, he patiently awaited her seductive dance that drove him wild. While she stared back at him and gathered herself, her sweetness tightened around him, and her heart began racing. Tony reacted by closing his eyes shut. That was when she began slowly riding him as the song *Ain't Nobody* by Chaka Khan played from the speakers. Out of all the times they made love over the course of their love affair, this night was different from all the others. And it was obviously because of the debacle, which not only threatened life and limb, it threatened their fairytale love story existence. This is why when Sugar reached her first climax on this night she held Tony tightly for several minutes and cried the entire time.

"Baby girl, are you okay?" Sugar paused to gather herself.

"Just promise me you won't ever leave me again."

"I promise, baby girl. I won't ever leave you again, and I love you."

"I love you more."

At the time, and in the heat of passion, making her that promise was the right thing to do. However, little did Tony know that the future had something else in mind. Unbeknownst to them both, there was another storm brewing in the horizons in which he had no control over nor the outcome. And in the midst and aftermath of this storm, Sugar would once again have to reach deep down inside of herself to protect and preserve everything that she loved.

CATO

Chapter 4
Family Secrets

Not long after the plane touched down on the Orlando International Airport runway, Tony's heart rate ticked back down to normal. He'd always had a fear of flying. Sugar and Horace could hardly wait to get back home to see their granny, who'd spent two nights in the hospital for observation. The good news was, everything checked out and she was therefore given a clean bill of health. The other bit of good news was the pain from Horace's reattached finger had subsided and it had even begun to itch, which meant the nerves had begun to regenerate.

The only thing that made this reunion a little awkward was Sugar's apprehension about having to explain why the people were there at her granny's crib to kill her. Ever since Sugar was taken captive, she played it over and over in her mind on what kind of story she would give her. The last thing she ever wanted, since she was a little girl, was to disappoint her in any way.

The time she ran with her stickup crew homies her granny never knew anything about it. As far as she was concerned, her granddaughter was beyond reproach and could do no wrong. But last week's drama could very well change all that. Tony had urged her to just put everything squarely on him to remove any blame from herself. But that would probably forever change her view of him. And that is something that she didn't want either, because her granny's acceptance of Tony was extremely important to her. Her granny would naturally forgive her and would even forgive him as well, but it would definitely destroy his mystique of being the perfect husband and grandson-in-law. Either way, she was going to have to tell her something.

When the white Infiniti QX56 rental truck pulled into the driveway of Big Roy's crib, Sugar saw her granny peeping out of the blinds and smiled. Like always when she came home to see her granny, she could barely contain herself.

"Hey grandma," Sugar said as she walked through the door. Her eyes welled up with tears.

"Hey baby!" The two headed towards each and embraced.

"I'm so glad to see you, grandmama!" Sugar held her tightly.

"Grandmama glad to see you too, baby."

"Well, is grandmama glad to see me too?" Horace said as he and Tony walked in the door.

"Of course I'm glad to see you, old long-headed boy," Granny said before they too embraced. "What happened to your hand?"

"Oh it's nothing. Just a l'il scratch. I'm fine." Granny stood there and analyzed both grandchildren before she looked over at Tony.

"How are you doing, baby?" She hugged Tony.

"I'm good, ma'am," he said. Sugar's granny reminded Tony so much of his own grandmother. Her mannerisms, demeanor, the way she spoke, even her pleasant smell was like that of his own granny.

"Where is Uncle Roy?" Sugar asked.

"He went to CVS to get my medication. He should be back directly."

"So are you okay, granny?" Sugar gently rubbed her head.

"Yeah, baby, I'm alright. Especially now that I see you and your brother."

After the greeting, the feeling in the room was kind of awkward as an eerie quiet settled over the living room. Sugar didn't wanna bring up what happened, but she knew her granny wanted some answers and she intended to give them to her, though reluctantly. Not wanting to kill the reunion, she really didn't know how and when to mention it, however. She didn't even wanna bring up her cousin Trent and the date on when the family decided to bury him. As she watched her granny's pleasant interaction with Tony and Horace, she concluded she would talk to her about it much later.

About a half an hour after arriving and settling into a jovial family interaction, Big Roy returned. "Hey up in here!" he said as he walked in the door with granny's medicine in hand. This was Roy's trademark greeting everyone had come to know.

"Hey Uncle Roy," Sugar said excitedly before giving him a tight hug.

"You alright, Sugar dumpling?" he said as he stood back as if to inspect her.

"Yeah, I'm good."

36

"What about you, old knucklehead boy?" Roy said to Horace.

"I'm good, old man."

"Old man? I bet I can still put you on your back," Roy replied with a raised eyebrow. Everyone laughed.

"Yeah, you would try a handicapped man, wouldn't you?" Horace replied, holding up his bandaged hand.

"Handicapped or not. You still couldn't do nothing with me, son." Roy then gave Horace a hard punch to the chest.

"Alright now, Roy! Don't hurt ya nephew now," granny said with a concerned look. "You see he already hurt." Roy was a rough, rugged, hardcore dude coming up. One of those types of old school uncles who would damn near knock your head off and claimed it would make a man of you.

"Awww, ain't nothing wrong with that nigga," Roy said with a chuckle before turning to Tony. "Mr. Stallworth, what's good with you? How's my niece treating you? Better be good." Tony laughed.

"All is well, my brother. She's treating me good so far. But seriously, we are just glad to be here with family."

"Yeah, I second that. Hey, since we are all here together, we may as well put some meat on the grill. I took out some meat to marinate after I heard y'all were coming. Y'all know I'm mean on that state of the art grill I got out there." Roy was also the type of uncle in the family who swore he was a grill master. If you told him that he wasn't, be ready for a fight, especially if he had too much of his E & J, aka Easy Jesus.

"Sounds good to me," Sugar said looking around at everyone.

"Unc, you still think you're a beast of a pit master on the grill, huh?" Horace said with a chuckle.

"Uh oh," Sugar and her granny said at the same time. "Don't get him started, Horace." Laughter broke out in the room.

"Son, I don't think it. I know it!"

"Yeah, I did happen to hear about Roy's grilling skills," Tony said looking over at Sugar winking his eye.

"See there!" Roy said. "This man lives way up north and knows about how I gets down behind that grill. I knew I liked something about this brother. Now don't worry, youngster. I will teach you how it's done and just maybe you will be as good as ya unc one day and carry on the family tradition. But it will come at a cost."

"And what cost is that?"

"Just like any apprentice. You will have to be my do boy for the day. Carrying my charcoal. Lighting the grill. Bringing out the meat and flipping it." The living room exploded with laughter. For the time being all was well in the in this reunion of sorts. Just to be able to laugh and see one another again after what took place only a few days prior was one of those blessings granny often made religious references to. And indeed it was a blessing for all sitting in that living room.

After the barbeque, Tony and Sugar volunteered to wash the dishes, against granny's stern objections. They were able to convince her that she needed the rest, and eventually she agreed and relented. Standing at the kitchen sink Tony washed while Sugar rinsed and dried.

"I just want you to know you're doing a pretty good job there, sir." Sugar chuckled before Tony bumped her playfully.

"You're not so bad there yourself, ma'am. I have never in my life seen a dish rinsed so thoroughly and dried so well," he joked. "Damn good for a boss, Queen."

Sugar burst out laughing. The two shots of hen and coke earlier had her feeling some kind of way. She was also relieved that she didn't have to have that talk with her granny. At least not tonight. Roy pulled her to the side earlier and informed her that he had already given her a story that the people who came to the house were robbers and that it was just a random situation they chose her crib. Sugar knew however, that her granny was no fool. She would just think about what Roy said, and conclude most of it as bullshit. But at least that gave Sugar a reprieve of sorts to have the most difficult conversation she'd had with her since she informed her she had lost her virginity.

"So, baby, did Ike go back after y'all took care of that business?"

"Yeah. He actually went back the same night. He said Samira demanded that he come back immediately." They both chuckled.

"Aren't you glad you have a woman who don't have tight reins on you like that?"

"I sure am." Tony kissed her. "And thank God. 'Cause, baby, I won't lie. If you were like Samira, I think I would have to tear out on you." Tony again chuckled.

"Oh, wait a minute. Maybe Samira has a reason to act the way she acts. Just maybe, it is because Ike was a ho at one time."

"Ike? A ho? Nah. He's super square." Sugar stopped rinsing and looked at him with her hands on her hips.

"That's right. Ike! He could be the ho-ish type. Women typically don't act the way Samira acts for no reason."

"Okay. Maybe so. And then again, maybe she's not the typical woman who has the normal jealousies and insecurities. Who knows? But I do know Ike cares about her a great deal. He gives her anything and everything she wants."

"As he should," Sugar said.

"Like I am with you?" Tony kissed her on her lips. Sugar smiled.

"Yes. Like you are with me. You are the man of my dreams, Tony. And I thought that dream would come to an end after that night in granny's new crib. I love you."

"I love you too, Queen. You too are the woman of my dreams." Again they kissed, but this time it was long and sensual. The kind of kiss that leads to one of their legendary lovemaking sessions.

"Unh umm." Horace cleared his throat. Tony and Sugar tried to pull back as if they weren't doing anything.

"What is it, Bug?" Sugar smiled and said in a dragging voice.

"I didn't mean to interrupt or cock block," he said with a chuckle. "But grandmama want you." Sugar took a deep sigh.

"Oh God," she said under her breath. She knew exactly why she was being summoned. She knew, however, it was better to go ahead on and get it out of the way.

"I will see you in a few minutes, bae." Sugar kissed Tony on the cheek and headed upstairs to where her granny was. When she walked into the room her grandmother was laying down watching TV.

"Hey grandma."

"Hey baby." Sugar lay down next to her. After about a minute her granny broke the silence.

"I'm sure you know why I sent for you." Sugar closed her eyes.

"Yes, ma'am, I know." Again, the room fell silent. "Grandma, what happened that night shouldn't have happened. It was sort of a case of a misunderstanding." Granny remained silent as if she was waiting for the rest of the story. "There were some people who tried to take over Tony's business. When he refused, they became upset with him and thought by kidnapping me, he would give in to their demands."

"Well, baby, what kind of business is Tony in that would attract people like that?" Sugar sighed as her mind raced for the right words that would put her granny at ease without lying to her, which is something that she did not do.

"Tony is in the diamond business." Granny paused before responding. She, too, was trying to wisely choose her words as not to seem overbearing and intrusive into her granddaughter's marriage.

"Oh, okay. I see. But why would people go to that extreme that they would kill over diamonds?"

"Well, Granny, diamonds are very valuable, especially the type and amount that he sells." Granny paused again. Her mind was definitely working. She was no fool.

"Baby, I'm going to say this. I like Tony. Better yet, I love him. And that is because he is the best thing that ever happened to you. With him at your side, I don't worry about you like I used to when you were with that ole no good boy what's his name. But you know grandmama ain't slow, now. Not by a long shot." Sugar couldn't help but chuckle at her saying ain't nothing slow about her. "Let me show you something," she said getting up from the bed. After going to the closet where she put some of her belongings, she grabbed her bible and walked back to the bed and laid it down on the bed. After plopping back down beside it, she opened it up to Luke chapter 15:31, which was the parable about the lost and found. Lying there on the page were some black and white pictures in pristine condition. There was her granny as beautiful as ever beside a man in a zoot suit standing next to an older model ride with gangsta white wall tires. Sugar noticed Granny was smiling endearingly at this man.

"Who is that, grandma?"

"Why that's your grandfather, Jim Henry, baby." Sugar looked at the picture again as she noticed the unmistakable look of a G.

"Wow! Granddaddy look gangsta." Granny smiled and flipped to the next picture.

"That's because he was. Your grandfather was as gangsta as they come. The man you knew was nowhere near the man in this picture. He was like night and day by the time you started growing up." Granny flipped to another picture that showed her husband with his suit jacket off and donning his two gun holsters strapped around his shoulders. To say Sugar was surprised was an understatement. She was downright amazed at what she saw. A tall man with his hair slicked back in a gangsta pose with men standing around him. He had the look of a boss. Seeing him brought back some memories that she had long suppressed. Her mind drifted back to when she was a shorty. Her grandfather took her with him to get ice cream as he did every Sunday after she got out of Sunday school, which was something he somewhat rejected and only tolerated to please her granny, who always had a strong religious foundation. She recalled as if it was yesterday that they stopped by this man's house that went by the name Bo Diddley. While she sat in the backseat enjoying her ice cream, she noticed her granddaddy had an angry look on his face as if he had been arguing. Being a shorty she didn't pay too much of attention to it. The only thing she cared about at that moment was that Oreo cookie ice cream and getting back home where Horace was who was on punishment, so she could brag about it and rub it in his face. As she sat reducing the once full to the rim cup of the delicious Dairy Queen ice cream, the song *Rock The Boat* by the Hues Corporation played from the speakers. At this point she noticed a mid-sized golden dog standing outside the car staring up at her. He whimpered as his eyes begged her for a bite of the ice cream. As she sat there watching the dog, somewhat amused and scared at the same time because of her recently acquired fear of dogs, she caught a glimpse of her grandfather who was now inside the house. He had some silver looking object in his hand that glistened when the sun hit it. When he swung it, it moved at lightening quick speed. When this shiny object came into contact with Mr. Bo Diddley's head, a loud bang that sounded like a firecracker went off that frightened the dog away. Mr. Bo Diddley lay there motionless on his back as her granddaddy went rummaging in his pockets. A couple of people in the neighborhood stuck their heads out the door momentarily and dismissed it as perhaps one of those bad ass hood kids popping firecrackers left over from the 4th. A couple of minutes later, granddaddy emerged from the house.

When he got in the car, he said to Sugar, "Sugar momma, what have I told you before to never play with stray dogs?" He then put the '69 caddy in gear and drove away from the scene. As the car traveled farther and farther away, Sugar looked back at Mr. Bo Diddley, who remained motionless on his living room floor. Although she didn't fully understand what happened to him and why he was laying there, she couldn't help but feel a sense of compassion and sympathy for him. She never told anyone about this incident even after the news traveled through the hood of Mr. Bo Diddley being taken to a nursing home where he never came out of his coma.

"Granny, I am shocked. Why you never told me?" Sugar continued to look at the pictures in amazement.

"Well, baby, cause I just didn't feel like that was something that needed to be discussed. See, baby, back during that time, people did what they had to do. And Jim Henry was no different. I never told you or Horace about his past because I didn't want y'all to view him differently. To y'all he was granddaddy. And that is the way I wanted it to stay."

Sugar continued to look at the numerous photos she never knew existed. As much as she had plundered through her granny's belongings over her teen and pre-teen years, these pictures somehow eluded her.

"The reason I showed you these pictures is because Tony reminds me a lot of your granddaddy. Since the first day I met him, I knew there was something about him. He had the same look and mannerisms just like him." She picked up the picture and stared at her late husband. "Your grandfather was a hit man and a gangsta, but he changed. Just like Tony can change."

Very little did granny know, her own granddaughter was a gangsta in her own right. Drifting back to that Sunday evening at Mr. Bo Diddley's house, Sugar thought just how much her grandfather had changed and laughed to herself.

"Whatever Tony is into, I hope and pray that he stop for both you and for his own sake. And maybe even for the sake of your children one day when y'all decide to have any. See, baby, when you are done doing what you have to do, it's time to do something else that you can sleep well at night." Sugar's granny then reached over and kissed her on her forehead. "Now let your tired grandmama get some sleep. We have to leave tomorrow to go to Panama City to be with the family for your cousin's services."

And just like that, Sugar's ordeal of having to explain the incident at the new house was over. And how relieved she was. However, she was pleasantly surprised to learn granddaddy was a gangsta.

CATO

Chapter 5
Road Trip to Trent's Home going

The next morning, before making the last minute decision to attend her cousin Trent's services in Panama City, Florida, Sugar got up from the bed and made a mad dash to the toilet. Tony, who was tired from the trip from New York and last night's family gathering, was still asleep, and didn't even notice that something was wrong with his Queen. Sugar's granny, however, who didn't miss much, noticed her grand-daughter looked as if she was suffering from some nausea sickness. Granny walked to the bathroom door and stood there.

"You alright in there?" she asked as she stood there at the bathroom door listening intently.

"Yeah. Yeah, I'm okay, grandma," she said as she tried to quickly gather herself before flushing the toilet.

"Are you sure you okay in there?"

"Yeah, grandma, I'm sure. Just had some acid reflux."

"Acid reflux? I have some milk of magnesia in the room, if you need any."

"No. I'm okay now. Just got choked up a little. That's all."

"Well, okay. Let me know if you need some."

"Okay, grandma." Sugar knew she didn't have acid reflux and so did her grandma who had dreamed about fish for the last three nights. There was something else going on here. Something that she'd never felt before. After gathering herself she walked out of the bathroom.

Later that afternoon, Tony, Granny, Horace and Roy all loaded up in the Infiniti truck and set off for their destination. A funeral was the last thing that Sugar wanted to deal with, but she knew that she had to be there for her granny and the family. The plan was to go there long enough for the funeral and come back the next morning.

While on the way there, Tony couldn't help but reminisce about the times he traveled with his father to visit their relatives in Alabama as they passed the country stores on the highway. The many signs advertising goodies such as peanut brittle, pralines, Gator jerky, beef jerky, fresh handpicked strawberries, grapefruits, and of course, Florida oranges were lined up and down the highway. Another typical sight in Florida was the ten-foot gator who was holding up traffic. As it slowly trudged across the highway trying to get to the nearest watering hole, an amused Tony took out his camera phone and snapped pictures of the reptilian. To a city cat like himself, this was a reminder that he was in Florida. A city cat like him had never seen a gator before in real life.

"Hey, Roy, can you please pull over to the next store?" Granny asked. "I gotta use the restroom again."

"I sure can. There is one at the next exit."

"Yeah, I done got hungry. I hope they got some chicken wings or something at this store," Horace said rubbing his stomach. Sugar smiled and shook her head.

"Boy, that's all you think about. Eating!"

"Sho' you right! I spent nearly ten years eating state food, soups and potato chips. I want what's coming to me." Everyone in the truck erupted in laughter.

"Don't put it on that. You were greedy before you went to prison," Sugar said. Tony smiled as he listened to brother and sister haggle. This was the most he'd been around family since he was a shorty. Soon his mind drifted back to the last family reunion he and his folks attended. He could still recall the conversation he overheard between his father and grandmother.

"Lett, what kind of life you providing for that boy in there?" Tony's grandmother said as she shelled her snap peas. *"Sooner or later you gonna have to make a decision about his future and what little you have left. We have all done things in life that we regret, but we have to show that we learned from it by leaving it alone at some point. You can't keep on running, 'cause sooner or later trouble catches up to you. And God forbid if Tony or your wife get caught up in it."*

"I know, momma. I know. Moving up north where Walter is at, is all in my plan to give them a new life. After we leave here that is where we are headed. I have already cleared it with him."

"Okay. That sounds like a plan, but your brother is just like you. Maybe even worse. I've heard the stories about him, even though he will just lie when I ask him. He lied to me so much I stopped asking him

and just pray to the good Lord that I don't get a phone call in the middle of the night, just like the one I got about your father. Y'all get that gangster crap from him."

Lett smiled as his mother studied him with a serious look on her face.

"I don't want Tony to turn out like y'all. You hear me, son? The cycle needs to end with you."

Little Tony lay there on the floor at the door steadily taking in an ear full of grown folks business. His heart pounded, because he knew if he got caught eavesdropping, he would get the ass whuppin' of his young life.

"Alright, ma. Don't worry. Tony isn't cut like me and Walt. That boy makes straight A's in school. None of us ever did that. I'm telling you, ma, that boy of mine is going to make something of himself and I have made a couple of moves to make sure of that. So don't worry yourself, okay?" Lett then placed a kiss on his mother's cheek, which still didn't allay a mother's fears. She knew her son would soon meet the same fate as his father. But she nonetheless prayed for the best outcome possible, at least for little Tony whom she saw hope for the future in to carry on the Stallworth name.

"Tony!" A voice yelled out. It was his mother. Little Tony knew this was his cue to ghost the scene before he got caught. After springing to his feet he tore out in the direction of his mother's voice.

"I'm coming, ma'am." As he made his way to the living *room, he wondered exactly what it was his father and Uncle Walt did that was so bad that granny objected to. As far as he was concerned, his father and Uncle Walt were rich and important men who could do no wrong. From what he saw, his father always dressed in suits, went on trips a lot and bought he and his mother nice things whenever he returned. The conversation left him perplexed and curious. He knew what a gangster was, but that couldn't be his father. He was too nice to be that.*

"Hey baby," Sugar said as she sat down beside him in the back seat interrupting his daydream of a time gone by. "You didn't need to use the restroom?"

"Nah. I'm good. What is that you got there in that bag?" Tony said staring down at the brown paper bag she held in her hand with a curious look on his face.

"This is peanut brittle. And it's sooooo delicious, bae. You ever had any?"

"Have I? My granny used to make the stuff all the time. People from miles around used to come buy it from her."

"Here try some." Sugar pushed the golden brittle towards his mouth, but he hesitated. "Go head, boo. It's really good and you know you want some," she said with a grin. Tony chuckled.

"Okay. Just a little piece. You know I'm abstaining from sugar right now to shed a few of these pounds," he said as she put the brittle into his mouth.

"You abstaining from sugar, huh? All sugar?"

"Nope. Just the kind that put weight on ya, bae." They both laughed.

After Granny, Horace and Roy returned to the truck with some food and refreshments, they resumed their trip to Panama City. About four hours later, they hit Highway 231 to see it crawling with State Troopers. They were pulling people over left and right for speeding.

"You better slow this here truck down, Roy," Granny warned.

"I see'em over there," he replied.

When the Infiniti truck pulled into the parking lot of Battle Memorial Funeral Home about four and a half hours later, Sugar and family noticed there were already cars there and people standing outside. Eager to see her sisters and other relatives, Granny had to be helped out of the truck. Although she could hardly contain her excitement on this solemn occasion, the long ride wasn't too kind to her already stiff joints. As Sugar and the others exited the truck, they were greeted by some family members with stares, that either suggested a curiosity and admiration or resentment, which Sugar had anticipated since some might lay blame on her for what happened to Trent.

After greeting the relatives, Sugar, Granny and Horace walked inside the funeral home while Tony and Roy remained outside. Though they didn't verbalize it, they had seen enough death in a lifetime. Battle Funeral Home, which had been an iconic landmark and black-owned family business for over half a century, was just like any other funeral home during a viewing. There was the floral incense smell permeating the air, soft gospel music playing in the background and the funeral director or one of his underlings standing at the door to meet everyone with a warm greeting, a low whisper, and a cold handshake.

Also present was something intangible that could not be seen with the eye. It was an invisible presence that Sugar felt every time she had ever gone into a funeral home. She vowed after her grandfather's funeral that she would never walk inside another one again unless it was for her granny's wake. And this time she would have kept that promise if it were not for her granny. She had to be there for her no matter what, especially since much of this she blamed on herself.

On the right, there was a room just passed the lobby, with Trent's body lying in a light blue and white casket. He appeared to be in a peaceful sleep. As Sugar walked closer, holding her Granny tightly, she mentioned that Trent looked as if he was smiling. Granny walked around the casket thoroughly inspecting him, which is something that older people have been known to do. Flashbacks of the night of the gun battle at granny's new crib and the instance one of the widow's killed Trent began to playback in Sugar's mind as she stared at him. The flashback was so vivid it somewhat shook her.

"They put Trenton away nicely," Granny said as she touched his gloved hand that was folded across his torso. This jarred Sugar and brought her back from that brutal night.

"He does look as if he's at peace," Sugar replied. "They did a great job on him." Horace remained at the doorway staring at his cousin who was more like his homey. He still blamed himself for his death. Little did they know, they were about to find out that there were others in the family who felt the same way. The age-old family dissention brought on by envy and jealousy was about to rear its ugly head and add to the already tense and potentially volatile situation with emotions running high.

Later that evening at Trent's mother's crib, the family had started to gather. She was only one of two surviving siblings of Sugar's granny, whom she really didn't get along with. When Sugar and her entourage had walked into the huge back yard, which smelled of barbeque, fried fish, cigarette smoke and weed, there were a scattering of different groups doing their own thing. Some played cards and dominoes, some danced to the music, others stood around gossiping, while some of the younger relatives stood in the far back near the fence smoking weed and congregating.

"Sugar! Bug!" one of the females who wore a half shirt, tight jeans and a purple weave, yelled. "What's up cousins?"

"Hey Thelma. What's good, girl?" Sugar said before they embraced. Thelma then embraced Horace.

"Ain't nothing, girl. You look good! Girl, gimme those boots." Sugar laughed.

"Girl, I got these from the Macy's in New York."

"And I need them in my closet."

"If you stay at auntie's house you better watch your shoes," a short cat with dreads interjected before he walked up and gave Horace some dap.

"Robert, what's up, cuz?" Sugar replied as they embraced.

"Not much, Sugar gal. Just doing what I do out here in the streets of Panama." Robert was a small time weed dealer who had big time ambitions. A three-time loser, he swore he would die first before he went back to the joint. Although he had a mean hustle, pussy was his downfall. He was what they called a *real cake daddy*.

"You stay outta my business too, nigga," Thelma warned him.

"Girl, you ain't got no business when everyone know yo business," he shot back. Sugar and Horace laughed as Thelma punched him in the chest.

"Sis, Imma go over here and see what cuzzo Bookie up to. I see him over there in the cut burning."

"Alright. Don't you be over there indulging," Sugar said with her hands on hips and eyebrow raised.

"Ummm, sis. Grown man status? Chill," Horace replied before walking over to his relatives who were burning one after another.

"Cuz, check this out. What happened to Trent?" Robert said under his breath. "I know he got shot and stabbed, but how did it happen?" Sugar sighed and closed her eyes tightly.

"You know, Robert, I really don't wanna get into that right now," she said, looking him directly into his eyes. Her once cheerful mood was now gone and she was now on heightened bitch mode alert. She had already decided the night before that she wasn't going to be made to explain anything to the family regarding Trent's death.

"Okay, cuz, I feel ya on that. But the family been tripping. Imma just go ahead and tell you that some even blaming you for his death."

"Yeah, I'm sure they are, Robert. And thanks for telling me, cuz. But I'm going to keep it real with you. Other than Auntie Teretha and his immediate family, I really don't give a fuck what the family thinks," she said with her voice rising. Her face now had that no nonsense look about it. Thelma's eyebrows raised as she looked away. Her body language suggested that she felt some kind of way about Sugar's comment, but she elected not to say anything not wanting any drama. By this time, Tony and Roy were walking out of the glass patio door into the yard.

"Unc! What up, man?" Robert said before giving him an embrace.

"Bob, ain't nothing up but the rent."

"Alright, unc. Bob left the scene when I was a little shorty. It's Robert now." Everyone laughed except Sugar, who was almost past the point of no return in her 'tude, which wasn't lost on Tony. Walking up to them, he noticed it almost immediately.

"Okay, Bob," Roy repeated. Laughter broke out again.

"Sugar, who is this fine nigga here? He ain't one of our long lost kinfolks, is he?" Thelma said, looking Tony up and down as if she was undressing him with her eyes.

Sugar stared at Thelma momentarily. At this time it wouldn't take much to set her off. She was counting in her head to calm herself down. If there was one thing in this world she hated was fake ass people, especially kinfolks sitting around backbiting their own. To find out that she or even perhaps her grandmother was the topic of a family conversation took her to a place she didn't want to be.

"Oh. Excuse my manners. This is my husband, Tony. Tony, this is my cousin Robert and his sister, Thelma."

Tony embraced them both then resumed monitoring his woman's face as he was trying to figure out why she was upset. Following the introduction, there was a cold vibe that filled the air and everyone standing there felt it.

"You alright?" Tony whispered in her ear as the others talked amongst themselves.

"No, but I'm going to be alright," she said matter-of-factly.

Finally recognizing the vibe and perhaps building up enough courage to walk away, it was time for Thelma to make her retreat.

"Well, cuz, I'm going to go back over here. Good seeing you, girl." She extended her arms and moved towards Sugar.

"Okay, cuz. Likewise. Good seeing you too," Sugar said as they embraced and kissed one another on the cheek.

"Alright, see you at the funeral tomorrow, Sugar."

As Sugar watched Thelma walk back over to where her family stood, she thought to herself, *I know this bitch is going back over there to gossip. She better not let me hear about it later though.*

Tony, Roy, and Robert, continued to engage in some small talk. The whole entire time, Robert was trying to pick Tony to see what he did. He knew his uncle Roy had that package. But to him, Tony fit the profile too. His mannerisms, the clothes he wore, the watch, the look in his eyes, he knew there was something about Tony that said big time gangster. Probably even a plug. His curiosity had gotten the best of him so much, he had made up his then and there he was going to step to Sugar and crack on her about her old man.

"Bae, I'm going to go in and check on grandmama," Sugar said.

"Baby girl, what's up? Is everything alright?"

"Nothing. I'm okay. Really. I'm good." Tony monitored her and gave her a cynical look. "No, really I am now." She then gave him a reassuring kiss on the lips.

"Okay sweetie." Tony watched Sugar walk back into the crib. Even before the trip he had a feeling that Sugar would catch some type of grief from the family for Trent. The one thing Tony knew with any grieving family, where there is alcohol, grief and someone looking to place blame, there was sure to be drama. He had hoped he was wrong in this situation.

Inside Trent's mother's house the older people sat around reminiscing about old family times and listening to a mixture of old school music and gospel. Trent's younger sister, Missy, who had been outside smoking weed with her younger relatives, walked right in behind Sugar and went and posted up beside her mother and folded her arms. Standing there as if she was her guardian protector, she stared over in the direction of Sugar and her grandmother. She clearly had an attitude and something on her mind. Perhaps she was one of the family members Robert mentioned who was upset about her brother's death and naturally wanted some answers.

"Mary, you remember this picture here?" a heavyset gray-haired lady said to Sugar's grandmother.

"Let me see." Sugar's grandmother leaned over to take a look at the picture. "I sho' do! 'Cause that's my picture." Everyone in the room cracked up laughing, all except Missy who continued to stand near her mother as if she was in a protective posture with her arms folded and lip poked out. Sugar stood there next to her grandmother grinning at the picture which showed her granny in some hip huggers, big hoop earrings and high heels standing next to her relatives. "Girl, you were the one in the family who swiped everybody's pictures."

"She sho' is," another relative said. "I bet we go over to her house she got a picture of everybody and every event under her component stereo."

"Gladys, how many more of my pictures do you have? Seems to me I am missing some," Granny said. The room again filled with laughter.

"Girl, these are my pictures. I don't know what y'all talking 'bout. I'm the one person in the family who just keeps up with and take care of pictures. That's all."

"Yeah okay," another relative said. "Don't let us go to your house and find our pictures."

"Whatever Tina," Gladys said. "Y'all look at these here." She passed the photo album to Sugar's granny.

"Umm hmm. Here are more of my pictures. Girl, the next time you come to my house, I'm gone keep my eye on you the whole time. I know damn well these are my pictures." Again the room filled with laughter. Sugar was amused at her granny. She hadn't seen her this lively and animated in a long time. Though it was a sad occasion, perhaps this funeral is just what she needed.

"Mary, just look at the damn pictures and pass them, will you?" Everyone continued to laugh. Missy continued to stand behind her mother, who was sitting in a recliner. Her arms were still folded and lip still poked out. She was obviously not in the laughing mood and Sugar noticed it, but ignored her. She was enjoying looking at the pictures of a young grandmother who many say Sugar got her curves and looks from. As Sugar looked down at the pictures that were being passed around, she couldn't help but to agree with that opinion. She and her granny looked nearly identical.

"Hey, there is Patricia. This is yo momma," Granny said to Sugar.

Sugar took the photo into her hand and looked at it endearingly. Her mother was beautiful just like herself. The big butt, the curvy hips, the voluptuous lips, now she could see where they all came from. This was actually the first time she had seen this particular picture of her dressed in a bathing suit and standing on the white sands of Panama City Beach. Sugar was a little girl when she and Horace's parents were killed in a car accident.

"Your mother was so beautiful, wasn't she?" Sugar nodded her head with a look of amazement. "She was a teenager in this picture here, on summer break hanging out at the beach." The next few pictures were also of her mother. From baby pictures to school pictures to wedding pictures of her mother and her father, they all evoked both joy and sadness in Sugar and her granny who never really got over her daughter's untimely death.

Part of the reason why she thought the world of Sugar transcended grandmother/granddaughter relationship. Sugar was granny's daughter reincarnate. Almost everything about Sugar, whether it was her mannerisms, her laugh, physical features, her feistiness, intelligence, and even her athleticism, was damn near identical to that of her mother.

Sugar was only 7 years old when the doorbell rang late one night two days before Christmas. Restless and unable to sleep due to her anticipation of all those presents under their Christmas tree at home, Sugar and Horace faked sleep even after Granny's admonitions that their eyes would burn something serious from the salt ole Saint Nick would be throwing in their eyes if he caught them awake. Laying there in the pitch dark room staring up at the ceiling and fantasizing about the gifts she would have to show off to her friends, Sugar's life as a happy little girl as she knew it, would soon come to an end with a high pitched scream that she could still hear loud and clear to this very day.

"Oh nooooooooooo! Oh my Lord! My God! Nooooooooooo! Why take my baby, Lord? I know you don't make mistakes, but I ask why my Patricia? My last child! You done already took my only son, Eddie. Now you take my only daughter? Why, Lord? Why?"

After Sugar awakened Horace, they both ran to the living room to see their grandfather holding his wife on the floor by the front door trying to console her.

This was one of those images Sugar remembered about that night more so than other happier times in her young life with parents who gave them everything they needed and wanted. Everything else prior to that night was like a blur or a moment in time that seemed to travel at the speed of light. When the baby picture of Trent was pulled from the album, the once jovial, happy mood in the room changed. The somber faces and silence had now taken center stage as everyone's sympathetic eyes shifted to the woman who birthed him into this world.

"Look at my baby," she said as her voice began to crack and her eyes began to well up with tears. As she looked down at Trent's baby picture, where he had a football sitting next to him that was nearly as big as he was, a testament to his father's dreams of a son in the NFL. She shook almost uncontrollably while her daughter held her tightly to console her. When Sugar's granny got up from her chair to help in consoling her sister, Missy who had been holding in her anger and resentment for Sugar and her family being there, snapped.

"Look! I got her!" she said in a raised voice. "She's going to be just fine! She still have children here for her!" Granny stood there momentarily speechless as the room fell silent. Everyone, including her, seemed to be caught off guard with the outburst as the spirit of family togetherness had now all but left the room. Sugar's body language was like that of a guard dog. The moment her cousin raised her voice at her granny perhaps marked the end of civility. No one talked to her granny like that, especially Missy.

The bad blood between she and Sugar was still obvious from the moment Sugar and her family walked in the door. The beef between them went way back when they were teens while Sugar was down on summer break. And of course it had to do with a young boy who Missy showed an interest in. He made it known to her, however, that it was her cousin, the young beautiful girl from Orlando that all the cats at the recreation center and in the neighborhood went crazy over that he wanted to holler at. This and other family dynamics that actually existed before either of them were born contributed to the bad blood.

Something similar happened between Missy's mother, Theretha and Sugar's granny when they were young girls. Sugar's grandfather ended up choosing her granny, although their mother had intended for him to be with Theretha. This was typical in most black families. Either a man, money or even petty shit like pictures, clothes, shoes or even dishes was the cause of beef between the female family members, even the older ones who no one would have thought was a trip in their day. The unanswered circumstances behind Trent's death, only exacerbated a family rift that already existed and opened up old wounds, although Trent was estranged from his sister and that side of his family, which is why he was in Orlando where he had been living on and off for a few years. He was closer to Sugar, Horace and Granny than he was with his own mother and siblings. Sugar may not have shown it, but she too grieved over his death and dealt with it in her own way, but she'd be damned if anyone was going to use his death as an excuse to disrespect her granny.

"Okay, Missy, I was just trying to help," Granny said in a low voice. She totally understood Missy's anger. She had never had that type of interaction with her before and just passed it off as her way of dealing with the grief of losing a sibling.

"Yeah okay! Y'all helped enough, don't you think? I tell you what! If you really wanna help, tell us why Trent is dead! That's the only damn help you can give us at this time!"

Sugar had heard enough. Distraught cousin or not, she wasn't going to go in on her granny and disrespect her.

"Hold on! Pump your breaks, Missy! Now I understand that you all are upset about Trent, but that gives you no cause to speak to my grandmama, your elder, in that manner. What happened to Trent is not her fault. Now, I have heard about the way you talk to your mother, but this woman here you will respect!"

"Bitch! Let me tell you something!" she yelled. By this time some of the relatives and friends outside heard the commotion and began walking in to be nosey.

"What? What do you have to tell me?" Sugar shot back before she could say what it was she needed to tell her. Sugar moved closer to her.

"You, your husband, prison-raised brother, and your grand mammy can raise the fuck up outta here and go back where you came from with your boushie asses!"

"Grandmama, excuse me. Come over here," Sugar said as she placed herself between her granny and her cousin. Her granny gave her a look as if she was making an appeal for her to be civil.

"What the fuck did you just say?" Sugar said as she moved closer to her, placing herself between her cousin and her granny.

"What? You hard of hearing? Take your grand mammy and get the fuck...." Before she could finish repeating her demand, a slap that sounded like a gunshot reverberated across the room, sending Missy flipping over the recliner chair. When she got her bearings, she stood up to her feet groggily.

"Bitch! I know..." Again, there was another slap that put her square on her back. By this time it seemed like everyone had rushed into the house, the living room was now filled to capacity. Tony, Roy and Horace ran into the house pushing everyone out of the way to get to Sugar who was standing over Missy while her granny tried to hold her.

"Cousin or no cousin. Bitch, I will drag your muthafucking ass up in here if you ever talk to my grandmother like that again!" Tony ran up and grabbed Sugar.

"Baby, come on! This is your family! Chill out!" he said pulling her back as Missy got to her feet.

"Missy, y'all cut that out," her mother said. "This ain't right for y'all to be fighting and y'all cousins." Ignoring her mother's plea for civility, Missy got to her feet and charged at Sugar screaming at the top of her lungs.

"Bitch!" she yelled as Tony nudged her and held her back to protect Sugar. The last thing he wanted to do was be a part of some family feud, but no one was going to hurt his woman, family included. Robert grabbed Missy, who was acting like she wanted to get loose. The first slap that reddened the entire left side of her face had stunned her, and the second one made her conclude that she didn't have any hands for Sugar. This is when she figured she would have better luck with her box cutter and now had her hand inside her purse reaching for it. Missy, who was the pure illustration of a hood rat, was a known cutter who once sliced her brother Trent's back. Box cutters were her weapon of choice. The cut was so deep that it came centimeters from piercing his lung, which could have proved to be fatal. When Missy broke loose from Robert, ran around her mother who was trying to talk some sense into her, she came out of her pocketbook with the box cutter and lunged at Sugar who had her back turned and was being led away by Tony. Horace stepped in and grabbed her hand and bent it back so far, everyone in the room could hear her wrist pop as the box cutter fell to the floor.

"Cuz! You think I'm gone let you cut my sister? What the fuck is wrong with you? Have you lost your muthafucking mind?" Horace said standing as he held her.

"Let me go, muthafucka!" she yelled.

"Oh bitch, you were about to cut me? You were about to cut me, huh?" Sugar said as she rummaged through her purse for her .38. Fearing that Sugar was about to pull strap, everyone in the room ran to the back patio door for their dear lives. Realizing that his woman had been taken to a place of no return, Tony intervened quickly and grabbed her hand. He had always told her that if she ever pulled her gun out, somebody had to be shot.

"Sugar! Baby! Come on! This is family," he said as he pulled her to the front door against her protests. Missy's boyfriend, who went for bad, had just walked up accompanied by two of his homies with a unit on his face. Seeing Horace manhandling his woman he stepped to him aggressively trying to play hero.

"What the fuck going on, nigga? Why you holding my woman like that?" he said moving towards Horace with his fists balled up and his feet planted as if he was positioning himself to fire off a punch.

"Slow your roll, potna. This is my blood and this family business," Horace said.

"Y'all ain't none of my muthafucking family!" Missy shot back at the top of her voice. "Let me go!" she demanded.

"Missy! Stop it, I say," her mother yelled as she tried to help restrain her. Finally building up enough nerve, Missy's boyfriend then charged Horace and swung at him. The overhand right he threw did not fully connect but managed to catch part of Horace's shoulder knocking him into the wall. Before dude could throw another shot, a pistol crashed into the side of his head, sending blood flying across the room. At this point everyone at the back glass door decided they had overstayed their welcome. The family gathering was now over. Missy's boyfriend lay there stretched on his back motionless as Roy clutched his chrome .357 Magnum.

"Awww hell naw!" one of his homie's said.

"Hell naw what?" Roy asked, placing the barrel of his gun on his forehead. "Y'all want some?" His homie put up their hands in a defensive posture.

"Naw. We cool."

"Alright then. If you ain't family, get your boy and get the fuck outta here!" Roy said with his pistol cannon down by his side. Missy's old man's friends helped him to his feet and led him out of sliding glass door. Missy went right in behind them, cursing every step of the way and consoling her old man who leaked all over the floor.

"Theretha, I'm sorry this happened," Granny said with her eyes welling up with tears. "I'm sorry about everything." Her sister who felt so ashamed of her daughter's actions, looked down at the floor and nodded her head as Roy, Granny and Horace walked out of the crib to join Sugar who was being calmed down by Tony.

"Aunt Theretha, kinfolk, friends, it's been nice, but we gotta go," Roy said after placing his pistol back into its holster. The entire room was left speechless and in shock. They had been used to family drama in the past at reunions, funerals and other gatherings, but nothing like this. This latest family drama brought on by a family tragedy in which many wanted answers, only added to the sadness of losing Trent. He seemed to be on the way to finally getting his life together with the start of his own lawn care business.

Sugar, who had misgivings about the trip, the one thing she did not play was someone disrespecting her grandmother. Once cooler heads prevailed, many present would probably take the opinion that she could have handled it better than she did. But they didn't know this Sugar. The young girl they once knew who talked to dolls and stayed to herself no longer existed. Over time she grew up like all children do as nature dictates. However, they had no idea of the person she had transformed into or what she was capable of. If Tony had not been there, they would have gotten a first hand glimpse of who and what she had become. As the song *Thicker Than Water* by Sarah D played from the Infiniti truck's speakers, Sugar stared out of the window at the darkness hovering over the waters as they crossed the Hathaway Bridge to head back to their condo at the Wharf. As Tony massaged her neck, she had one last fleeting thought about the family drama that took place in her great aunt's living room. She handled that shit exactly how it needed to be handle. Fuck'em.

Chapter 6
Wedding Bells for a Boss

Since Sissy's death at the hands of Lavrov's twin killers, Angel and Blaze, Genie's attitude towards women and the idea of settling down had changed dramatically. He was now seriously involved with the other woman in his three-way love affair. He had even given her a diamond ring that would have cost him at least a million dollars if it were not for his best friend who was now a former diamond kingpin. After he had informed Tony of his plans to tie the knot and hang up his player hat for good, Tony was so elated that he gave him the ring on the house as a gift.

He had always advised Genie that having a good woman would give him stability, which would make him a better boss of their crime family that had now grown so big that he had to hire more workers and soldiers. He even wanted to make Macky Boy his underboss and eventually transition him to take the throne, but Tony urged him against it for the time being. Although he knew better than anyone that Macky was definitely boss material, it was his opinion that Macky would be better served keeping him as a silent underboss that no one reported to or knew about, and Genie agreed. And little did he know how much that wise decision would pay off in the end.

"Bae, this ring is so beautiful!" Genie's girl, Tracey, said. Her eyes sparkled as she marveled over the ring on her finger. "Thank you, bae." She placed a kiss on his lips, followed by a tight embrace.

"You're welcome, darling. Nothing but the best for my woman and future wife."

"Future wife?"

"Yes. You don't think I would give a ring like that to just a girlfriend. Would you marry me?"

"Really? Are you serious? You know you play too much already."

"Not this time, sweetie. I am serious as a case of Ebola."

"Really? You really wanna marry me?"

"I said it, didn't I? Do you think I would give you a ring like that on GP? Woman! You better go ahead and accept before I change my mind," he said with a chuckle.

"Yes! Yes, I will marry you!" she yelled. Her eyes welled up with tears of joy as the restaurant patrons looked on endearingly. Genie's stone-faced soldiers, sitting a couple of tables over, looked on with a wary eye. They were unmoved and on high alert for any issues after the incident at the park a few days ago.

"Okay. It's settled then. We go to the courthouse tomorrow and get married." Genie downed the glass of cognac before motioning for the waiter.

"Courthouse?" she replied with a raised eyebrow and animated tone. "I don't want to get married in no courthouse!"

"Why not? All that matters is if we get hitched, right? The bill please," he said to the tall waiter who looked like Phil Jackson, former head coach of the Chicago Bulls and LA Lakers.

"No sir! My first wedding is not going to be in some small back room in a courthouse!"

"Well, if not in the courthouse, then where? I ain't trying to go in no church. You know me and Jesus made a deal a long time ago on that."

"Although I grew up in the church and always dreamed of a church wedding, it doesn't have to be in a church. But it definitely can't be in a courthouse or city hall either. Maybe we can have it in a neutral place like a park or something. Maybe even a beach." The mention of a beach elicited an immediate objection from Genie.

"And you can strike a beach from the list too." Genie placed the tip down on the table, motioned for the soldiers and stood up.

"What you got against beaches? I love the water."

"Long story," Genie replied as he and his woman walked to the door and waited for the soldiers to make sure the coast was clear. After they cleared it, the two walked out arm in arm to the Bentley. As the Bentley drove off from the curb with the two SUVs of soldiers following in behind him, Genie peered out of the window and tuned Tracey out as she carried on excitedly about their coming wedding. He thought to himself, *What the fuck am I doing? I must be losing my damn mind to be marrying this broad, or any other broad for that matter.*

CATO

Chapter 7
The Rules in This Game Aren't Made To Be Broken

When Tony was the head of the empire he built, he lived by certain rules and guidelines regarding the sell of his top quality product. One of which, was the prohibition placed on his men from chopping up and adulterating it. How he gave it to them was how it was to be sold which is why he set it at a low price. This, consequently, would be the eventual cause of the mini war between he, Nathan Ward, and the syndicate cats that led to their demise.

If Tony found out that his men violated this rule, he would cut them off. There were other rules, however, which were enforced with a heavy hand, such as setting up traps near schools and inside the hood. This was one of those killable offenses, as these sacred places were off limits no question, no exception. This typically meant that most of the deals within the city limits started on the phone and culminated at a mall, while others were over dinner, over drinks, or a package left inside a parked car. This operation of Tony's wasn't the traditional armed project or hood takeover and occupation that brought with it the inevitable wanton violence. This thing ran as smooth as any legitimate business, which is why it did so with near complete impunity from federal, local, and state law enforcement.

Another rule Tony had established under his leadership was regarding doing business with gangs, which was of particular importance since many of them did dumb shit like shoot up innocent people, which was obviously terrible for public relations, and attracted too much heat. This aspect of Tony's hustle was so important that quite some time ago, he had established a gang council, who set out an agreement of peaceful coexistence and cooperation, which meant no petty squabbles or turf wars over bullshit. In exchange, they would get the best dope with the lowest price tag possible and an endless supply. If anyone violated this agreement, Tony would completely cut them off and out to where they wouldn't even be able to buy an 8 ball in the city or anywhere else in the tri-states. This was Tony's way of keeping the peace, reducing violence in the boroughs, and setting into motion his greater goal of making way for an era of black underworld organizations that could have long term benefits and ramifications for themselves and their hoods for years to come. It was similar to the Italians and Russians who took dope money, cleaned it up to do worthwhile things with it for their people.

After Genie took over, some of these rules had not been consistently enforced. Here and there, there was an oversight and it wasn't that Genie was sloppy. He just wasn't so enthusiastic about Tony's vision for the hood. Not being the diplomat and strategist like Tony, if Genie found out that a rule had been violated, there wasn't going to be a meeting or some sort of arbitration in some council setting. Someone was just going to get bodied, no questions. And this was keeping true to his gorilla mentality, which meant that if shit became too complex and it required too much thought, time, energy and input, his response was just to send in the hit teams and end all discussion. It didn't matter if it was a crew or gang members or a gang leader. Genie didn't give a fuck. His organization carried power because they had the best dope for the best price that put most wanna be bosses out of business. Not that Genie was a bad boss, but he just had his own way of doing things that worked in the short term, while Stallworth on the other hand, was obsessed with the long term. In one of these oversights there was the growing threat from a young ruthless gang leader who had his own set of ambitions. He went by the name of Supreme.

Chapter 8
The Young Lion Has Arrived

Supreme, or his government name, Roberto Clemente Scott, as a young kid began running errands for the late Nathan "Natty Boy" Ward who taught him many things regarding the streets. He even used the police as a necessary tool to get rid of a rival. Eventually, Supreme graduated to bigger and better things like enforcer, and soon thereafter, hits. After doing a ten-year stint in a Florida prison for manslaughter, he came out educated in both criminality and academia.

While inside, he ran with an older inmate named Rush who was a walking encyclopedia and prison philosopher, not to mention killer on the streets. Taking notice of Supreme's above average intelligence, Rush urged him to become book smart by reading everything he got his hands on, and taught him some things that are lost on this generation, such as organization and adhering to rules. This, Rush convinced him, would help him in his quest to rule the streets. The O.G. Rush had such an impact on Supreme, he took college courses and learned the Spanish and Italian languages from his two cellies during his bid. However, there was something in Supreme that could not be amended by education or enlightenment. It was just in him to be a thug. His idea of getting out of the joint and making something of himself was to be a powerful gang leader. And that is exactly what he did before he decided to upgrade his hustle and formulate an ambitious plan to become a boss.

Supreme's legend was etched in gang lore after he traveled all the way to Florida from Brooklyn to hit 3 former gang members who robbed, tortured, and murdered one of his young underlings and his girl. Taking the slight to his authority and his gang personally, he traveled to Miami and took care of that business himself. He tracked the 3 traitors to a house party in Miami Gardens. Without saying one word, he walked in and murdered them at a card table in cold blood where they sat. He then calmly walked back out, passing some of the witnesses who were frozen in place from fear. After the first-degree murder case against him had begun to fall apart for lack of cooperation by the frightened and intimidated eyewitnesses, his high-powered lawyer was able to get the charge reduced down to manslaughter and he copped out to ten years. And if it wasn't for the only piece of evidence, a security camera that caught him going in and out of the house just before and after the murders, he would have gotten off scott free. This incident, however, not only won the respect of the youngsters he did time with in Florida, but he became a legend to the youngsters in the five boroughs of Brooklyn who pledged their allegiance and loyalty to him.

After being released, Supreme stayed in Tampa with a prison guard broad he was fucking during his bid at Martin Correctional. There in Tampa is where he started his own gang named Supreme Beings, the S.B.'s. from Tampa. This gang grew in numbers like wildfire, and eventually spread to other parts of Florida, and even back in Brooklyn, the place of Supreme's childhood. This gang's influence also reached the smaller Florida towns like Panama City, where interestingly enough, Supreme had family ties, like Sugar. Supreme's ultimate aspiration as a gangland don was not to sell dope, but to shake down street level hustlers, and better yet dope kingpins, and make them pay tributes. After making his triumphant return to New York and hearing about these cats Tony Stallworth and Genie Smalls, who carried power in the city and beyond, he set his sights on them.

Trinidad, or Trini as his homies called him, who was a runner for one of Genie's best workers, Keeno, had long dreamed to graduate from his current position of taking packages from point A to point B and picking up money. His job was filled with risks that included being rousted by the Pigs or worse yet, kidnapped, robbed, shot, given an acid bath inside a chest, and thrown into the Bay weighted down with cinder blocks. These occupational hazards inspired Trinidad to conclude he would do whatever it took to climb the career ladder. With his sights set on a lieutenant's position that had just opened up with the untimely demise of the man who once held that position, he knew that one of two ways to climb that ladder was to do a little enterprising on his own by finding new customers who would buy major weight. The other was to get a few bodies of those who made the organization's shit list. The former was the better option since Trinidad was by no means, a killer. He was a young kid of privilege raised in an upper middle class family who attended private schools like Staten Island Academy. That is until he decided one day that he wanted to be a gangster.

While at the mall waiting on a phone call to pick up and deliver a package, he met this fine ass redbone in the food court. What really surprised him about her is that she seemed to seek him out. After he asked her what made her interested in him, she told him that she had her eye on him the entire time he was sitting down eating. From that day on, he and the broad whose name was Jazz, fucked daily. Being the square ass, off brand type of nigga that he was, he had never dealt with a girl of Jazz's caliber, who was a former dancer and call girl. After she did what she did best and put it on him, he was indeed pussy whupped….so much so, he violated a rule by taking her on his runs.

If Keeno found out, he would cut him loose immediately, and perhaps end his dream of becoming a gangster. If Genie found out, there was a good chance that he would have both Keeno and Trinidad clipped. Involving a civilian on dope runs was a serious offense because of the ramifications. The obvious reason was, if they got caught, the civilian would bend to the extreme pressure and would more than likely spill his or her guts to the police, or worse to the Feds. Or something far more sinister, like the runner and even the supplier being set up for a robbery. Between that pussy and that fire ass head that he'd never experienced before in his square ass, off brand life, Trini was gone. Jazz knew everything and everyone he picked up and dropped off too, while she remained out of sight. The slick bitch would even go through his phone after she put him to sleep with that fire snapper of hers. While Trini was trying to impress her, little did he know she had run through a gang of green ass niggas like him. At the age of 26, she was already a vet.

One evening after sucking his dick so good he told her that he loved her, Jazz brought up something to him that would change the course of his life.

"Bae, you remember when I told you that if there was any way that I can help you, I would?" Trini lay on his back smiling and staring up at the ceiling like he was on some good dope, as she softly caressed his balls.

"Yeah, shorty. You always trying to help me. But I told you the people I work for, if they find out that I be taking you on my runs, they would cut me loose. Or worse, body me."

"I know, bae. I'm not trying to get you cut loose or killed. I just wanna help you." Trini rolled over to face her and gave that goo goo eyed smile that only a pussy whipped nigga can give.

"So how you wanna help me, shorty?" He kissed her on her lips before he began licking on her ears.

"Bae, stop," she said in a playful voice. "I'm trying to talk business here and you wanna fuck."

"Yeah, I do wanna fuck. But okay. What kinda business? I wanna hear this."

"Alright. Listen. I have a cousin who trying to buy some real weight. I told him about you, and no, I didn't give him your name." Trini raised up and sat erect in the bed and looked at her menacingly. The smile was now gone and replaced with wrinkles and a frown.

"You didn't tell that nigga who I was, did you?" he said as he grabbed her arm.

"No!" she yelled, jerking her arm away. "I told you I didn't! You think I'm that green or something that I would put you out there? I know about the streets. I been on my own since I was 14." Just that fast, Trini softened up on her.

"Okay, baby, I just wanna make sure you didn't put me out there. The niggas I'm running for is serious. Deadly serious. They don't play nothing. So you say this cousin wanna cop some weight, huh?"

"Yeah. He got the money."

"Okay. Well, you get back with him and ask him what he talking about and I will see what I can do. What's your cousin's name?"

"Supreme."

Chapter 9
Thicker Than Water

After Trent's funeral, which lasted 3 hours, and was without a doubt the longest funeral Sugar ever attended, the family and friends set out for the cemetery. As the more than 60 cars in the funeral procession, led by a sheriff deputy's squad car, drove through the neighborhood where Trent grew up, the people standing on the side of the road who knew him waved and paid their respects as they passed. When the family finally arrived at Hillside cemetery, Sugar, Tony, and Horace decided to hang back away from the family, while Roy accompanied Granny. From a distance, Sugar stood there arm in arm with Tony watching the final phase of the funeral take place. The winter winds blew her fur coat. She could hear the faint sobs from Trent's mother and other family members while the preacher read a verse from the New Testament. Remaining her stoic self, a tear, blended with mascara, rolled down from underneath her dark shades and down her cheek as she played back in her mind some fond moments with her cousin during their childhood.

Within minutes, Trent's funeral was over. Not wasting anytime in the 45 degree weather, the friends and family members quickly walked back toward their cars, leaving Trent's casket sitting atop the straps that would soon lower him into his eternal abode. After his sisters, Missy and Stephanie, helped their grief-stricken mother to the limo, they climbed into the backseat with her before the limo slowly pulled out of the cemetery. After everyone was gone, Sugar walked over to the casket and said her tearful goodbyes to Trent before she, Tony, Roy and Granny headed back to Orlando. They had decided the night before that they would forgo the repast to avoid being involved in any more family drama. After Sugar had cooled down, she had promised her granny that she would eventually make an effort to patch things up with her cousin Missy, but only if she was receptive to it.

After getting back to Roy's crib in Sanford, Tony decided to chop it up with Horace about his future as he had promised Sugar he would.

"Horace, come take a walk with me," Tony said. Horace's finger was healing almost miraculously, which was perhaps a testament to his clean living and his youth, not to mention the topnotch surgeon who reattached it. The itching and burning sensation had become more frequent, which was a good sign that the nerves were regenerating. He even had some movement in it, but he was told to be cautious with any movement as it may rip open the incision.

Walking into Roy's huge billiard room, Tony began racking up the balls.

"Do you play?" Tony asked smiling.

"Do I play? I have mastered this game. But I'm a little handicapped right now. So if you beat me it doesn't count." Tony laughed. After Tony broke the balls, he went straight into the reason he pulled him to the side.

"I want you to know that I was impressed by the way you handled yourself during that incident at your granny's crib. Sugar told me how everything went down." Horace struggled to shoot the balls as he was careful not to injure that index finger.

"Yeah well, they came to touch my family and I did what I needed to do without even thinking about it. I just hate my cuz and my homie, Marco, had to lose their lives over it."

"I feel ya, man. That was definitely unfortunate. Especially knowing that they were going at your sister to get to me. But unfortunately, those things happen in my line of work," Tony said before he banked the 11 ball into the side pocket.

"Yeah, I feel ya," Horace said as he looked at the table to plot his next shot.

"What do you have in mind to do for a living now that you are in the free world?" Horace smiled as he looked at the table to see the perfect set up.

"To keep it real with you, I don't know at this time. I was fighting and wildcatting so much while I was in I stayed in the box most of the time. Those crackers shipped me to 8 different camps in one year. I was what they called a *hard case*," Horace smiled and said before he knocked in the eight ball. "Game over. Rack'em."

"Damn! I got beat by a one armed man." The two laughed.

"Well, let me ask you this. Are you on any probation?"

"Nope. I got a straight dub with no papers." Tony nodded his head as he finished racking the balls.

"Okay. Cool. How would you like to come work for me or my partner, Genie?"

"Well, that depends," he said before he broke the balls.

"Depends on what?"

"Depends on the pay of course and what I have to do."

"Good question. How about security?"

Horace laughed.

"Security?"

"Yeah, security." Tony smiled.

"I was hoping for something that was a little more exciting than guarding things."

"Okay. Something like what? What did you have in mind?" Tony tried a bank shot and missed.

"Maybe something like a problem-solving position." Tony smiled.

"A problem-solving position, aye?"

"Yeah. Someone who solves a problem that arises. You do run into problems sometimes, right?"

"Oh yeah. We do run into those every now and then. So do you know how to solve problems?" Horace made a beautiful double bank shot that caused Tony's eyebrows to raise.

"I told you I was an expert," Horace said with a confident smirk. "And yes. I know how to do that too. Why did you think I had those tools that we used in that incident?"

Tony smiled and nodded his head. He was impressed with the mini arsenal he saw lying scattered on the floor of Granny's crib after their gun battle with Lavrov. After Sugar voiced her suspicions about what he did before he got caught up on that manslaughter charge, he had a feeling all along about Horace. The story of how he killed that neighborhood bully with such casualness was also a dead giveaway to a man like Tony. He knew that Horace was a killer for scriller.

"Okay. We will see," Tony smiled and said before he sank the eight ball on a 3 cushion bank shot.

CATO

Chapter 10
I Need Some People To Go Away

Not long after Macky returned from a vacation in the Bahamas with his girl, Nicola, he was summoned by Genie to meet him at his crib. The purpose for the visit must have been one of urgency since past meetings would often take place at a cafe or some other public venue. When Macky walked in, Genie was sitting at his bar smoking a Black and Mild.

"What's up, youngster? How was your vacay?"

"It was straight."

"Okay cool. Catch a seat," Genie said smiling. "Can I get you anything? Something to drink or snack on?"

"No, thank you, Mr. Smalls."

"Okay. The reason I called you here is I need something handled. I don't babysit grown ass gangsters who know the rules. I send late night hit teams to set things straight. I want a couple of folks to go away," Genie said as he took a sip from his drink and pushed a picture towards Macky. Macky looked down at it to see two gang members and a third cat. One of which was his homie out of Yonkers that somewhat jolted him. He then looked up at Genie as if to get the rest of the story. Genie took another sip from his drink and a drag from his Black and Mild.

"One of my men's runners was robbed and killed yesterday. Your man was seen hanging out with these two niggas before and after they robbed the runner. We got word who carried it out and we will be seeing them in the coming days. Now I don't have to spell out for you the nature of their association. Your man here was in on setting up the robbery and getting the youngster killed." Macky nodded his head. He knew what it was and didn't need to have an interpreter to explain the situation. He didn't really know Danello, only that he was from the same hood and knew people he knew. However, he had always gotten a vibe from him, since the first day he got hired on to the team.

"Okay, sir, consider it done," Macky said before walking out.

So this business he now had with him was just what it was - business as usual. Nothing personal. And just like that. In less than a two-minute conversation, the decision was made to clip Danello. But that is how it was with Genie. He was a man of few words, but when he spoke those words were absolute.

Danello Braxton who had done time in New York, as well as California's notorious Pelican Bay, which was something he often boasted of to gain some street cred, had a secret that he kept in the closet at all costs. He was who some call a down low cat, while others just call it straight up gay. The only person who took notice that there was something suspect about him regarding his sexual preferences was Macky, who had a knack for seeing things that others either could not or ignored. And like Tony, this is what made him such a prolific killer. An apex predator who always killed his intended prey.

After sitting back in the cut a short distance away in his ride, Macky's suspicions were confirmed when he saw Danello coming out of the gay bar hand in hand with a tranny. After they got inside the Hummer, they kissed before pulling out of the club's parking lot.

After the Hummer pulled into Danello's apartment complex and parked, he and the Puerto Rican punk named Fe Fe exited the truck with grocery bags and went into his apartment.

"Damn, Nello! You have a really nice apartment, but you must allow me to decorate it," the slim feminine looking punk said excitedly. If one didn't know what to look for, they would swear Fe Fe was a woman. He had a slim waist, hips, lips, eyebrows and long hair weave like a female. He even had breasts that looked as real as any woman's. Nothing about him appeared masculine, other than the slight Adam's apple that one would have to look real hard to notice.

"My apartment is fine as it is," Danello said as he started putting the groceries up. "I didn't bring you here to decorate. I brought you here to fuck," he said before they resumed where they left off and started kissing wildly. Forgetting all about the groceries, the action transferred into the bedroom where they continued to swap saliva. When they finally came up for air and turned on the light, the punk took a deep breath and placed his hand over his mouth. Standing there with his eyes stretched and fixated on something behind Danello.

"What is it?" Danello asked. When Fe Fe didn't answer him and remained standing there with a petrified look on his face, he turned around to see Macky sitting in a chair.

"Umm, Macky. What...what...what...what are you doing here?" a startled Danello asked with a nervous stutter.

"I think you know why I'm here," Macky said with a calmness in his voice that matched the calm look on his face. Danello then turned and looked at Fe Fe.

"Oh. Is this about her? I mean, him? I can explain. It's not what you think. See...."

Before he could finish his sentence, a shot rang out from the tip of the silencer and hit him on the top of his head sending blood and parts of his scalp across the room. After his limp body collapsed to the floor and began to twitch, again the deadly whispers from the silencer spoke twice more when Macky hit him off with two shots in the head to finish the deal.

Recovering from the initial shock, Fe Fe was finally able to let out a high-pitched scream before Macky grabbed him and led him straight to the bathroom.

"Please! Please don't hurt me! I will do anything! I will do anything! Please don't! Please don't hurt me!" Fe Fe pleaded. With lightening quick speed he came out of his purse with a straight razor and took a swing at Macky who quickly stepped back and grabbed his arm and twisted. With his off hand he grabbed a handful of Fe Fe's weave and dunked his head into the toilet and held it down. Struggling for air and dear life, Fe Fe mustered enough strength to pull his head up.

"Please! Please!" he pleaded frantically for his life in between deep breaths, but again his head was viciously slammed back down into the toilet as Macky bared all his weight down, this time to finish the business. Soon the struggling began to subside, all except for some faint gurgles and air bubbles, followed by silence and stillness as Fe Fe's body became limp and his eyes stretched wide under the water. His face displayed both shock and horror as Macky held him down a few seconds longer to make sure that the deed was done. In Macky's mind, there was no way he was going to let this punk live to I.D. him. So unfortunately for Fe Fe, it was just a case of him being at the wrong place at the wrong time with the wrong nigga. Nothing personal. But nonetheless, his days of masquerading as a woman and fooling the various men who didn't know he was born with a dick and a pair of nuts was now over.

After Macky cleaned up, he walked out of the apartment as if he lived there. Cognizant of the lone security camera on the west side of the building from previous trips to Danello's crib, he stayed close to the walkway with his ball cap down over his face and his hands inside his bomber jacket pocket. This business with Danello was somewhat disappointing, but not half as much as to find out that a fellow Yonkers cat had not only dishonored himself by betraying the organization, but by being a faggot.

The killing didn't stop with Danello, however. A day later, and true to his word, Genie's wrath continued as the two decomposed bodies of the Brim gang members, who robbed and murdered the young runner, were found inside the trunk of a car in the Bay. They were bound and gagged with their severed dicks and balls stuffed in their mouths, and shot twice in the back of the head. This was Genie's way of making a statement to all those involved and those who even dreamed of fucking with his money and product. However, he wasn't finished yet. Not by a long shot. Other gang members would have to pay for their comrades' transgressions to make shit understood and it didn't matter who it was or whether or not they were involved. Genie realized that he had made the mistake of taking his eyes off some things and shit had gotten out of hand, but he intended to give it a quick fix.

The next evening, two of Genie's goons walked into a known hole in the wall Brims hangout in the Bronx where four members were shooting pool. The two men dressed in suits, looked around and walked back out without the gang members taking notice. They were too busy smoking weed and talking shit about whose broad was the finest and which one had the best pussy while the song *Used To This* by Future, featuring Drake, blared from the jukebox's speakers. When the two men returned, they stepped in and immediately lit the entire bar up with AKs. After unloading their clips, they reloaded and sprayed it again. The gang members never knew what hit'em. Their bullet riddled, bloodied bodies with exit wounds so big you could put your fist in them, lay stretched out on the floor throughout one corner of the club. Two lay face down on the pool table, one underneath and the other, who had tried to flee and managed to strike out for the exit, lay sprawled at the backdoor. After Genie's killers were sure their mission was completed, they turned and calmly walked out. Luckily for the owner, a Vietnam vet, he was on the shitter at the time when he heard the explosions of the choppers. Thinking he was back in a war zone, when the shooting started, he jumped off the toilet and dove on the floor with his pants down to his ankles and began crawling to the next stall. Nothing inside the club escaped the destructive wrath of the 7.62s. Everything had multiple bullet holes in it.

For all intents and purposes there was an undeclared war going on now. And depending on the Brim's leadership's reaction, it could turn into a full blown war in which they had zero chance of winning going up against a powerful boss like Genie, who had hundreds of soldiers eager to deal with any and all drama, not to mention killers for hire in other states. And if shit got too real, all it took was a phone call to his plug, Armando, to enlist the skills of the paramilitary killers on his payroll. It remained to be seen whether or not the gang members acted on their own to take from Genie. However, if that was the case, the leader had better hurry up and let it be known, because taking Genie's shit, especially some disorganized gang of blunt toting, po butts with their pants hanging off their asses, was not something a boss like himself was going to let ride.

***

After Tony, Sugar and Horace arrived back into town, Tony decided to take Horace and introduce him to Macky and Genie.

"Bae, I'm going to get some rest. I am mentally and physically exhausted." Sugar plopped down on the bed.

"Okay, baby girl. Me and your brother going to run to a few places. Introduce him to the city." Tony kissed Sugar on her forehead.

"Okay, bae. Take care of my brother," she said smiling.

"I got him, sweetie." Tony again kissed her before walking downstairs where Horace was chilling.

"Come on, youngster. Got a few people I want you to meet."

After Tony rang Genie's doorbell, Tracey answered the door.

"Hey Tony! Come on in. Genie is in the back," she said giving him a hug before quickly walking to the back to grab Genie. Tony and Horace went and sat down at the huge bar. Moments later, Genie walked in.

"My brother! I see you made it back alright! Where is your tan?" Genie said as he and Tony embraced.

"Believe it or not Genie, it's cold as hell there right now. Not New York cold, but colder than you would expect in the Sunshine State. But hey bruh. You have a female answering your door now?" Genie smiled and shook his head before heading to the bar.

"Yeah. Yeah. Yeah. And I think that calls for a drink." They all laughed. "I'm just doing what you and that wife of yours wanted me to do. I'm getting hitched."

"What?" Tony said out loud then held his mouth. "Real talk?' he whispered.

"Yeah. Real talk. And don't act like you didn't know when you gave me the ring." Genie looked at him side eyed. Tony laughed out loud.

"Well, to keep it real with you, bruh, I honestly didn't think you would go through with it when I gave it to you. But congratulations, my brother. It's about time and long overdue....so much so I should take a drink right now," Tony said with a chuckle. Genie looked at him with a raised eyebrow and a grin before downing his drink.

"Alright now. Don't pick with me. I'm already having second, third, and fourth thoughts about that shit." Tony nearly fell off the stool laughing.

"Noooooo. Trust me, bruh. I'm not ridiculing. I'm happy for you. This is what you need to become a complete boss." Again, Genie gave him that look.

"Yeah, but for real for real, T, she's a good girl. I may as well reward her with a life with me," he said jokingly. The three laughed.

"Hey, bruh, this is my brother-in-law, Horace, Sugar's brother. Horace, this is my man, Genie." Genie and Horace exchanged firm handshakes.

"I heard how you handled yourself in that drama in Florida. Much respect."

"Thank you, sir. But we were all in survival mode that day and it came natural."

"Yeah, I feel you, youngster. T, speaking of drama," Genie said turning to Tony. "I had some to come my way while you were gone. But you know I handled it."

"What's that, bruh?" Tony sat back down on the bar stool looking at Genie intently.

"Yeah, I had to check a few gang members and one of our own."

"Who was it?"

"That nigga Danello and a few of those Brim punks over in the Bronx. They robbed the young cat who ran for Danello and took a few of those things and murked him. I found out Danello was involved and took care of him."

"The same Danello out of Macky's hood?"

"Yeah. In fact, for that reason I let Macky handle it." Tony cringed inwardly momentarily. He knew better than anyone about Genie's gorilla tendencies.

"Okay. That's what's up. It didn't get messy, did it?"

"Nah," Genie said before downing a shot.

"You sure, bruh? You know your hand can be a little heavy at times," Tony said with a raised eyebrow.

"Yeah. I'm sure. I handled the shit as lightly and quietly as I could."

"Okay. Cool. Speaking of Macky, we're headed over to his crib when we leave here."

"Well, if y'all sit tight he should be here in a few minutes," Genie said as he poured himself another shot. Tony looked at Horace.

"Okay. We can wait on him."

A few minutes later, Macky was walking through the door.

"Mr. Stallworth. What's up?" Macky said, smiling as he shook Tony's hand.

"Not much, youngster. How was your first ever vacation in the Bahamas?"

"It was good and everything I expected. We really had a good time. And how were things in Florida?"

"Everything went alright. Speaking of Florida, I want you to meet my brother-in-law, Horace, Sugar's brother." Macky and Horace gave each other dap.

"Good to meet you," Macky said.

"Likewise, folk." By this time Genie was walking back into the living room.

"What's up, youngster. Talk to me."

"I think they got the message, Mr. Smalls. Their leader wants to talk with us now. He said his people acted on their own and he had no involvement." Genie smiled.

"Good. Well, let him know we can do that over the phone. I'm not cut out for those damn meetings." Tony smiled and shook his head. The one thing about Genie was, boss or no boss, he remained the same and sometimes to a fault.

"Genie, did you tell Macky you were tying the knot?" Genie waved Tony off. "What? You don't want people to know that you're marrying the love of your life?" Tony laughed out loud.

"Is that right, sir?" Macky asked. Genie shook his head.

"Yeah. I'm getting hitched. Go ahead and tell every damn body then, Stallworth." Tony laughed even louder.

"But seriously. Do you have a date for the wedding?" Tony asked trying to hold a straight face.

"Yeah, man, we have a date for the wedding. You call ya self trying to be funny."

"Nah, bruh," Tony said laughing. "Serious business." Genie smiled and monitored him.

"Okay. The shit gone be next month. Alright? And the sooner the better before I change my damn mind." Tony, Horace and Macky all laughed.

"Well, fellows, the reason why I dropped by was to see if you had a spot open for Horace. He would be an invaluable addition to the team." Genie looked at Macky.

"Yeah. Well, Danello's spot is definitely open now," Genie said with a chuckle. Tony and Macky grinned. "Danello also needed a lieutenant. So we definitely have openings."

"Umm, I was thinking more of something along the lines of problem solving. That's more in Horace's line of work, so to speak," Tony said. Genie and Macky analyzed Horace as if to size him up. To them and everyone else he sure didn't have the look of a killer for scriller, but neither did Macky or Tony for that matter. Both Macky and Horace could easily walk onto a high school campus and pass for students, which is partly what made them so dangerous. Their enemies and marks could never see them coming.

"I have a feeling we will have some work for him real soon," Genie said. He was referring to the growing tension with the young hungry gang members who wanted what he had. Before Tony and Horace left, Tony pulled Genie to the side to make sure he had that talk with the Brim's gang leader to clear the air and avoid any further drama.

"Hey, bruh, don't forget to have that talk with that gang leader so you two can have an understanding. The last thing you need is more drama, my brother." Genie nodded his head.

"I will handle it."

CATO

Chapter 11
The Young Man with the Proposition

Once the hostilities with Yuri Lavrov began, Genie relocated his Bronx office to upper Manhattan. And since that time, the white people in the building knew there was something about him that did not say Fortune 500 businessman. His rough around the edges demeanor, the cold stare in his eyes and the mannerisms belied any legitimate business dealings that he pretended to have. That, coupled with an innate judge first suspicion of black men, there was often whispers and backroom conversations among them about the black tenant. Genie, however, didn't give a shit. As far as he was concerned he had just as much right to be in that building as anyone of them and perhaps the only one who could buy the entire building with cash and become their landlord if he chose to. But he didn't have to do that nor did he want to do that. The Jewish cat who owned it, Genie owned him. Every week he bought no less than a quarter of a brick of those fish scales from Genie's folks.

When Genie walked into his office, there was a young brother dressed in a red suit with a black turtleneck underneath sitting at his desk. At first it caught Genie off guard then he became somewhat angered by the intrusion.

"Are you lost or something, son?"

"No. I don't think so. You're Genie Smalls, right?"

"Yeah, I am he. And you're sitting at Mr. Smalls' desk. What's your business here? And who the fuck let you in my office?" The young man laughed.

"I used to make a living breaking into things. No one needed to let me in then or now."

"Okay. So you are a burglar. Good to know you have a hustle to make a living. Now get your l'il narrow ass out of my chair." The youngster with the tattoo on his neck grinned and then immediately got up and walked away from the desk and sat down in another chair facing Genie. Genie then walked over and sat down at his desk, sat back in his chair, and began studying him.

"Okay. Again, what's your business here?" Genie asked before he pulled out a Black and Mild and fired it up.

"I came here to give you a proposition." Genie chuckled.

"You came here to give me a proposition?" Genie asked condescendingly.

"Yes, sir."

"What kind of proposition you came to give me?"

"Survival. Protection. I came here to offer you both." Genie paused for a minute then laughed out loud.

"So, let's get this straight. You came here to give me protection? Really nigga? Protection from who and what? Youngster, are you fucking high on something?"

"Yes, I'm high. But it's all natural. I'm high on ambition. I am fresh out of the joint and I'm hungry." Genie studied him for a minute. If they weren't in an office building filled with white folks, he would blow his brains out on GP.

"Okay. I get it. You are hungry and I'm on the menu, right? You go do a bid, come out angry at the world as if it owes you something and now you think you're a gorilla? Little nigga, please. I murdered 10 niggas like you last week. You better take your ass to the Italians with that boo game." The youngster laughed.

"Oh I will. I'm stepping to them next. I just thought since I was in the area I would come by and pay you a visit first."

"Perhaps you should have paid them one first, because this ain't what you want. I could have your entire bloodline erased talking like that. But I'm in a good mood right now. So why don't you go somewhere and play. I've got grown folks business to attend to." The youngster laughed out loud.

"So, you don't even wanna hear my proposition in its entirety?"

"Not at all. Because if I do, I may become upset and change my mind about killing you. Now again, I have some very important grown-up business to take care of, so run along." The youngster smiled and looked away before he stood to his feet.

"Okay. Get atcha later," Supreme said before strolling out of the office. Genie leaned back in his chair and smiled. He kind of admired the nerve of this youngster who reminded him of himself. However, the direct challenge to his authority was obvious and something he considered disrespectful, and thus a killable offense. Picking up his phone, he called one of his soldiers downstairs.

"Hey, you see that young lanky nigga in the red suit come out of the building? Get his tag number and follow him to see where he goes. If he drives all the way to Coney Island I want you to stay with his ass to see where he goes." Genie then hung up the phone. Something told him that this visit was tied to the small drama with that Bronx gang and was therefore not a coincidence. There was something brewing and he planned on getting to the bottom of it and deal with it, starting with the arrogant, overly confident nigga who just walked out of his office.

After the 2017 BMW A7, pulled into the parking lot of the 4th Avenue Pub in Park Slope, Supreme stepped out of it and strolled inside. When he walked in, sitting at a back table were four cats with a pile of hot wings and beer, making small talk.

"'Sup gentlemen?" Supreme greeted them.

"Not much, kid," one of the men said as he stood up and gave him some dap. "So how did it go with the O.G.?" Supreme chuckled and grabbed a wing from the pile.

"It went just like I expected. The only reason he didn't body me was because we were in an office building with witnesses," he said laughing.

"Well, did you even get to tell him?" one of the cats who wore a mohawk haircut interjected. Supreme's face wrinkled up at the question.

"No! I didn't get to tell him," he said, soliciting an eye roll from the dude. "Hey, Hassan, who the fuck is this clown ass nigga here who talking out of line?" Supreme asked, mad dogging him. If his glare could kill he would catch a body.

"Oh, he cool. That's Diesel. My folks."

"Well, tell your folks to not speak out of turn. And why is he here any muthafucking way? What stake does he have in this?" Diesel's facial expression looked as if he was about to have a stroke. To say that he was pissed was an understatement. The last nigga who talked to him like that was knee capped with a .380.

"He's got a stake in it. He's my lieutenant and enforcer." Supreme laughed so loud it could be heard clear across the restaurant. The few white patrons inside gave them that look all niggas get for being the least bit loud and obnoxious.

"Enforcer, aye? Okay. Well, Mr. Enforcer. I didn't get to tell Mr. Smalls because he didn't give me the opportunity. But here is where you can come in at. You can send him the message to make him feel what we are trying to say. I did my part for now and you niggas are going to have to show me that you are up to this shit. I'm not going to commit any of my people to do nothing until I see how serious you are about this, you feel me?" Hassan looked at his partner, Diesel, and the other two cats, who nodded their heads.

"Okay. We will handle it," Hassan said before taking a sip of his beer.

Chapter 12
In This Life, Everybody Is a Snake

Antwan "Diesel" Jemison, a former stick-up kid and strong arm out of New Orleans was once reported to have filled a bathroom sink up with water and dunked the head of a 1 year old baby down in it to teach the kid's father a valuable lesson in the perils of being delinquent on the funds of a Dominican heroin kingpin named Saulo "King Saul" Rodriguez. Amid the screams of the baby's horrified mother, every time the kid looked as if he was about to drown, a laughing Diesel would pull him up long enough for him to catch his breath. Even a gorilla like Diesel didn't have any intentions of killing a baby. He just wanted to scare his father shitless to teach him a lesson. Eventually, the father somehow came up with the money he had been holding out on the entire time and much to the mother's anger. As a lasting reminder to never fuck with King Saul's emotions and his money ever again, Diesel took a gun butt to the father's right hand, crushing it so badly it had to be amputated above the wrist.

Diesel was as violent as they came. His understanding was zero and his fuse was even less. His one major weakness, however, he was a big dumb brute who had very little going for him up top. In school, he was one of those special needs kids who only had to show up for class to get passed through the system. He was also the type of student who not only bullied other students, but one who was so big he intimidated teachers and staff alike. Being as dark as night, only added to his intimidating persona.

Outside Trini's apartment, Diesel and four of his goons sat chilling in a black and gold Range Rover with black tints sitting on 24s. As the men talked and laughed amongst themselves, Diesel's eyes were glued to the townhome.

When Trini and Jazz came out of the crib hand in hand, Jazz's eyes shifted around from east to west as if she was on the lookout for something or someone. Sprung and in love, Trini was totally unaware that the slick bitch, who was a seasoned vet, had straight larceny on her mind.

"Ight. Y'all niggas shut the fuck up and get ready," Diesel barked with his eyes still glued to his mark. His voice sounded like a continuous thunderclap. After Trini opened the car door for Jazz like a gentleman, she again scanned the area one last time before sitting down. When the silver Audi with the black rallying stripes sitting on 22s pulled off, Diesel's driver pulled behind them and hung back, so as not to be detected. While Trini received his pick up instructions over the phone, Jazz texted furiously with someone.

"Okay. Okay. Already. Be there in a minute, bruh," Trini said before hanging up. He then turned up the volume on his car's stereo and began bumping to *Can't Trust Thots* by Wash, featuring French Montana, while rubbing Jazz on her leg, but she continued to text and didn't pay him any mind. As the silver Audi got off the exit and drove into Crown Heights, Diesel and his goons crept slowly in behind them without Trini even noticing them. When the Audi pulled into the Home Depot parking lot in King's Plaza, the Range Rover pulled in and went around, still unbeknown to Trini, who was too busy trying to impress Jazz.

"Okay, baby. You know the routine," Trini said to Jazz. "Sit still and chill so the spotters they might have out here won't see you."

"Okay, bae. I know. I know," she said in a dragging voice. Trini leaned over and kissed her before heading to the pick up point. When he got out of sight, Jazz began texting again.

We're here. Where are you? the text said.

Okay. I'm nearby. But don't worry. My people are on him. Is your period on?

Huh?

Is your period on?

No. Why would you ask that?

Why don't you take ole boy home and fuck him. Jazz paused a second before responding.

K.

When Trini returned from inside the hardware store with a Home Depot employee rolling a dolly with a huge box on it, all four pairs of eyes in Diesel's ride were locked in on him as they sat off in the cut amid the many vehicles in King's plaza. After the Home Depot employee placed the box into the trunk of the Audi, Trini shot him a $50 tip and got back into his ride.

"Told you I wouldn't take too long," he said kissing Jazz. "These people I'm running for are straight business. They run this shit like a fucking Fortune 500 company," he boasted. "The only difference is, you fuck up, they don't send their team of lawyers to sue you. They send a team of killers to see you." Jazz smiled and began rubbing him gently on his dick.

"I know, baby. But you smooth with your shit too, though. And that's what really turns me on about you." She continued to rub his manhood, which had now begun to harden and jump around in his pants. As he drove out of the parking lot, Diesel waited for him to turn the corner.

"Alright. Move," he commanded his driver. The driver then maneuvered the Range Rover slowly behind Trini's Audi.

"Bae, I'm horny as fuck," Jazz said.

"Girl, you always horny. What else is new?" he said smiling.

"I'm serious, bae. I didn't really get enough of this big dick earlier. You know how much I love it," she said as she began stroking his manhood again before unzipping his pants and pulling it out. After crouching down in the seat, she slid it into her mouth and began doing what she did best. She gave him some fire top right there in the ride while he drove. As his Audi slowed down, she continued to bob up and down as Trini turned down the stereo's volume so he could hear the sound effects her voluptuous lips made.

"Alright, baby, we have time to go back to the crib 'til I have to make the drop off," he said in a low exasperated voice. Known by the hustlers and ball players she's tricked with in the past, as Brooklyn's version of Super Head, Jazz was definitely putting in work on him properly. She was sucking his dick so good, his foot let up off the gas as the Audi began slow crawling up the highway like an old man was driving. The angry motorists honked their horns and sped around him while Diesel and his men continued to patiently hang in behind him.

"Damn! She must be sucking on the nigga's l'il dick or sumpin," one of Diesel's men said.

After Trini pulled into his apartment complex, he and Jazz got out of the ride and went into the crib. And before they could get in the door good, their fuck session began right there in the living room as they kissed wildly. From there, they kissed all the way to the bedroom and quickly began stripping down.

"Okay, baby, this gone have to be a quickie," Trini said as he took off his underwear.

"They're all quickies," Jazz said with a chuckle. Trini smiled sheepishly.

Outside, across the street from Trini's crib, Diesel began running the game plan down to his goons who were high on Kush. They were hungry, eager to take something and ready to put in work, if necessary.

"Okay, y'all niggas listen up. We go in here and straight gorilla this fuck nigga, you heard? But don't murk him. We need him to tell us where the stash is." After exiting the Range Rover, Diesel and the goons headed to Trini's crib where they found the door left unlocked. When they walked inside, they could hear the headboard of the bed slamming into the wall and Jazz doing what she do best, which is to make lame ass dudes think they are the best fuck she ever had.

"Ooooooo yes! Fuck this pussy! Oooooo bae! Ooooooo! I love this dick!" When Diesel and the goons walked into the room, Trini's ass was going up and down with Jazz's legs wrapped around his back. Her antics only encouraged him to fuck her harder while Diesel and the goons stood there taking in an eye full and seeming to enjoy the spectacle of this fine ass woman being piped. After a few moments of allowing his goons to get their thrill, it was time to get down to business. Diesel slapped Trini on the ass so hard it sound like a firecracker going off in the room. Startled and with his ass stinging as if a bullet hit it, Trini rolled over to face Diesel.

"What the fuck, nigga?" he yelled. Before he could make a dash for his pistol on the nightstand, Diesel slapped him on the left side of the head with his Glock 40. It sounded like a gunshot going off. The lick sent a blood splatter across the room and onto the wall and sent Trini crumbling to the floor. Jazz cringed and quickly pulled the comforter over her naked body while the four goons stood there eyeballing at her like two crazed perverts. What they had on their minds was not

apart of the plan. They wanted to fuck her. As Trini tried to shake off
the blow, again, Diesel's Glock cut through the air and crashed into his
mouth, knocking out two of his teeth. Lying there on the floor, Diesel
straddled his large body over him with a menacing look on his face that
would scare the average off brand like Trini.

"Okay, dope boy! You know what the fuck this is and I ain't gone
ask you but one muthafucking time. If you don't tell me what I wanna
know, I'm gone kill you and your bitch! But before I do, we gone fuck
both of y'all with your pretty ass," Diesel said, once again slapping him
on his ass. By now Diesel's goons were nearly salivating at the prospect
of fucking Jazz who was as fine as they come. In a sense, they actually
hoped Trini didn't spill his guts so they could have their way with this
beautiful high yella girl who had curves everywhere. This was the only
thing they had on their minds as they stood there smiling waiting for
the word to take some pussy from her.

"Bae, tell him!" she urged Trini. Diesel reached down and pulled
Trini's scrawny body up from the floor with one hand and slung him
over the bed before sitting him up. Still groggy from the pistol whip-
ping, he began pleading his case incoherently.

"What? What was that?" Diesel asked with his ear up to his mouth.
"I can't hear you!" Diesel pressed the Glock to his head. "You got five
seconds to tell me where the money and the coke at or I'm gone blow
your muthafucking head off! One. Two. Three. Four." Jazz winced and
pressed her body up to the bed's headboard in anticipation of an explosion from the pistol.

"Okay. Okay," Trini grunted with his hands in the air. The threat
of having his head blown off seemed to bring him to his senses. "The
money is out in my trunk."

"And where the coke at?" Diesel said grinning.

"It's in my storage unit."

"Alright. We 'bout to take a little ride then. You and your bitch put
your clothes on, and hurry your asses up!"

After arriving at Treasure Island Storage in Park Slope, Diesel, accompanied by one of his goons, walked Trini at gunpoint to his storage
to retrieve the coke while the other two goons waited in the Range
Rover with Jazz. Unfortunately for Trini, he had just received a load

from Keeno and had to make a pick up of cash, so he was about to lose dope and money. If he survived this robbery, it was a good chance he would be murked anyway for this loss, especially if it was found out that he was set up by the broad he had been taking on his runs.

"This it right here," Trini said. As he opened the storage, Diesel gave him one final warning about any heroics.

"Looka here nigga! If you try anything, word on my mother, you and that bitch is dead! You understand?" A terrified Trini nodded his head profusely. There was no way he was going to buck this robbery with no weapon. Even if he had one, he wouldn't do shit, because he knew better than anyone that he wasn't no gangster. The only thing at this time that was on his mind was survival. As Diesel stood there with the Glock still trained on him anxiously waiting to get his hands on the coke, Trini opened the climate-controlled storage unit, before walking inside followed closely by Diesel. After walking over to a huge roll of brand new carpet, Trini knelt down and unrolled it, revealing four big duffle bags. Inside the first duffle bag was at least ten keys and the same number in the other two bags, which was a total of 30. In a brief-case, in a fourth duffle bag, there were stacks of cash. Diesel had hit the jackpot. His eyes rolled inside the sockets like pinballs and lit up like a Christmas tree. A petty poor hustling ass dude like him, he had never seen that many bricks at one time before. Peering down at them, and almost to the point he could not contain his excitement over this haul, he placed a hasty call to one of the goons who were inside the truck with Jazz.

"Alright, nigga, come on!" he said excitedly.

"Alright! Hey, be right back," the goon said to his partners before tearing out to the storage unit. As Jazz sat there she thought to herself, *Where the fuck you at, Supreme? You should have been here by now.*

"Damn, baby girl! I wanna tell you, you fine as fuck!" the goon said smiling and undressing her with his eyes. Sitting in the backseat, Jazz rolled her own eyes, but she decided to play along with him until her cousin showed up and peeled his cap.

"Thank you," she said, smiling flirtatiously.

"Yeah, you welcome, shorty. I really dig you. When this shit is all over, I wanna holla."

"Oh yeah? We will see. You probably tell all the females that." Again, she said putting on her smile that was between a hungry croc and little innocent girl in convent school. *Ugly muthafucka make me wanna throw up. Kill yourself!* she thought.

"Well, yeah. But only the fine ones," he said with a chuckle. "But for real for real shorty, I wanna holla at you. That fuck nigga you got is too slow and lame for you. He ain't even in your league." In total agreement with everything he said, his partner smiled and nodded. As the goon continued to make his pitch that he was the better man for her, Jazz caught a glimpse of Supreme and three of his masked men steadily creeping up to the back of the truck in a crouch out of her peripheral vision. Not wanting Diesel's men to see what was unfolding a few feet away, she continued to make small talk with the goon to distract him.

"Oh, so what you saying? You in my league? You think you can handle all this?" she said gesturing to her beautiful body. "I'm high maintenance, now. And you gone pay for every inch of this."

"Fuck yeah, shorty," he replied. Her words only seemed to excite and encourage him. He just knew he was in there. "I can take care of you better than that nigga ever could. He shouldn't have never put you in harms way like this anyway. It says a lot about his judgment and how lame as fuck he is." At this point Jazz stopped talking and slid down in the seat in anticipation for the next turn of events. "Why you got so quiet back there, shorty?" he asked, looking in the truck's interior mirror.

Suddenly, the truck's passenger door swung open and before the goon could react, two shots rang out from a pistol, equipped with a silencer, into the side of his head. Simultaneously, the same happened to his partner from the other side of the vehicle. Three of the masked men then quickly pulled their lifeless bodies out of the truck and onto the ground before dragging them behind the storage building. Supreme looked at Jazz and put his finger to his mouth and motioned for her to keep quiet. "What took you so long?" she whispered. Waving her off, Supreme and his masked killers continued onward to the storage shed where Diesel, his two remaining goons, and Trini were.

When Supreme arrived to the unit, Diesel and his homies were just about to leave with the duffle bags thrown over their shoulders.

"Supreme, what you doing here, bruh?" Diesel asked in surprise. Supreme's eyes narrowed as he stood at the entrance of the shed with his two men standing behind him. "And why those niggas masked up?"

"I just came here to make sure you didn't fuck nothing up, homie," he replied. "Good job. You passed the test with flying colors," he said before the short burst from the tip of the silencer spoke its deadly whisper, followed by three more. Diesel's huge frame slumped to the ground as his two goons were killed instantly with shots to the head. With strained eyes and a grimace on his face, Diesel looked up at Supreme as he desperately clutched his pants leg. Coming to the painful realization that he was the victim of the old double cross, as his killer stood over him smiling, he knew this was it.

"Fuck ass nigga! I knew you was a snake," Diesel blurted out followed by a blood vomit. Each time his struggling heart pounded, his lifeblood flowed from the two wounds to his chest like a water fountain.

"If that was the case, why did you let a snake get close enough to sink his fangs into you?" Supreme replied coldly. "In this life, everybody is a snake," he said before finishing Diesel off with a shot to the temple as Trini looked on in horror. Although he was given a temporary reprieve, Trini knew this wasn't going to end well for him either. With his killers posted up at the door as lookouts for any drama, Supreme knelt down and opened the duffle bags. He then smiled menacingly and looked up at Trini who was about to shit on himself.

"I can't believe anybody would be dumb enough to let a lame ass young nigga like you handle this much weight. They must be sitting on Peru." Supreme zipped the duffle bag and stood up.

"Alright, y'all grab this shit and let's flex," he said to his men.

"What about this nigga, here?" one of them asked. The storage unit was so quiet you could hear a mouse piss on cotton as a lump developed in Trini's throat. Awaiting his fate, and facing his own mortality, surprisingly, his concerns were still with Jazz and what would happen to her. But little did he know, Jazz was with the man standing in front of him with the pistol in his hand. Supreme stared at him momentarily as if he was trying to decide what to do with him.

"Young nigga, today is your lucky day. Fortunately for you, my cousin like you so much she made me give her my word that no harm would come to you. For what, I don't know," he said looking him up and down in contempt. Besides all that shit, I just saved your people's money and product, and I think they will be hella grateful for that." As they were walking out of the unit, Supreme smiled and led Trini with his hand tightly clasping the back of his neck. "I actually have a new friend," he said. A confused Trini had no idea what he was talking about and didn't care. He was still alive and that's all that mattered at this point.

As Supreme, his men followed by Jazz and Trini, drove away from the scene, the unit and Diesel's vehicle burned on with the charred bodies inside. With the gas used to accelerate the fire, the coroner would probably need dental records to identify them. Supreme's plan worked like a charm. All the schooling he learned in prison from the O.G. Bobby Rush, on how to be a better criminal, had paid begun to pay off huge dividends. He used his wits, his cunning, and not mention a big butt and a smile, to get that much closer to the boss of bosses. It was time for phase two of his plan.

The next evening, as Genie sat back in his office chair smoking a Black and Mild, one of his soldiers walked in.

"Mr. Smalls, some dapper don cat say he's here to see you. He said that it's urgent."

"Alright. Let him in," Genie said as he took a puff from the Black and Mild.

When the soldier returned with the visitor who was being escorted by another soldier, Genie realized it was the same ambitious youngster who dropped by a few days ago with a smile and a proposition.

"I see you made it back alive," Genie said, smiling as his eyes shifted down to the two suitcases he held in both hands. "And in one piece too. I guess the Italians didn't take you serious either." Supreme laughed.

Just as Supreme was about to sit down he caught himself. Looking over his shades, he asked, "May I catch a seat?"

"Sure. Go ahead. What's on your mind?"

"Well, the last time I was here, I didn't get a chance to tell you the nature of my visit. And I think you took it the wrong way."

"Alright. You're here now. Let's hear it."

"First of all, it wasn't what you thought. I wasn't trying to gorilla you or extort you." Genie smiled and took a toke from his cigar as if to say, *I wish you would try me, young nigga.*

"I came through to inform you that you have some pretty ambitious and hungry folks out there who want what you have. Some unscrupulous, wayward YGs who have sat down and plotted to make a move on you." Genie chuckled dismissively.

"Tell me something else I don't know. They can get in that long ass line that stretch from here to Baltimore." Supreme grinned.

"Well, you don't know who they are, or what they are capable of, but I do."

"You talking about like the ones they found in the Bay last week? Or the ones they found shot up at that hole in the wall joint over in the Bronx? I have seen them all and dealt with them all." Genie smiled as he thought about the Russian Mafioso cat who he and Tony just gave an early retirement.

"Nah. Nothing like that. Those fools were amateurs. I'm talking about a couple of gangs who have consolidated just for you." Genie studied him momentarily as if he was trying to determine if he had an angle or to take him serious. "As far as they are concerned, you are the old gangster on the block who had his time." Hearing this, Genie couldn't help but to recall the clash of eras he and Tony had with Nathan Ward and his old guard black syndicate. They too were passed their time.

"And you know who they are?" Genie asked.

"Sure I do. I know everything that's going on in the streets and most of the time before it materializes. I was one of them at one time in history. I even knew about this and retrieved it for you," Supreme said as he clutched one of the suitcases and placed it on Genie's desk. Almost immediately, Genie's soldiers quickly stepped in to protect their boss, but were waved off by him. Supreme smiled and shook his head.

"I didn't come here on some suicide mission to try and harm you, Mr. Smalls. I ain't that stupid." Genie smiled confidently and sat back in his seat and fired up another cigar then motioned for Supreme to continue opening the briefcase. When he opened it, there were several wrapped bricks of coke. Underneath, were stacks upon stacks of $100 bills. Supreme then opened the second briefcase, which contained the same thing. Genie realized it was his shit after seeing his trademark crown with two AKs above it, stamped on them.

"Someone misplaced this, aye?" Supreme said smiling.

"Yeah. We didn't miss it though," Genie said downplaying it. "I guess someone dropped it by mistake or sumpin." Supreme laughed out loud. *This OG is one tough customer*, he thought.

"Oh no doubt. I know this ain't nothin' to a boss like you which is why I thought long and hard about keeping it," Supreme joked.

"And maybe you should have," Genie replied as he sat back in his seat studying him closely.

"Nah. I couldn't live with myself if I did that. I ain't the type of po hustlin' ass nigga who take things that don't belong to him."

"So how did you happen to come across it?"

"Well, like I told you, I know everything that's going on in the streets. One of your green ass runners, let's just say he's a little weak for a big butt and a smile that happens to belong to my cousin, luckily for him." Genie continued to study him carefully. He wanted to know why would a cat fresh out of the joint, would return the type of weight and money that would put him on his feet in a major way?

"Okay, youngster. Good looking out. Now let's cut through the shit. What is your angle, here? And don't insult my gangsta by telling me you don't have one." Supreme smiled and briefly looked down at the floor.

"I won't lie to you, Mr. Smalls. I do have an angle."

"Okay. I'm listening," Genie said, leaning forward in his chair with his elbows on his desk.

"I want a job."

Genie smiled, leaned back in his chair and fired up another cigar.

Chapter 13
Back On Familiar Grounds

"So bae, you show my brother around the city?" Sugar said as she lay in bed on her side facing Tony. The flame from the candle that provided some light to a nearly pitch dark room, flickered as the cool air from the air conditioner blew from the vents.

"Yep. I gave him a grand tour of the city. Even introduced him to the family," Tony said before kissing her on her forehead.

"Mmmm hmmm. You didn't take him to the strip clubs, did you?" Tony smiled.

"Now since when have you known me to hang out in places where naked women are shaking their asses?"

"Nope. I never have. I won't lie. But I know how men get when they trying to impress other men while giving them a tour of their city."

"Well, not me. Horace don't strike me as the strip club type. I did take him by the ho stroll, though." Sugar playfully punched him in the chest as Tony laughed out loud.

"Y'all probably did go to the stroll."

"So what, you think I would corrupt your brother?" Sugar laughed.

"Hell, he would probably corrupt you." They both laughed.

"Who? Horace? That quiet, baby face looking dude with the school boy looks, corrupt an old seasoned cat like me?"

"Yes. Don't let that innocent look fool you."

"Oh I'm sure."

"But seriously, bae. I appreciate you bringing him here and taking him under your wing. Florida is a not exactly a good state to live in for black men with records, and especially those who are fresh out of prison."

"Yeah, baby girl, don't mention it. We got him. Horace has a lot of potential and I have a feeling he will fit right in. I introduced him to Genie and Macky."

"I sure hope he can adjust. I mean, he's been in Florida all his life. In fact, I don't think he's ever really been outside of Florida, other than going to a couple of family reunions." Tony lay there looking up at the ceiling while Sugar rubbed his chest.

"Are you sure about that?" he asked.

"Sure about what?"

"Are you sure he hasn't been outside of Florida before? He seems like the type of cat who slides in and out of places. And I have a feeling he's been here before." Sugar stared off into space momentarily. She, too, had long suspected that Horace got around, although he never uttered a word to her regarding his business, nor had he ever let on that he was anything more than an antique car enthusiast. The day of the incident at her granny's new crib with Lavrov, gave her insight into her brother when she found the mini arsenal he had stashed away at the old crib.

"Well, I don't *think* he's been here before," she replied with a less than confident tone.

After the nerves in Horace's reattached index finger had started to regenerate, the pain at times would be constant, particularly at night. He was told by the surgeon that this would happen and that it was actually a good thing since it was a sign that he would regain mobility and full use of it. Refusing to take the Percocets prescribed to him, because of the way they made him feel and his dislike for medication, the pain would often keep him up most nights. Tonight however, he had a replacement for the Percocets. From the moment he settled into his room in his sister's mansion, he had been taking straight Hennessy shots to the head. The once full fifth was now reduced to only a couple of shots. Before long, the much needed elusive sleep that he had been hoping for on this night, finally overtook him.

Sitting outside in the parking lot across the street from the King Spa in Palisades Park in Newark, New Jersey, Horace sat back in the seat totally relaxed and staring at a picture of two white men on the golf course while the old school joint, Street Fame by Tupac played from the satellite stereo. It had been two months since he received the paperwork on the two brothers who had closed shop rather abruptly in Orlando and fled up north. The rumors of their whereabouts put them in California and even all the way in Europe. After one of those angry Facebook rants by a jilted girlfriend of one the marks regarding his side broad, less than a week later, Horace was able to track them to Newark. Within one week, his homework paid off as he narrowed down their movements and the places they frequented. This popular bathhouse was the one and only place they normally frequented together without the usual bodyguard or two tagging along. This bathhouse served as both their meeting place and place of leisure. The first mistake these two brothers made was to fuck with Carmine Assante's bread. The second mistake, which would be their last, was to flee to the same city to hide out in.

When the two men pulled into the parking lot in separate vehicles, they found the 24-hour spa empty. After a tight embrace, they both took one last cautious look around to scan the area before walking inside, while unbeknownst to them, the interested observer across the street continued to sit back in his seat monitoring them.

After about twenty minutes of waiting for the two men to get settled inside, Horace calmly exited his vehicle and made a straight line to the bathhouse. As he approached the building, he could clearly hear the two men talking.

"I think we have gone past our stay here in this city, Simon," the short and brawny white man wrapped in nothing but a towel said to his brother who had one streak of gray that went from the front to the back of his head as if someone drew it with a wide paint brush.

"I'm with you on that, Pete. Lately, I have been having a bad feeling about being here. In fact, just last night I dreamed that I woke up with some asshole in a ski mask standing over my bed holding a bloody knife in one hand and my Dorothy's head in the other. I'm telling you, bro, I just cannot deal with this anymore. I think what we should do is give Carmine every fucking penny of his money back with interest, even if it breaks us." Pete chuckled and shook his head.

"Okay. So we give the Wap back his money. What happens after that? I mean, what about his brother, Geno? Do you have a way that we can retrieve his body from the stomachs of those alligators in that swamp so we can put him back together? Even if we gave him his money back we can't give him his brother back."

"Yeah and thanks to you. We weren't supposed to kill him. We were only supposed to take the shit from him and that was it. But you had to *go and waste him!" Simon said angrily. Pete smiled and looked up the ceiling as if he was becoming agitated.*

"Here we go again with this bullshit! How many times do I have to tell you that what's done is done? If I could bring the Wap mother-fucker back, I would do so just to shut you up!" Pete said loudly. "But obviously I can't because I'm not fucking Jesus, here! But you know, Simon. Maybe it's just time for us to part ways. Like you go your way and I go mine." Simon sat there staring off into space pondering the frightening prospect of life on the run on his own. Since they were ba-bies, he and his brother had been together. They dressed alike. They fucked the same women. When they were in the juvenile facility upstate, Simon was about to be raped in the shower and his big brother got word that it was about to go down and stormed inside with two locks in a sock and began pummeling the pervs and saving him from the man-killing indignity of becoming somebody's bitch, and not to mention a gutted out asshole. To say Simon was totally lost without him was an understatement. And he knew it.

"Well, listen, bro. We don't have to go that far," he said in a low humble tone. The base that echoed off the walls was now conspicuously absent from his voice. "For some reason, my nerves have turned to shit lately. That's all. I didn't mean anything by that."

"Yeah, and it wouldn't have anything to do with that dumb cunt bitch you were with putting your business all on social media, would it?" Simon put his head down. His brother had always been critical of the type of women he seemed to fall in love with, which ranged from the bipolar to the psychotic.

"Yeah, I know, Pete. I don't need you to remind me again for the thousandth time." The echo of Pete's mocking laughter bounced off the walls of the bathhouse.

"Hold on. Did you hear that?" Simon said as he froze in place and listened intently for what he thought were footsteps.

"Did I hear what?"

"Shssssh!" Simon extended his neck out like a Snapping Turtle and raised his head in the air so he could hear better.

"What? What the fuck is it now?" Pete whispered.

103

"I heard someone coming inside." Pete froze in place to see if he could hear what his startled brother was talking about.

"I think you're just hearing things again, baby bro. You are going to worry yourself to fucking death, man!" Again, Pete's laughter echoed off the walls and this time traveled outside the bathhouse, which made an approaching Horace stop dead in his tracks.

"Man, let me get my ass out of here. You are so jittery you are scaring the fuck out of me too," he said grinning and shaking his head. Just as he was about to get up to end his steam session, a shadowy figure wearing all black quickly appeared out of the smoke like an evil spirit looking to cause fright, and before Pete could react, three explosions opened up his chest cavity. Pete let out a guttural yell before crumbling to the floor. When a petrified Simon nervously fumbled for the .38 revolver he had under his towel, a shot ripped through his neck sending him to the stone floor next to his brother. As he clutched the gaping neck wound in a desperate attempt to tourniquet off the blood flow from his carotid artery, the shadow was now in full view.

Standing there menacingly and looking down at his frightened quarry whose eyes were stretched as big as saucers, Horace calmly took careful aim and said, "Carmine Assante sends his regards."

He then pulled the trigger over and over. One shot followed by three entered into Simon's forehead and exited out of the back leaving a greasy smear of brain matter and blood on the bathhouse floor. Pete, who had been hit first, mustered up enough strength to make a futile attempt to slowly crawl away, but was shot in the back two times before taking one last coup de gras to the back of his head that blew his right eyeball clean out of the socket. Kneeling down over the bodies of the two brothers, a grim faced Horace took out a knife and began methodically cutting away at their ears. After taking his souvenirs as proof of death as instructed by Carmine, he calmly walked out of the bathhouse leaving the corpses of the two Lehman brothers behind. Their days of taking shit that didn't belong to them were now over.

After climbing into his ride and typing his destination into the GPS, a knock at the window startled Horace. It was a female cop standing there wide-eyed and clutching her Glock. She was just as startled as Horace, who after composing himself, let his window down.

"Hello officer," he smiled and said politely. "You scared the shit out of me. Is everything alright?" After gaining her own composure and trying to catch her breath, she took a step back. She was obviously new at this.

"Yes. I was about to ask you the same thing. Can I ask you where are you just coming from?"

"Sure. I pulled off the highway into the parking lot to type in my destination. As a man, I hate to admit, I'm a little lost," Horace smiled and said as his right hand clutched the pistol equipped with a silencer at his side.

"Oh okay. I see. You're a tourist," she said smiling. "Where are you headed?"

"I'm headed back to the Waldorf Astoria in New York."

"Okay. Well, you are all off course. You're going to have to pull out of here and get back on I-95 and head north and it will take you straight to the city."

"Oh wow! Thank you! I am an embarrassment to the alpha male world getting lost like this," Horace joked. The cop laughed out loud. She seemed to be at ease now. Before, she was such a nervous wreck she probably would have shot herself by mistake if Horace moved the wrong way. The back up she called seemed to take their time getting there. And perhaps it was because of her male chauvinist colleagues who resented a female being on a male dominated force in the first place and gave her a hard time in the hopes that she would fold up and quit.

"It's okay. You aren't the first man to ever get lost and have a woman to help you find your way." They both laughed.

"Right! Well, thanks once again, officer. You're a real God send."

"Oh, don't mention it." Just as Horace's heart rate seemed to decrease and he was about to put the car in drive and pull off, that one dreaded question came that no cat doing dirt wanna hear. "Sir, before you go can I see your I.D.?"

Horace clutched his gun tightly and briefly closed his eyes as the trigger finger tightened. Damn! I've got to kill this bitch, he thought.

"I just want to make sure you don't have any warrants."

Although his license was under an assumed name, Horace knew that he couldn't allow her to run his I.D., because that would surely bring him back up to the scene. This thing would definitely get out of hand if another pig showed up and decided to go inside that bathhouse to investigate. With time running out, and this situation quickly spiraling out of control, he had to think fast.

"Officer, is this really necessary? I mean, I'm a little tired and wanna get back to my room." The officer studied him momentarily to monitor his body language for any furtive movement or nervous twitches just as she had been trained to do. Not seeing any signs of nervousness, she responded.

"Well, sir, I promise you it won't take long," she said politely.

"Okay, ma'am. Sure." Horace relented, gave a disarming smile and handed her his I.D. As soon as she took it in her hand, her face exploded and her body dropped to the pavement like a sack of bricks. Calmly leaning out of the window, the silencer once again spoke its deadly whispers as he gave her two more shots to the dome to seal the deal. Her lifeless body jerked with each burst from the Maxim 9 with the built-in silencer. Just as he was about to drive off, in all directions, marked and unmarked squad cars rushed into the parking lot with sirens blaring and lights flashing.

Suddenly, a frantic Horace quickly rose up in the bed in a cold sweat and began looking around the dark room. His heart pounded and his mouth was completely dry as if he had taken a hit of crack.

After finally regaining his composure he realized this was that same recurring nightmare regarding a real life situation that took place a year and a half before he went down on the manslaughter charge. The case of the murdered female rookie cop and the Lehman brothers was ruled as a mob hit gone wrong. The case had never been solved and became what's known as a cold case. And luckily for Horace, the pigs didn't have so much as a lead on it. He never uttered a word of this incident to anyone, not even to Sugar, and he knew not to. This hit and others inside and outside of Florida, was something he was going to take with him to the grave.

Chapter 14
A Son to Carry On His Name

Genie Boy Smalls had always wanted a son to carry on his name. He vowed that if he ever became a father, he would do the things for his son that his own absentee father failed to do with him and his younger brother. The years of being hooked on that Boy heroin was perhaps the reason he could not bear children. At first, and being in denial, he attributed it to the infertility of the older women that he dated, who were typically around his age or older. But after kicking it with Sissy, and now Tracey, who were in their twenties, he concluded that it was he who was infertile, or as the older folks used to say, shooting blanks. This longing for a son made him once consider adoption, but he concluded that he was too involved in the gangsta shyt for that type of thing and so he blocked that thought out of his mind as he did with other things that he concluded as being unrealistic.

There was something that he saw in Supreme, however, that seemed to reignite that longing for a son to carry on his name. This is perhaps why he had begun doing something uncharacteristic of himself, like developing a relationship with people outside his circle that was tighter than Stud pussy. He took Supreme under his wing in the same way Tony did with Macky.

"So tell me some things about yourself, youngin'?" Genie said to Supreme as they both walked on the pier, while the soldiers hung behind them a few feet away with their rotating heads scanning the area. Supreme smiled and looked out over the relatively calm water's subtle ripples slowly surging in and out to sea. This was his opening. The OG Rush once taught him that to get next to an enemy or even an ally, find out what makes them tick, what their weaknesses and strengths are and build rapport. Genie was giving him exactly what he looked for.

"Well, there isn't anything comparable to your life, O.G." Genie smiled and took a toke from his Black and Mild.

"That's okay. I'm still all ears."

"Okay. I was raised in Bedstuy before my mother was evicted and forced to move to the Bronx with some relatives who didn't much like the idea of us intruding on them. Eventually, I did like any other kid and got caught up in the gang shit. Running for a couple of the OGs, let's say my quick temper and penchant for violence became very useful to them. After moving up the ranks, I eventually became even more useful to the OGs and formed my own gang. There was nothing spectacular about us other than doing the typical hoodlum shit in and around the hood. We extorted some folks and made others feel like the OGs were their protectors. One day, some fools got their own ideas and murked my young lieutenant and understudy and his broad. Kids wasn't no more than 17 years old," he said with a pained expression on his face as if he relived the incident all over again.

"I took the shit extremely personal and so I dealt with it personally. My emotions ended up costing me my freedom for the next ten years in some of the finest gladiator camps in Florida before I got sent to a cozy little prison called Martin, where niggas get shanked for breakfast and white boys get raped in the shower. While inside, as the old folks used to say, I put some skin on my head, took some college courses, learned some world culture and some social etiquette from an OG who was like the father I never had. After jumping out, I hung around in Florida long enough with this C.O. broad to sow some oats and spread my wings. When that shit ran its course, I flexed and came back to the crib. And here I am. Hungry, ambitious and ready and willing to pay my dues." Genie smiled as he seemed to stare into Supreme to study him carefully. His life somewhat mirrored his own.

"So where are your folks? Are they still here in the city?"

"Well, my ole girl got cleaned up, got her shit together and married some wealthy wall street cracker she used to trick with. We see each other every now and then when she can sneak away. My other folks are scattered here and there. Some live in Georgia and others live in Florida. What about you, OG? Your folks live here?"

"I don't have any family left. At least not here in the city. The last I recall, there are some in Atlanta and Louisiana. I had a brother, but he was killed in some dark alley in Harlem back in the day. Other than my brother from another mother, Tony, and my beautiful wife to be, I'm all I got."

"You mean you don't have any shorties, O.G.? Surely, a man of your stature got some mini-mes running around the city tearing up shit." Genie smiled and looked out over the water as they continued to walk aimlessly with the well-dressed trench coat wearing soldiers behind them scanning the area. Unbeknown to him, Supreme's words struck a painful chord.

"Naw. No shorties. At least not yet. And what about you? I didn't hear you mention any kids." Supreme smiled endearingly as he thought about his seeds.

"I have four. Two in Florida and two here in the city."

"Any sons?"

"Yep. All four of them are me all over again."

"Well, is that right? Four boys. Wow! You are one lucky man, youngin. But surely, you don't want them to be a repeat of you, right?"

"Naw. Not in the least….which is why I didn't lay down with any hood rats. Well, let me take that back. Three of my sons I have no doubt they are going to break the cycle. One of them however, that little muthafucka is me all over again. I can see it in his eyes. He doesn't blink nor does he smile much. He would just stare at you as if he was looking through you. I mean, even when he was one years old, right before I caught that case, what I saw in him kinda scared the fuck out of me. And coming from a cat like myself who have lost all fear after coding twice from a gunshot, and a stabbing, that is saying a lot. It was like I was standing outside of my body looking at myself. He's fourteen now and my oldest. His mother was a beautiful, yet crazy, homicidal project raised Puerto Rican bitch. Believe it or not, she had two bodies on her resume. Both of them were old abusive boyfriends."

"Damn! You lucky she didn't body your ass up too." They both laughed.

"She almost did," Supreme said, rubbing the long keloid scar on the side of his neck where she hit him with a box cutter.

"Do you take care of your seeds?"

"Oh no doubt. They want or need for nothing. With my oldest, our relationship is a little complicated to almost nonexistent. He blames me for his mother's death. She got stabbed by a couple of broads from a rival gang while I was in the joint. It doesn't help matters that his grandmother be filling his head up with shit about me. All those letters I wrote him, which was two a week for damn near my entire stretch, I don't believe he received one due to the grandmother's meddling."

"Have you tried to connect with him since you been out?" Genie asked as he walked with his hands in his trench coat pockets.

"Yeah. All the time. In fact, the day I touched down in the city from Florida I tried to see him. I'm not going to give up on him. I can't. As long as I have breath in me and as long as he's living I will continue to reach out to him." Genie nodded his head.

"Respect! The last thing our people need is more sorry ass absent fathers. My pops, or better yet my sperm donor, I saw him two times. Once when he came to the house and slapped my mother, and the second time on an obituary." Supreme chuckled.

"I don't mean to laugh, but did you ummm…"

"Did I kill the nigga?" Genie asked with a raised eyebrow. Supreme looked at him without breaking his gaze and nodded. "Sure I did. I killed him a thousand times in my mind. In reality, someone else beat me to it, because I vowed that I would take him out of his misery as soon as I was old enough to use a gun. But you know, over time that type of shit subsides and you forget about it. In fact, sometimes you have a change of heart. Strange enough, I had a longing for his deadbeat ass. I wished that he had lived so we could reconcile and do the father and son thing, even if it was late in the game. This is why it is important that you do all you can for your shorties and spend as much time with them as possible, even when you are knee deep in dirt. Your oldest, he will come through. Just watch. No matter what his messy ass grandmother is filling his head up with, none of that will keep him from his natural male instincts to gravitate to his pops."

"That's true, OG. My father was there until my mother ran him off. So I understand that I need to be all I can be to my seeds."

"Respect! Do you do any fishing, youngin?"

"Huh?" Supreme replied with a bewildered look on his face. Genie laughed.

"Do…you…do…any…fishing? You heard me right."

"Oh. Not since my father was around. We fished a couple of times while visiting his folks in Florida. But that was probably when I was about 7. Until you brought it up, I had actually forgotten about it."

"Is your father still alive?"

"Yeah. Last I heard he was. I think he's in Florida or somewhere. My mother dogged him out and he left here a broken man. He was a good man, but to her he was a pushover. And she ran over his ass like a Mack truck."

"Well, maybe we can go fishing one of these days. For now, let's go grab a couple of drinks at the tittie bar. I feel like seeing some ass tonight," Genie said before motioning to the soldiers.

CATO

Chapter 15
A Long Awaited Night of Passion

Since the Lavrov problem was solved, Tony and Sugar had not had any quality time to themselves. The 48 hours his Queen was away from him while a guest of Lavrov, was perhaps the longest two days of his entire life. Even more so than when he and two Marines in his company were cut off from the rest of soldiers and trapped behind enemy lines after a failed mission to kill a local Taliban commander. With all the business with Trent's funeral and the visit to Sugar's grandmother, they finally found the time to show how much they missed one another. As with most of their sessions, it started off with a subtle kiss here and there before it turned into a full-blown night of passion. Sugar's favorite time to make love was late nights and in the wee hours of the morning.

When Tony began kissing her gently, starting at her feet before slowly making his way up to her curvaceous hips then up to her belly button, she cracked open her eyes and started taking keen notice of his tongue. Straddled over her, he was caressing her nipples that were now hardened from the excitement. The moisture from his tongue left every part of her body that it touched shiny and wet. As he continued to run it up and around her neck and ears, he occasionally blew a cool breeze that sent chills throughout her body. Now fully awake and fully receptive to his seductive onslaught, she parted her legs in excited anticipation for a pleasure that was second only to the deep penetration of his long muscular manhood. After reaching her sweet spot that seeped a nectar that was even sweeter, Tony took in a mouth full of her before slowly releasing it and making a smacking sound with his lips. Taking all of her back into his mouth again, her body tensed up as if a jolt of electricity surged through it. Clutching her pillow with both hands, she bridged up in the bed lifting her voluptuous brown sugar bottom off the satin sheets as Tony moved with her not missing a beat and continuously licking her softly.

"Ooooooooh bae, your tongue is so damn soft!" she said in a low whisper.

"Ummmm," Tony kept saying over and over as he caught a steady rhythm. Moments later, Sugar let out a deep hiss and grabbed his head. Her body tightened and bristled as her pussy quivered and began throbbing uncontrollably. She had just released her first heavy load leaving a puddle underneath her ass. This didn't stop Tony who continued maneuvering his tongue inside of her and going as deep as he could while he held her plump ass in his hands as if he was eating a whole pie. No longer able to take it, Sugar pushed back and crawled to the head of the bed on her elbows. Before she could catch her breath, he gently pulled her back and commenced to licking her before she once again pushed away. Turning her body in the opposite direction, she crawled toward his feet and placed her sweetness down on his face. This was his cue that it was dinner time once again.

As Tony laid his hands on her round bottom, her head methodically bobbed up and down while her tongue swirled softly around his manhood as if she was licking on a candy cane. Pausing momentarily to fully enjoy the pleasure she was giving him, Tony paused to moan and take a deep breath before resuming his own work. When Sugar came once again, this time more intense than the first, running, she inched forward, grabbed his dick and positioned it before baring herself all the way down on it slowly until she couldn't go any further. Feeling all of his firmness deep inside of her, her eyes rolled and her legs shook as if she suffered from Parkinson's. As she picked up the pace and began riding him wickedly from the back, the slaps to her ass sounded off around the room. When she came yet a third time in less than ten minutes into their lovemaking session, she shrieked and froze in place before laying her head down on his legs to rest and regain her composure. Wanting to show his woman just how much he missed her, Tony held back on his own climax. Gently rolling her over, he climbed on top of her while taking the time to kiss her neck passionately before easing himself deep inside of her slowly. Staring into each other's eyes, their bodies moved in synchronized gyrations as Tony's full, firm and pulsating manhood constantly traversed in and out of her sugar walls. The look in their eyes spoke volumes about the love they had between them without the agency of speech. When Sugar once again released her burdens for the fourth time, at the same exact time Tony finally released his, the tears streamed down her face while she held him tightly as if it was the last time she would ever see or make love to him again in this life. Her body shook and her sweetness quivered and pulsated as the last drop of her honey streamed down onto Tony's pelvic area leaving it soaking wet. Lying there in a tight embrace looking at one another with dreamy eyes, they fell asleep in each other's arms.

CATO

Chapter 16
No Loose Ends Left Untied

Sitting inside the semi-packed Peyton's Gentlemen's Club on Second Avenue in Brooklyn, Genie and Supreme sat at a table in the back, while the soldiers sat at a table nearby surveying the club with a discerning eye. The big booties pranced back and forth on a mission to attract and mesmerize the various big money cats that ranged from gangsters, blue collar cats coming off a hard day's grind to square ass white collar businessmen. Some were there seeking to fulfill their fantasies and hoping to get some ass at the end of the night from some stripper down on her luck. Some were there to supply many of those same strippers with their drugs of choice that would enable them to cope with the various pervs they were forced to suffer, while others were there to chill and unwind after a long day inside and outside corporate America.

"O.G., I didn't take you for a tittie bar man," Supreme said amidst the loud music that bounced off the club's walls. The song *Rack City* by Tyga played from the DJ's speakers.

"Who me? Hell, I like pussy just like any other man," Genie replied before he downed a drink and motioned for the waitress to bring him another one.

"I hear ya, O.G. Goddamn! Would you look at that over there?" Supreme said, nodding his head towards a tall light skinned girl who had an ass like a Clydesdale horse. Noticing the several pairs of eyes honed in on her moneymaker, she smiled and gave them a show as she walked back into the dressing room.

"Yeah, she damn sho' is toting sumpin' back there," Genie smiled and said before downing his drink. "I have to admit, I hadn't seen this much ass at one place and at one time in some years, youngin."

"I can tell," Supreme said laughing. "No disrespect, but you look totally out of place, O.G."

"You know, youngin, you might be right about that. I haven't been out to a spot like this in at least ten years. I used to live in places like

117

this. Don't worry. It will all come back to me soon." Genie again motioned for the waitress. "Let me get another round, baby. And get my partner one also." The waitress smiled and rushed away to get the next table's order.

"Hey daddy," a short, thick, dark-skinned girl said as she walked up to Genie's table. "Can I sit in your lap?" Genie looked over at Supreme as if to ask what should he do.

"Nah baby," Genie replied. "You sit on daddy's lap, you might have to go home with him." The thick beautiful girl with the deep dimples revealed each time she smiled laughed out loud.

"Well, we can arrange that," she said in a sexy tone before easing down in Genie's lap, nearly causing him to spill his drink.

"I think it would be a little crowded with my woman there and all."

"Well, hell, we can all get in the bed together if she get down like that," she said rubbing on Genie's chest. Supreme looked over at Genie smiling with a raised eyebrow as if to say, *your move, O.G.*

"Is that right? My woman would murder us both," Genie said with a chuckle before taking a sip from his drink.

"How do you know? She might like what she see when I peel off these clothes."

"Yeah, well she just might, but I ain't trying to find that out." Genie handed her a crisp fifty dollar bill. "Now run along, sweetie," he said. Grabbing the fifty dollar bill with no hesitation, she cuffed it, kissed Genie on the cheek and strolled to the next table as if she was a model walking on the runway.

"Youngin, I have a question for you."

"Don't tell me. You wanna take that trick bitch home?" Genie laughed.

"No. Nothing like that."

"Okay. She ain't what you want? There's plenty more to choose from, maybe not as bad as her though, O.G." Genie smiled and shook his head.

"No, youngin. Nothing like that. This is business related."

"Okay. Then, shoot."

"How did you say you came across my shit, again?" Supreme smiled and took a sip from his drink.

"A young lame ass nigga who been pushing up on my l'il cousin, who claimed he was a runner for one of your men. Some cat named Keeno."

"Is that right?"

"Yeah. He took her on a run and they got robbed by some jack boy gang bangers. She texted me her location and we got there just in time. Whoever had that little off brand running for them, they be slipping big time. And you know better than anybody, O.G, that in this day and age, in this game we are in, one slip could take down the entire kingdom."

Genie took a sip from his drink and peered at the other side of the club at the very man who they were talking about who put that off brand on the team. As he fired up a Black and Mild, a dark sinister smirk started to appear on his face.

"Yeah," Genie said as he continued to smirk and stare to the other side of the club at Keeno who was being his typical life of the party wild self. He had no idea that his placement on the shit list was just signed, sealed and delivered. Soon he would know the meaning and importance of gangsters obeying rules.

When a knock came from the door followed by a couple of rings, Keeno jumped straight up in the bed and looked around with a confused look on his face. The two naked strippers who came home with him from the club, continued to lay there asleep and not making a sound. A night of partying, drinking, popping zanny bars, and wild sex collapsed them into comas. A bomb could be dropped in the same room they were in and they wouldn't hear shit.

From the sound of the constant ringing of the doorbell at that time of the morning, Keeno just knew it was the police. Easing up from the bed, and pushing the two naked women to the side, his feet gently came into contact with the carpet. As he crept to the door ever so slightly as not to be heard, just in case it was the police, the doorbell continued to ring, followed by a few strong knocks. Whoever this was, they meant to see him. *Surely this is those crackers,* Keeno thought. Looking through the peephole, a sense of relief came over him when he saw that it wasn't the police. It was his boss, Genie, and some cat he never seen before. Probably one of the soldiers. Just as the relief set in, now a new concern went through his head. *Why is he here this time of the morning?*

"Maaaaan damn! I thought y'all was them folks, G," Keeno said, shaking his head after opening the door. Genie chuckled as he walked in, followed by Supreme who didn't even crack a smile.

"Thought we was them folks, huh?" Genie said before sitting down at the bar.

"Yeah, man. Scared the fuck outta me too." Keeno let out a nervous laugh. "What's good? Is everything alright?" he asked before dropping down in his lounge chair and firing up a cigarette." He then looked over at his wall clock, which showed 4:49 am, before shifting his eyes to Supreme who wore a hardness on his face that a wrecking ball couldn't crack. *What is this shit about?* Keeno thought.

"Yeah. Everything good on my end," Genie said smiling. "I just dropped by to check on you to make sure everything was good on your end." The shape of Genie's eyes had now changed to narrow slits as they zeroed in on Keeno whose nervous level immediately went up several points.

"Yeah. Everything is everything on my end. Just selling coke, as usual." Keeno smiled nervously and again cut his eye over at Supreme who, from the time he walked through the door, his expression never changed. And this only added to Keeno's uneasiness.

"Oh okay. Cool," Genie replied. "Are you sure everything's okay? Because I heard that it wasn't." Keeno hesitated as if to choose his words wisely. Genie's comment kind of threw him off. Before answering, his eyes once again shifted to Supreme.

"Huh? Yeah. Yeah. Everything is straight."

"Okay listen. As my number two runner and earner behind Danello, you already know that I don't like beating around the fucking bush. You also know that I know everything that goes on in the streets, you dig? So I also know about one of your flunkies, what's his name?" Genie asked, looking over at Supreme.

"Trinidad," Supreme replied. This caused Keeno's eyes to stretch. He knew exactly what and who he was referring to, but had hoped it wouldn't get back to him.

"You know him?" Genie asked.

"Yeah. He's some kid I have running for me. What happened?" Keeno asked, nervously as he began to shift around in his seat.

"What happened, you asked? He fucked up. That's what happened. And you fucked up too. You know the rules on that. We don't bring in green ass kids to do our jobs, especially those who are weak for big booty hoes and bring them along with them on business. I mean, there is a reason why we have rules, Keeno. If he or that broad got rousted and snatched up by the Feds they would have told on you, and you would have told on me. Now I know that didn't happen, but it could have. But what did happen, I, you, lost my shit. I mean, that is like adding insult to injury."

"Yeah, I heard. But I can cover it, Mr. Smalls."

"You can cover what?"

"I can cover what he lost." Keeno again cut his eyes over at Supreme who smirked and looked down at the floor.

"Oh yeah? You can cover it, huh?"

"Yeah. No doubt. I can cover the loss."

"Okay. That's all good. But when were you going to tell me about what happened? I mean, you lose thirty bricks of my coke and you don't tell me? You know why you didn't tell me? Because you knew you violated. Other than the obvious reasons I just mentioned, you should know by now that you don't put bricks in the hands of eight ball niggas. The shit we are doing is much too serious than to bring someone in who could potentially sink the whole ship. Which is why we have a rule against it. My hustle is serious and it ain't no out on the corner operation, you dig? It's so serious, I came here personally to make sure you understood this can never happen again."

"I know. I know. Yes sir. You are right. That was my fuck up. And like I said, I can cover the loss." Genie looked at him with disgust and shook his head. Keeno just didn't get it. What he did not seem to understand was, no amount of covering with money, apologies or explaining was going to fix this.

"Alright. Now you said you could cover the loss?"

"Yeah. I can cover it."

"Okay. Well, then cover it." Genie looked at him with a deadly serious look on his face.

"You mean right now?" Genie's right eyebrow raised.

"Ummm yeah. Right now. When did you think, next year?"

"Well, I can't cover it right now. I can make a few moves in the street, but I can cover it." Supreme again smiled and looked down at the floor.

This shit is becoming more and more pathetic by the minute, Supreme thought.

"But you just said that you can cover it a few minutes ago, right?"

"Yes sir. I got it. I mean I can get it," he said with a confused look on his face.

"But I want my money now."

At this time Keeno's legs were visibly shaking and he was now on his third cigarette. Now a man lost for words and seemingly all out of chances, his mind raced to come up with something that would defuse this potentially explosive situation. He knew that his boss didn't pay him a personal visit that time of the morning for a conversation, which was a real cause for concern since he typically never saw Genie. The late Danello was the only person within the organization that he always answered to.

"Mr. Smalls, word on my mother and everything that I love, I will have your bread in no time. Word is bond. Please give me the opportunity to clear my face." Genie smiled and looked away.

"Okay. Well, what's no time? When will you have my money? These things have to be covered, you know."

"Give me two weeks."

"Two weeks? You can get me taken care of in two weeks?"

"Yes sir. Maybe even before then," Keeno said with an eagerness in his voice, as if there seemed to be a glimmer of hope. In his mind, he had just talked his way into a reprieve.

"You think I should give him two weeks?" Genie looked over at Supreme and asked.

"Yeah. I think he's good for it," Supreme replied, looking over at Keeno who was now on cigarette number four.

"Alright. Two weeks it is," Genie said as he stood up. "But only two weeks." Keeno's once tensed body had now relaxed somewhat. He was off the hook and given his reprieve.

"Thank you, Mr. Smalls," Keeno said as he stood up to see them out. "My word. I will have your money in two weeks, maybe less." He then looked at Supreme and whispered, "Thank you." Supreme smiled and turned away.

"Okay. That's what it is then," Genie replied as he walked to the door with Keeno following. Just before Genie reached for the door-knob, the back of Keeno's head exploded like a watermelon. Blood and scalp pasted the wall and ceiling as his body collapsed to the floor and began twitching. Supreme lowered his pistol, equipped with a silencer, downward and gave him three more in the head to finish the job before casually tucking the pistol back inside his coat. Standing there stone-faced, Genie wiped a speck of blood from his right cheek with his pocket handkerchief as he looked down at Keeno's body like it was a doormat on the floor. When Keeno's body ceased twitching and his lifeless eyes stared up at the ceiling, Genie walked out with Supreme, leaving him there to have his last thoughts about how he fucked up his life.

A couple of weeks ago, Genie decided that there were a few loose ends that needed tying up due to some oversights on his part. With the demise of Keeno, Danello and a few enterprising Brim gang members, the last loose end had just been tied. Now it was time for things to go back to normal with a new addition to the team. Supreme had just proven his worth to be a part of a deadly serious major crime family that stretched from the east coast all the way to the west coast and in parts of the dirty south. When it came time to kill, he did so without hesitation or reservation, which is a necessary asset for this life. He was now inside and up under the boss of bosses, just as he had envisioned.

CATO

Chapter 17
Between Old Lovers

One of Angela Washington's mother's last wishes was to be cremated and have her ashes, along with her late husband's, blended into a special paint that would be used to paint their portrait and hung on Angela's wall. Although this seemingly macabre concept of burial wasn't the traditional method to black people, or even white ones for that matter, it was nonetheless what her Italian mother wanted.

Just as he had promised, Tony showed up to her mother's memorial services. It had been two years since that painful day at JFK airport when they said their goodbyes. Now Angela was back.

When Tony walked into the community center wearing a black suit with a matching gangster hat, Angela was standing near the people in the food line. As he began greeting a few of her many friends and family members sitting down at the tables eating their food, Angela's tired eyes seemed to perk up and become rejuvenated at the sight of the man she was still very much in love with. After making his way to her, their eyes locked on to each other as the two former lovers smiled.

"Hello, Angela," Tony said in a low somber voice as he embraced her. "Under the circumstances, how are you?"

"I'm fine. Just a little burned out with this whole process." Angela's eyes began to slightly well up with tears. Although she tried to present herself as a picture of strength, Tony could clearly see that she was still grieving, which wasn't hard to do since he knew her better than anyone.

"I can tell," he replied. They both sat down at a table in the back away from the others.

"I reached out to you earlier in the week. I've been here for a few days now. But I'm sure you didn't get my message."

"I know you did. And I would like to talk with you about it later."

"Okay. That's fine," she said smiling. The schoolgirl look of infatuation in her eyes when she looked at Tony had not changed. She was still head over heels about him even after a two-year separation. The feelings she still had for him were as if that separation never took place.

Just as darkness had fallen in Brooklyn Heights Promenade, it felt like old times to Angela as she and Tony walked aimlessly amid the groups of locals walking to and fro while the tourists were viewing the Statue of Liberty and the Empire State building in astonishment. The old emotions she thought she had long since suppressed had started to resurface. Before she came back into the states she had vowed to not allow herself to become caught up in a hopeless situation with a man who had obviously moved on with his life with another woman.

"So how long have you been married, Mr. Stallworth?" Angela asked as they continued to walk. The very question produced a lump in her throat. She knew that in her heart of hearts she was supposed to have the title of Mrs. Stallworth.

"About a year and a half now. That's partly what I wanted to talk to you about," he said as he looked down at the ground with his hands inside his coat pockets. Angela put on a smile and looked straight ahead.

"Wow! You know, I had no idea until I called you and spoke with your wife. She definitely let me know that you were her man now," she said with a slight grin.

"I know," he said smiling. "I was told. But I want to apologize for not telling you myself. This is why I wanted to talk with you."

"Yeah, it's cool. I didn't expect for a man of your caliber to remain single for too long. After all, I was the one who left you behind. But I never imagined that you would marry anyone else but me. I guess I was wrong. And now I know that is why I never allowed myself to go beyond the dating stages with anyone I met while abroad."

"I know. I thought the same thing. I have never met a woman that I would marry except for…"

"Sugar?" Angela said cutting him off.

"Well, yeah." Tony looked over at her as they walked.

"I know if you wanted to marry me you would have, Tony. I guess I wasn't the one and I'm kinda okay with that. I realize that what we had never reached that level. But it wasn't for a lack of me trying. I really wanted that for us. I had never met a man whom I loved as much as I loved you."

"I understand. But it wasn't your fault. It was me. I was the one with the hang up."

"And what hang up was that?"

"Well, I was into some things at that time that I didn't want to involve you in." Angela looked at him with a bewildered look. The entire time she and Tony were together, he never told her about his hustle. Only that he was a traveling salesman of imported goods.

"Oooookay. I'm listening. What were you into that you didn't want to involve me in?" Tony stopped in his tracks and faced her.

"I was into some dirt at that I could not stain you with, Angela."

"Dirt? But you were a traveling salesman, right?" Tony grinned and shook his head.

"Well, not exactly. Well, I was a salesman of sorts, but I was into some other things that I didn't tell you about."

"Like what, Tony?"

"That's not really important now, Angela. All you need to know is, I concluded this is why I never wanted to take things to the next level with us."

"Okay. I see. So basically what you are saying is, it was bad timing."

"Yes. That is what I'm saying." Angela nodded her head as if she understood.

"So I take it that by the time you met this girl, what's her name? Sugar?" Tony nodded. "You were no longer doing dirt."

"Yeah, well, kinda."

"Okay. So are you in love with her?" she asked bluntly as she stood directly in front of him face to face.

"I think that's obvious, Angela. I'm married to her."

"That's not much of an answer," she said with a chuckle. "If you are in love with her why can't you say it." Angela was holding out hope that this new woman of Tony's was just someone who filled the void in her absence. Or in other words, just something for him to do.

"Okay. The truth is, I am very much in love with her." His straightforward reply seemed to jar her and deflate her hopes.

"Wow! Okay. I see. Does she know you are meeting with me here today?"

"Yes. As a matter of fact she does. She kinda demanded it." Angela's head slowly turned away to look at the city's lights.

"Well, I guess all I can do at this point is congratulate you. So congratulations, Tony. I sincerely mean that."

"Thank you, Angela. That means a lot to me." As the two former lovers embraced tightly, Angela could immediately feel the distance. Tony's touch wasn't the same anymore, although she had hoped it would be that she would have a chance to rekindle a flame that once burned as bright as the sun. The fact that it just wasn't there any longer, only added to her grief. It wasn't enough that she had to come home and bury her dear mother. She also had to bury a past love affair and perhaps for good. Although there was an air of finality to his words, she would still take him back if he just said the word.

As they began making the trek back to the car, Tony noticed a suspect looking white man off to his left walking about forty feet away as if he was tracking them. His instincts told him that something about the man didn't say tourist or local, although he was obviously trying too hard to pass himself off as one. After opening the door for Angela to get in his mustang, he went to the driver's side, acting as if he didn't see the man meandering around. Before climbing in, he took an inconspicuous scan of the area and saw that the white man had stopped to take a cigarette break at the gate of the *Promenade*. After cranking the car and driving away from the scene, Tony kept his eyes glued to the rearview mirror to see if this man was going to do what he thought he would. And sure enough, the white man was now on the phone and walking hastily away from the park. His body language and footsteps spoke both urgency and authority.

"Is everything alright, Tony?" Angela asked as she noticed the look on his face as he continued to look behind him.

"Yeah. Everything's alright," he replied as he caught a gap and quickly bolted his way into the oncoming traffic.

"Are you sure everything is alright?" Angela now had a concerned look on her face. She could tell something was wrong.

"Yeah, I'm okay, but I think we are being followed. If we are, can you make it back home?"

"Ummm yeah. But why would anyone be following us, Tony?"

"I'm not exactly sure. But in short, while you were gone I became a very important man, so to speak. And for that reason, I made a few people's shit list. But never mind that right now. If this car continues to tail me, I'm going to let you out at a public place like a hotel or something. And if that happens, I want you to go inside and call one of your friends or a cab to come scoop you up, okay?" Tony continued to look in the mirror intently as if he was anticipating the next turn of events to transpire.

"Okay," she said hesitantly. "If something is going on, Tony…"

"Angela, just do what I tell you, please," he said sternly. "I'm going to get off on this exit and if they are still behind me I'm going to let you out at the nearest safe place. Be ready to jump out." As Tony made his way off the highway and onto an exit, the two vehicles trailing him remained right behind him. As far as he could see there were a total of six men, three in each car. He couldn't make out whether they were Feds or some other hostile actors. His fear was that they were Russians looking to settle an old score over Lavrov. But that was unlikely since he got word from Armando that Lavrov's uncle, the boss of bosses, wasn't interested in pursuing any kind of vendetta. But that still didn't mean shit in the underworld, where revenge and making statements, were just as important, if not more, than making profits.

After pulling into the parking lot of the Ritz Carlton hotel, where the tourists were walking inside with their luggage to be checked in, Tony stopped in front, still looking into his mirrors for signs of the trailing vehicles.

"Angela, I'm going to let you out here. Walk inside like you are a guest and get on an elevator as if you are going to your room, okay?"

"Okay Tony," she said with a serious, but confused look on her face, "Are you going to be okay?"

"Yes, I will be fine. You just do like I said, sweetie. Call your friends, not a cab, to come pick you up and I will touch bases with you later." The two hugged and before Angela got out of the car she kissed Tony on the cheek. As she walked inside, Tony watched her through the lobby's glass doors until she got on the elevator with a crowd of guests and the door closed shut. Sitting there momentarily, all kinds of thoughts went through his mind about Angela's safety if these men who trailed him were in fact hostile actors.

Chapter 18
Dirty Cop

"Sir, do you need valet parking?" a male valet attendant asked Tony as he continued to sit in front of the hotel.

"No, thank you," he said before pulling away. Just as he was about to pull out of the parking lot onto the freeway, and thinking that the men pursuing him were gone, three cars rushed him and blocked him in. Not being able to react to it and avoid being blocked in, immediately he placed his hand on his two gold-plated .45s. Just as he was about to pull them out and go for broke, a tall white man emerged from one of the SUVs that had been trailing him. He held a badge in the air. Two men were beside him and two others sat off in their vehicles looking on intently.

"I'm sure I wasn't speeding," Tony said. "And I know I didn't miss court lately. So what is this?" The tall man holding the badge laughed before putting it back into his pocket.

"No, you weren't speeding. And you haven't missed court that I know of. But try racketeering, drug trafficking and murder. But you didn't do any of that either, did you?"

"Of course I didn't. You obviously have the *wrong* man." Even with the Feds standing around his ride, Tony remained his stoic, cool-headed self. Most cats would have been scared shitless at the very sight of them. Some would have been already spilling their guts even regarding shit they have no knowledge of.

"You *are* Antonio Stallworth, right?"

"Yes. That is me. Am I under arrest or something? Because if I am, let's get the bullshit part where you read me my rights and try to convince me that it is within my interests to cooperate, over with."

"No. You're not under arrest. But it would be beneficial to you and I if we go somewhere and talk. Off the record, of course. Do you have time?" Tony looked around as he wondered what was this man's angle.

"Who are you again? I didn't get your name?" Tony said, monitoring him closely. He had heard about the Russian mafia's tactic of posing as cops to lure in their targets.

"I'm agent Moresco, DEA."

"DEA, huh? Sure. I guess I will attend this off the record meeting. As long as it's off the record." Moresco laughed before waving his men back into their rides.

"Believe you me. It will be off the record. I don't think my people would like the idea of me having a cup of coffee with a black gangster like you they have deemed not only public enemy number one, but a real threat to the quote unquote status quo and balance of power. That's not a good optic for a career fed cat like me who understands that his bread is buttered on both sides of the law." Tony grinned.

Sitting inside a popular Manhattan cafe where they make their own ground hamburgers from scratch, two fed agents who had all the hallmark G-man looks, sat at a table far in the back near a juke box. As they kept a wary eye on the table up front where their superior and Stallworth sat, they took occasional sips from their coffee and made small talk.

"So how is life treating you, Mr. Stallworth, since you were retired?" Tony showed no emotions to the question. He didn't even break a smile. Although he knew that the news of his retirement wasn't exactly a military secret, he wasn't going to confirm anything this Fed pig threw out at him.

"Excuse me?" Tony said with a serious look on his face. Moresco chuckled and shook his head before taking a short sip of his piping hot cocoa with the shot of Hennessy he added to it from the miniature shot bottle.

"You can relax, Stallworth. This is not a roust and it is certainly not a covert proffered interview. Like I said, it's strictly off the record."

"Would you like to order something?" a short blond waitress walked up, smiled and politely asked.

"No, thank you, ma'am," Tony replied.

"Would you like anything else today, sir?" she asked Moresco.

"Yes. Give me one of those cinnamon rolls over there in that case."

"Yes, sir. Coming up."

"Ma'am. Can you warm it for me just a little, please?"

"Sure I can," she said before retrieving his order.

"Listen, Stallworth. I am an expert on you. I have been keeping a tab on you for the last 3 years." Again, Tony remained stoic and unmoved as not to show any worry or concern.

"Is that right?"

"Yes. To give a little background on you just in case you thinking I'm trying to pull that old time cop shit on you. Your father was murdered by a syndicate out of Detroit who tracked him here. Your uncle Walt, who I knew personally, was also murdered by these same people as part of their revenge. Your dear mother died shortly thereafter from a broken heart. And you showed your uncle and father's stock by taking care of the people who harmed them. You are a Marine like me. You were one of the most prolific killers in the Corp while serving in Afghanistan. While in Afghanistan, you were suspected of killing an army soldier who you caught raping an Afghan girl, but they could never pin it on you. Those killing skills you learned in the Corp, you carried with you on the streets and placed them on the open underworld market. The word was, if you wanted someone killed, call Stallworth. I lost track of the marks you took out or those whom I suspected were your handy work. Unlike other arrogant hitters, you never left a calling card or a clue that you were there. The investigators called you Phantom." Tony smiled and nodded his head. "Okay. Recent history - you brought to a tragic end, Nathan Ward and Cat Eye Jones' gangster days, which hurt my pockets a bit, I'm here to tell ya. And you just did the entire state of New York and beyond a favor by ridding the streets of that Russian maniac, Yuri Lavrov, and those genetic defect female attack dog widows of his. Yes, son. I could write your life story I know so much about you." Tony smiled, but did not acknowledge anything he said.

"So what is this about, if you don't mind me asking?"

"It's about you. Your present. Your future. Your survival. See, all this time I have been a friend to you of sorts. In the background, of course. Like a guardian protector angel, if you will. I've been a friend to you by keeping you off the radar screen. I won't lie. It wasn't easy with all the ambitious field agents in the DEA and those arrogant and hungry fed prosecutor fucks in the US Attorney's office looking for a snack to cut their teeth on. But I did it. The moment you knocked Ocho

Rios off the chessboard, to fill the void and take over the city, I was there watching you the whole way. Protecting you."

"Okay. So let's cut through the chase. You wanna be rewarded for your efforts? Or as you say, for being my friend from afar." Moresco chuckled and sipped his laced hot cocoa.

"Yes. Something like that. But the protection and our friendship will be maintained as long as I am fully appreciated of course. I will keep you off the radar screen." Tony laughed and peered out of the cafe's window.

"Hey, I thought you knew all about me to know that I am retired."

"I know you're retired. And I also know that Genie Smalls, your childhood friend and former underboss, is now the boss of bosses, thanks to you."

"Well, assuming you are right, shouldn't he be here sitting in this cafe having this talk with you instead of me? I mean, I'm done." Moresco laughed out loud this time, so much so he spilled some of his cocoa on his white shirt.

"Mr. Smalls is not the type of individual I could approach. He's more of the throwback relic from the past. Or as you guys say, the gorilla type. You, on the other hand, are more of a thinker. More calculated. Not that you are any smarter than he is. You are just the type of man who will always see the bigger picture." Tony paused momentarily before he replied. This man was right 100% about everything he said thus far. Especially that part about Genie's demeanor. Genie was indeed boss material, but he still had a lot to learn about other nuanced dynamics of that title few men enjoy in a lifetime. He had to think more versus reacting first.

"Okay. I tell you what I can do. I will relay this message to Genie for you. Now, I can't make any promises here, but I will do my best." Moresco stared at Tony without even blinking. It was obvious that he was the type of man who didn't take no for an answer. If his terms were not met, someone's life was going to undergo some serious changes.

"Okay, Mr. Stallworth, you do that," Moresco said as he and Tony stood up and shook hands. Just as Tony was about to walk away, Moresco stopped him.

"Hey. What you said earlier about being done with the life. Men like you and me can never be done. It's in our blood. Remember that." Tony stared at him for a second as the profoundness of his words struck him like a bolt of lightning. The question of him being done was something that he had been wrestling with since he decided to once again step aside and let Ike reassume his diamond trade.

As Tony got back into his Mustang and watched Moresco and his fed entourage, which was nothing more than a government commissioned gang, get back into their rides, the magnitude of what just took place was something that he did not take lightly. This was the shakedown of all shakedowns by a seasoned veteran agent of a government agency created to be on the front lines of President Nixon's drug war. A war, which was in reality on black people, according to that war's chief architect and Nixon's domestic policy head, John Ehrlichman. This was one of those situations unlike the run of the mill NYPD cops, Metro pigs, and DA's who were on Tony, and now Genie's, payroll. This was the Feds. The talk Tony was about to have with Genie was the most important one of all. Up until now, Tony only advised him on organizational matters and shit that was street related. This talk was going to be about survival.

For the past 3 weeks, Genie and his woman attended wedding rehearsals and much to his chagrin. A man like Genie who could become bored at a 1980's era Laker's game, didn't take too well with being coached on anything by some pushy white woman who was a perfectionist freak. But he promised his woman that he would attend at least a few of them. This was her thing. If it had been left up to him, they would be saying their vows down at city hall in some room with two people residing over it.

"Mr. Smalls, I'm going to need you to walk upright this time as if you are before the King and Queen of England," the white lady said in an English accent. "Right now you are kind of walking with your head down as if you are picking berries like some immigrant worker from Mexico." Genie's girl chuckled as she looked over at him, just as he was about to blow his top.

"Okay lady. My head is up this time. See?" Genie said with some base in his voice. *A Goddamn drink is what I really need, bitch*, he thought to himself.

"Okay. Now let's try this again," she said. "And remember, not to lean to one side when you walk. We are not out on the street corner hanging with the homies, you know." Before he proceeded on, Genie gave her a look that, if it could kill, he would have a murder rap. *Well, that's where I'd rather be, bitch. On the corner with the homies,* he thought to himself again.

"Okay. Okay. That's it!" she said excitedly. "Keep walking sir and slow down. This is your wife's dream wedding. We don't want to walk to slow and make it seem like you are apprehensive about marrying her. And we don't want you to look too rushed as if you are trying to get the whole affair over with. Steady. Steady. Keep that head up and pretend you are staring at your maker."

Apprehensive is right. That is because I am apprehensive. And everyday that passes I'm becoming more and more apprehensive, Genie thought to himself. His woman was getting a real kick out of watching he and Mrs. Shank's interactions. They were both headstrong people who didn't bite their tongues or have any reservations on barking orders.

"Okay. Splendid, Mr. Smalls! It's about time. Now let us do it again."

"No! Let us not do this again," Genie firmly objected. "Let us, as in *me*, go have a drink. I've done enough tonight. I got to go tend to some business."

"No, Mr. Smalls, you are nowhere near done. I think we should do this at least four more times."

"Lady, I know you are a perfectionist, as I am, but I *said* I'm done for tonight. And when that happens, it's a don dada. End of discussion, you dig?" Genie then made that type of eye contact with his girl that said, *you better get this bitch.*

"Mrs. Shanks, I think Mr. Smalls has had enough for the evening," Tracey said laughing. "I can work on my part some more, however."

"Well, alright. I guess we can stop here with Mr. Smalls tonight," she said reluctantly.

"Alright baby," Genie said before placing a kiss on his girl's forehead. "I will see you back at the crib later on.

"Okay, bae. See you later tonight." Just before Genie walked away he whispered into his woman's ear.

"I'm so sick of her ass." His girl cracked up as he walked away.

Once outside, Genie's soldiers rushed up to him and assumed their protective barriers on each side, in front, and behind. As he was about to climb inside the pearl white Bugatti, he saw Tony's ride sitting across the street.

"Hey, I will be right back," Genie told his main bodyguard, Crenshaw, who held the door open for him to get in.

After walking across the street to Tony's car, Tony rolled down the window.

"How is the rehearsal going, almost married man?" Tony said smiling. Genie cracked a smile, took one last drag from his cigar and threw its remains across the street. When the cigar hit the concrete, the sparks jutted forth before dying a quick death, like a falling star.

"I'm hating every minute of that shit. That's how it's going," Genie said before opening the passenger door and climbing in.

"What's going on, bruh? I know you didn't come all the way here to see how the rehearsals are going?" Tony nodded his head.

"As a matter of fact, I didn't. I have something pretty heavy to lay on you."

"Okay. I'm listening."

"Earlier this evening I had an encounter with this certain fed agent named *Moresco*. Obviously he's been doing his homework on us for some time now. He made a proposition that I think you ought to think long and hard about. Better yet, I think you should accept."

"Oh yeah? And what proposition is that?"

"The kind that you don't refuse, my brother. This agent isn't like the ordinary run of the mill flunky pigs whose palms we have greased over the last few years. This is the DEA we are talking about. A higher up and seasoned vet who been around for a while shaking niggas and Italian mobsters down probably since he was a young field agent." Genie looked unmoved as he looked out of the window at the passing cars.

"So, I take care of him and he will take care of me, aye?"

"Yep. That is the reality. You already know how these things work, bruh."

"Yeah, I know. Seems like every time I turn around some other muthafucka is looking to get his hands in my pockets." Tony chuckled.

"Well, such is the life of a boss, bruh," Tony said grabbing his shoulder. "Here is the fed pig's card." Tony handed Genie Moresco's business card that had the DEA symbol of an all seeing Eagle clutching arrows in one talon that symbolized war and an olive branch in the other that symbolized peace with the title *Department of Justice* ribbon underneath. As he held the card in his hand, Genie stared at it and thought about the utter hypocrisy of it all.

"Are you alright, my brother? Seems like you have some shit on the brain. What's going on?"

"Nothing. Just the life of a boss, I guess," he said in a distant voice before opening the car door. "I will get back at you later, bruh." Genie bumped his partner's fist, stepped onto the pavement, and closed the door as Tony looked at him through the passenger window.

"Okay, bruh. But more importantly make sure you get at that pig. You don't need his kinda drama."

"Yeah. Okay," Genie said dismissively before Tony's car shot from the curb and disappeared up the dark block. As Genie slowly headed across the street to the Bugatti where his men were standing and the SUV that sat behind it with four more men sitting and waiting patiently, he crumbled up the card and threw it to the ground. This was perhaps his answer to Moresco's offer of protection.

Chapter 19
The Chains That Once Bound Us Together

Two weeks later, Genie's bachelor party took place at a huge banquet hall and ballroom in Upper East Manhattan. Over two hundred male guests, including some gangsters, pimps, hustlers, and other square ass civilians, including some politicians and off duty law enforcement, all gawked and made cat calls at the teams of naked females walking around like fantasy French maids up in the private rooms off limits to the public. The only clothing they had, if one would call it that, was a small sequin cloth the size of a half dollar that covered their nipples. These women were all dimes. Some were serving drinks, while others did lap dances. The real go-getters were in back rooms serving up their male guests with pussy and the best fire top head that money can buy. Genie, Tony, Macky Boy, Supreme, Horace and the rest of the family occupied one side of the hall. Amidst the jovial chatter, the music and the other noise pollution inside the ballroom, Tony was about to begin toasting his main man and brother. Standing at the long banquet table while all the others sat, he began.

"Although I thought this day would never, ever, ever, ever come in my lifetime," Tony said as a few chuckles had broken out. "It is none-theless here and it is better late than never. Every King needs a Queen to help rule the kingdom and Genie found his. Sometimes it takes that King a lifetime to find that one woman who can assume the throne next to his. Genie took almost two lifetimes." Again, the entire side of the room broke out in laughter. Genie sat there totally amused puffing on his high priced Cuban cigar that cost as much as dope. "But nonetheless he found her. So to you, my brother, Tracy and maybe a couple of little Genie's running around the castle, I toast and salute." The applause that broke out overshadowed the outside noise. Genie stood up and em-braced his best friend as if this was the last time he would see him.

"Thank you, my brother," he said among the applause and shouts from the distinguished guests. "I love you, man."

"I love you too, my brother," Tony replied. Macky Boy, Horace and Supreme, although they were there for personal reasons and there were enough bodyguards present to protect the gangsters in the building, the three men could not help but to scan the area for possible danger. They looked like three highly trained German Shepherds on high alert and poised for any and all drama to pop off. As with any setting of this type with high-level crime figures in attendance, there was always that air of danger looming over such functions. But there were enough fully armed soldiers there to go to war. Therefore, anyone would be a damn fool to try some gangsta shyt on this night.

While the party went on, a stationary Horace stood near a fountain punch bowl in which a fruity mixed drink flowed in a stream like a waterfall continuously for the guests to imbibe. When Supreme walked nearby aimlessly scanning the room, he caught a glimpse of him and walked up and posted up near him. For a couple of minutes, the two men stood there in silence as if they didn't notice one another as the party rocked on. Finally, Supreme broke the silence.

"Don't I know you from a past life, kid?" Horace casually looked over at him and took his time answering.

"Hey, I'm straight. All the way straight. No offense." Supreme laughed out loud.

"And I should hope so. I don't associate with punks in the joint or out here in the outside world. They're bad luck." Horace gave a cynical nod. "What I'm saying is, I think I know you from the pen. You do time in Florida?" Again, Horace hesitated before answering as he looked around the ballroom at the different people mingling. He also took notice of this cat who had a little too much to drink, harassing and manhandling one of the strippers.

"Yeah. You?"

"Yep. As a matter of fact I have. Attended some of the very best gladiator schools DOC had to offer a young impulsive nigga like me."

"Is that right? Hold on. Be right back," Horace said as he shot across the ballroom in the direction of the drunk dude who was by now, holding the stripper against her will amid her loud protests. He'd had enough of dude and wasn't going to allow his new boss's party to turn into some ghetto hood spectacle.

"Hey, bruh!" Horace said sternly to dude with his hand firmly fixed on his shoulder. "She doesn't want to be here with you. Let her go."

The brother with long dreads, dressed in a white suit and bow tie, turned and looked at Horace with utter contempt.

"And who the fuck are you? Her old man? If so, did you know you got a trick bitch stripper for a woman?" he said laughing belligerently.

"Look, bruh, I know you had a little too much of that oil, but that doesn't excuse rude behavior. This is not the strip club or some hole in the wall function in the hood. Look around you. There are upscale people in here. Important people. Look at yourself. You're even dressed in a nice suit for this occasion. All groomed up with ice on every finger. Act like you have some class, okay? You may luck up and get a job offer."

By this time, Tony, Genie and Macky were all looking on waiting for the next turn of events to transpire. Macky motioned for two security guards to intervene, but Genie waved them off. He wanted to see how Horace carried it.

"Maaaaan, fuck all that! Fuck you and fuck this bitch here!" he said before he attempted to push Horace. The first vicious kick landed to his kneecap made a cracking sound like a board being broken at a karate exhibition. His right knee was no doubt shattered. Then came the bloodcurdling scream as the nerve centers of the brain registered excruciating pain. Then another vicious kick followed to his midsection that folded him over and caused him to vomit up alcohol and the hors'doeuvres he ate earlier. Horace then grabbed a handful of his dreads, viciously slamming his head into a table, disturbing the drinks and food that set atop it. The people in dude's entourage jumped back from the table. Some acted as if they wanted to intervene on their friend's behalf, while others who knew the association of the man who was assaulting their friend waved them off with a warning that this isn't what they wanted to be involved in. After one more hard bang to the table with his head to let him know just how serious he was, Horace immediately dragged him straight to the exit past the guests who all parted ways, giving him a free path to the door to rid a relatively peaceful event of a silly nigga who couldn't handle his liquor or a stripper.

As Horace walked back into the club, the people standing outside stared at the unconscious man lying there on the pavement as a couple of homeless junkies eyes honed in on him like a predator on its prey.

All the jewelry he wore attracted every scavenger in the vicinity. When Horace cleared the door and went back inside, the two junkies didn't waste any time making their move. They made a mad dash to him and within seconds, he was nearly naked. Stripped down to his floral pattern boxers and dress socks. And he managed to sleep through the whole ordeal. Finally, one of the cats in his entourage went outside, gathered him up and took him away from the scene.

"Bravo!" Supreme said to Horace as he walked back in and posted up in the same spot near the streaming liquor fountain. Tony looked at Genie who smiled and gave a nod of approval. Horace had passed the test. He was no doubt a real nail. "I see you handle yourself well. Let's see. If we were at still at Martin Correction, you would have shanked that nigga, right?" Horace looked at him and didn't say a word. "Yeah. That's where I know you from. That quickness, agility and that kung fu shit jarred my memory."

"So you were at Martin, aye?" Horace said chewing his gum and looking around.

"Yeah. Just not long jumped. Well, it's been a little over a year. But it still feels like yesterday. I was the cat who used to run with OG Bobby Rush. Martin CI guru. I was also cool with the cat who you stuck out on the rec yard." Horace gave him a look as if he was expecting some hostilities. The young thug he stuck was one of Supreme's gang underlings. The thought of it seemed to take Horace back to that day when dude tried that gorilla hard con shit with him to impress and prove himself to his homies and ended up being life flighted out. The last thing Horace wanted to do was catch an outside charge with only a few months left before he reached his end of sentence. He even tried to reason with him, but that was only perceived as weakness and capitulation. And in the joint that is the wrong way to be perceived. So after all efforts to avoid the inevitable failed, Horace ran that steel off in him several times with lightning quick speed before dude realized he was being murdered. All that begging he was doing for his life seemed to snap Horace back just as he was about to give him one last coup de gras to the heart. Fortunately, for both he and Horace, he survived the ordeal to learn a valuable lesson in life. The only reason Horace didn't catch an outside charge was because dude carried it like a G and kept his mouth shut.

"Okay. So what's next between you and me? You here to keep it real for your homie and ride for him?" Supreme laughed.

"Hell no. What happened in the joint stays in the joint, you feel me? I'm out here to seek my fortune, not some bullshit gang code. Besides, it looks like you and me are on the same team," Supreme said as he noticed Genie motioning for him to come to his table. "We will catch up later. Maybe chop it up about old times at Martin."

"Yeah. Okay. Later," Horace said with his eyes trained on Supreme as he walked away. Although he didn't let on, he knew exactly who Supreme was, or at least had heard of him. Many of the young cats like the one he shanked, idolized him. He had also heard how the OG took him under his wing and civilized him. But as far as Horace was concerned, a snake never loses his fangs unless someone pulls them out from the root.

At Genie's bachelor party, which was one of those who's who of the gangster world events, Genie decided to introduce his new prospect to Tony.

"Tony, I want you to meet Supreme, one of my new men who is like the son I never had. Supreme this is Tony."

"Yeah, youngster. What's up? Good meeting you. Heard a lot of good things about you," Tony said shaking his hand and looking him directly in his eyes as he seemed to study him.

"Yes, sir. Likewise. I've heard a lot about you, as well. Almost like I know you I've heard so much." Tony smiled.

"Well, don't believe half of it. My man, Genie, here is a great storyteller." By this time Horace had walked over to them as the last guests were being escorted out by the security. Macky Boy had also walked up.

"Hey, Horace, I absolutely loved how you handled that shit earlier," Genie said. "I guess the real nigga shit run in the family, huh?"

"Oh don't mention it. He was drunk, so it wasn't no thang."

"Yeah, no doubt. Have you met my new hire, Supreme here? You and him might be working together on some things."

"Yeah, we've met," Horace replied dryly.

"Yeah," Supreme said smiling. "Come to find out, me and karate kid go way back."

"Oh yeah? How is that?" Genie asked. Tony and Macky looked on with a keen interest.

"We did time together in Florida. This kid here was as quiet as they come, but commanded mad respect. Damn near bodied one of my young protégés," he said with a grin.

"Is that right?" Genie said, looking at Horace.

"Yeah, something like that," Horace said. "But that is all in the past. The one thing I vowed when I left the joint, I left it all behind. Even talking about it." Tony and Macky continued to study the body language between the two men.

"Yeah, I can dig it," Genie said. "Well, that's enough of that shit. Everybody know everybody now, right? Are y'all hungry?

"Nah, I'm good," Horace said.

"I'm good also," Supreme replied.

"Tony? Macky? Y'all hungry?"

"Well, I can use a bite to eat, "Tony replied. "What about you, Macky?"

"No, sir, I don't eat this time of the night." Tony smiled.

"Yeah, there used to be a time I didn't eat this time of the night either, but I guess my old age is making me less disciplined."

Just as they were about to walk out, two white men dressed in tan London Fog trench coats walked in as Genie's soldiers strolled in behind them with a helpless look on their faces. Agent Moresco soon followed.

"Mr. Smalls. Mr. Stallworth. Sorry to barge in and crash what's left of the lucky groom-to-be's bachelor party, and I really would have called ahead of time, but Genie here is a man who don't like to reach out."

"Who the fuck is this? And how did he get in here?" he asked angrily looking at his soldiers. Tony whispered in his ear.

"This is that Fed pig I was telling you about."

"Oh Tony, you didn't tell Mr. Smalls about me? I was certain he knew all about me by now. Well, since you didn't I guess I'm going to have to introduce myself. I'm Brandon Moresco. DEA."

"I know who the fuck you are!" Genie shot back. "Now couldn't you have chosen a better place to see me at?"

"Well, I thought about that. I really did. But I don't think coming to your crib where you and your woman live would have been a good idea. At least not at this point. I mean, where a man lays his head is sacred and should be off limits. That is unless that man's crib has a search warrant signed by a federal magistrate that would believe I had confidential information that Elvis was being held against his will inside your basement." Realizing he was just threatened, Genie gave a smiling Moresco a deadly stare as Moresco's men kept their eyes glued on Genie.

"Okay. I catch your drift," Genie said. "Now what the fuck do you want?" Moresco looked around the room at the men standing around.

"Here? You wanna talk about all that here in front of everyone?"

"Yeah. Why not? I have nothing to hide? Do you?" Genie smiled wickedly.

"What you and I have to discuss is best talked about in private, you catch my drift?"

"Yeah, I catch your drift and you're gonna have to catch me in traffic. I got things to do," Genie said as he got up from the table. "Here is my card."

Genie threw his business card down on the table in front of Moresco before walking out with his men forming a protective barrier around him, with Horace out in front. Supreme took one last look at Moresco and his men before catching up with his boss and mentor. An incensed Moresco picked up the card and looked at it as if he was examining it. He then peered over at Tony with a look of both frustration and resolve on his face before Tony and Macky walked out leaving Moresco and his two men there with the ballroom's clean up crew.

Tony knew Genie was making a big mistake by refusing to play ball with Moresco. But Genie was his own boss now who was just as headstrong and stubborn as ever. The one thing that somewhat concerned Tony was that Genie had failed to make certain adjustments needed to be the boss of the most powerful crime family in the tri-states. All the talking and advising he gave his best friend and brother hadn't quite had the impact on him to finally turn that corner. This alone was a growing cause of concern for Tony. However, with this new element of a persistent DEA agent looking to retire off Genie's success in the streets, only added to his growing anxiety, which had now been magnified tenfold.

Chapter 20
Then you have to keep your eyes on him. All three.

Horace sat at the kitchen table in the darkness taking sips of his steaming hot black coffee and looking down at his reattached finger. It had pretty much healed completely. The pinprick sensations from the nerve regeneration sent intermittent pain signals throughout his body. Luckily for him, the pain had begun to dramatically subside, although the surgeon who repaired it cautioned him that this regeneration process could go on for a year or even years.

Since Horace was a small child, he appreciated darkness and solitude when most kids were afraid of it. Because of this, many thought he was weird or unhinged.....even some in his own family. So while in prison, it was no surprise that he did his best time in solitary confinement, which is known to drive the average minds insane. Breaking the solitude that the dark, quiet kitchen had to offer, Sugar walked in dressed in her pink and white robe.

"What you doing up this early, boy?" she said, playfully pushing his head before walking over to the coffee pot and pouring her a cup.

"I'm up for count," he said jokingly.

"Oh, I forgot you were in the army," she joked. The two chuckled. "But is everything okay? How are you liking it up here in the city?" Horace took a sip and smiled.

"It's just like it was when I was here before. Heavy traffic, assholes and opportunity."

"You know, Tony said he believed you been here before, but I didn't believe it. When did you come here? You didn't come see me?"

"Well, it was some time ago. Like ancient history. And I didn't come see you because I wasn't here on personal time. I was here on let's say, unofficial business."

"Ummm. Well, excuse me then," she said as she punched him in the arm. "So what do you think about Genie?" Horace paused for a second as he again took a sip of his piping hot coffee.

"He's cool. You can tell he's a clone of Tony in some ways. In other ways I question."

"And in what ways you question? Like what?" Sugar said as she analyzed him.

"Well, it's just a few things I noticed about him that is un-Tony like."

"Such as?" Sugar gave him that look as if she expected an answer.

"His circle. I think he needs to do a better job at vetting it. But that's just my opinion. But who I am to question? He's the boss of bosses."

"Okay. That's your observation. But give me some specifics. Is there anyone in particular you are referring to in his circle?"

"Yes."

"Then who?"

"When I was nearing the end of my sentence, I had to stick this fool, as you recall from my letter. I tried everything I could to avoid it. The last thing I wanted to do was catch an outside case and have to do more time. But this crash dummy just kept on trying to lay down the extortion tactic on me on the orders of this ambitious cat who the young gees called New York. Others called him Supreme, a very influential dude with above average intelligence. A pseudo-mastermind type cat. So, eventually I gave the young crash dummy what he was asking for and called out his handler afterwards. I issued him a challenge he had to answer or lose face with the young Gs. But before I got out of the box, fortunately for him and me, he was released, so that ended that drama. Last night at Genie's bachelor party, I walk in to see this mastermind serving as one of Genie's soldiers. Small ass world, aye? From the looks of it, I believe he is being groomed to be Genie's right hand."

Sugar sat there for a minute trying to take in what she had just heard.

"Have you said anything to Tony or Genie about this?"

"No. Absolutely not. It's not my place. I am a newcomer. Besides, Genie seemed to be pretty fired up about him. He's got him pretty close up under him for some reason. Other than that, I can't truly judge him on how he was in prison, because that is not necessarily indicative of what and who he is now. I never knew the man personally to form an opinion about him other than that situation. I just knew of him. He was just like any other cat inside who wanted to get through captivity, including myself. The only difference between me and someone like him was he hungered for power even inside. I just wanted to do my bid and get the fuck back home to my peeps."

"So although you don't know this person, what is your gut telling you about him? I asked that because during the time I ran things for Tony in his absence, if there was a question about a person in the organization, he would often asked me what was my gut telling me. What is your gut telling you about this Supreme, bruh?"

"My gut is telling me that he is just as or more ambitious than he was inside. And that isn't something that changes just because you're out here on the turf."

"Then you have to keep your eyes on him. All three. Right now you don't have anything else to go on but your gut instincts. Listen to them, okay?" she said placing a kiss on his forehead. "And you take care of yourself and take nothing for granted and underestimate no one." Horace nodded his head.

"Hey sis," he said before she walked out of the kitchen.

"Yes?"

"You still haven't told me the story about how you were once a boss Queen," he said with a chuckle. "I wanna hear every detail."

"Maybe one day you will read about it," she joked. "Then again, maybe you will see it for yourself live and in living color." Sugar winked her eye and exited the dark kitchen, leaving her brother to resume his solitude.

CATO

Chapter 21
Your Problems Is My Problems

Inside his huge heated Olympic size pool, Genie laid back relaxed on a float, sipping on some yack, as his soldiers dressed in suits and armed with assault rifles and machine gun pistols strapped across their shoulders, stood guard with a wary eye. As the music played the old school 2 Pac joint, *Thug Mansion,* Supreme walked up and took a seat in one of the patio chairs next to the pool.

"What's good, O.G.?" Supreme said as he bumped his fist. Supreme marveled over the spectacle. This was the life he dreamed about in his bunk every night and that he was hell bent on having.

"You see it! Enjoying the fruits of my labor. What you got going, youngster?"

"Hell, hustling and trying to get like you." Genie chuckled.

"That may be a mistake trying to get like me. I've got all kinds of problems, especially as of late."

"Oh yeah? And what's that, O.G.? What kinda problems is that? You already know that your problems is my problems." Genie fired up a cigar and took a couple of drags from it.

"I got this agent on my heels. Fed fuck boy." Supreme's right eyebrow raised with concern. The mention of the Feds to any drug dealer would get that type of reaction every time.

"The Feds? What the Feds want with you, O.G.?"

"Hell, what all those muthafuckas want? A pig is a pig to me. He wanna eat off the fat of my labor like the others."

"Damn! So is he leaning on you or sumpin'?"

"Yeah. Kinda."

"Well, why don't you go ahead and grease the cracker's palms? Ain't but one way to handle that."

"Yeah, I considered it, briefly. But if I do that, what other enterprising pig gonna come outta the gutter to dig off in my pockets? See, the direction I'm leaning, I ain't going to give that pig shit! I don't like the idea of giving any of them my money as it is already. That is something that Tony put into place when he was running this thing."

"Yeah, O.G., I feel ya on that. But we aren't talking about some ambitious gang leader laying down the extortion bit. Or even the regular pigs. We are talking about the Feds here. And sooner or later you're gonna have to handle that, right?"

"Yeah. Sooner or later I'm going to have to handle it alright," Genie said with a maniacal grin as he sipped on his yack and looked off into nothingness. What went through his mind regarding how he was thinking about handling the situation was actually something that went against all the rules of the street among gangsters of all stripes, save the Mexican cartels who didn't have any compunctions or rules against killing DEA agents. At that moment Genie had visions of violating that rule and doing away with that situation altogether, the old fashion way. In other words, he was considering murking the agent rather than pay him.

"O.G., Listen, mayne! I know you are the boss and had this whole thing figured out way before I showed up, but what I saw in your eyes just then, I wouldn't feel right if I didn't advise you against it. Not even the Italians murk fed boys. NYPD or metro, yes. But to body a DEA agent, that might be the end game for you and everyone else involved. So respectfully, I strongly advise you against that, if that is what you are thinking." Genie smiled. He admired Supreme's willingness to speak up to him bluntly. To him, that showed leadership.

"Son, I ain't gone lie. That is exactly what I was thinking," he said laughing. "But it was just a fleeting thought. But here is what I want you to do. I want you to trail this cracker and find out everything about him, just in case I change my mind. From his family to his friends to his side bitches and even where he tricks at. I want you to find out, you dig? And take pictures, videotape the transactions, or whatever. Imma keep an ace in my pocket just in case."

"Yes sir. Already. Consider it done." Just as Supreme was about to walk off, Genie called him.

"Hey, youngster."

"What's up, O.G.?"

"Way to think on your feet and see the bigger picture. I need thinkers like you on my team."

"No doubt, O.G. I didn't get this far by not using the skin a wise old O.G. named Bobby Rush put on my head."

Over the next couple of months, and after finally seeing the wisdom in Tony's example of paying the pigs off to rest easy at night, Genie put agent Moresco on the payroll and true to Moresco's word, no heat from the Feds came his way, even though a few more bodies entombed in burned out cars showed up in alleys around the city. Other than that, all was well. The state of the streets was relatively quiet and prosperous, thanks in large part to Supreme and Horace who had more than proven their worth to the family. Genie had even paired them together on a few occasions, sent on missions as a team to put in work on a few enterprising niggas out of Baltimore who had watched one too many episodes of *The Wire* and tried to set up shop on the east side without Genie's blessing. And they handled it like the consummate professionals they were. Although Horace had become somewhat used to the idea of working with the man who tried to have him extorted back at Martin, and even warmed up to him enough to hang out with him from time to time, he kept his guards up and his third eye open at all times, just as Sugar had urged him to.

CATO

Chapter 22
Friends, Enemies, and Allies

At the Gentlemen's Club on Surf Avenue, the music blared from the club's speakers as teams of big booty girls walked back and forth from the dressing room to the stage while the security kept their eyes peeled for niggas getting out of line. Taking in an eye full of the fleshly creatures of all shapes, sizes and shades that swarmed around the club to separate dope cats and square ass niggas alike from their bread, Supreme and Horace sat at the table in the back corner with a bottle of chilled Dom in front of them.

"Horace, you look as out of place as the O.G., Mr. Smalls, was when I took him to another spot," Supreme said laughing.

"Bruh, you are right on that," Horace said with a chuckle. "I haven't been to a strip bar since I took a trip to Miami."

"And how long ago was that?"

"Shit, right before I did that ten year stretch."

"Yeah, I can tell. Loosen up, man. You kinda cramping my style, here." Horace chuckled. "Here. You want one of these big booty bitches? Take your pick. Hey baby," Supreme yelled and motioned to a Rican girl who would put Jennifer Lopez to shame. "Come here a second." The Rican girl, walking on red pumps that made her look like one of those legendary Amazon warrior females, sashayed her way over to them as if she was walking the runway.

"Hey Papi! What's up?"

"Shiiiid. You baby," Supreme said as he inspected her from her head to her toes. "Give my man here some attention."

"Sure Papi. But is he lame or sumpin?" she said looking at Horace flirtatiously. "Like, can he talk?"

"Hell yeah my man can talk. Girl, you are in the presence of a very important man. You better recognize."

"Okay, daddy. So how important are you? Are you too good or too important to get a private dance in the back?" Horace took a sip of his Dom and looked over at Supreme. Supreme smiled, shrugged his shoulders with his hands in the air and took a sip from his glass as if to say, *your move, son.*

"No. Not all," Horace said before she immediately took him by the arm and led him to the back rooms where broads were either giving the customary lap dances or giving a l'il sumpin' sumpin' extra.

While Horace was in the back, Supreme went to the bathroom to make a phone call.

"Tomorrow night at the Home Depot off DeKalb in Brooklyn," Supreme said into the phone as the song, *Devils* by L'il Boosie played from the club's speakers.

One of the investments that Genie made after he assumed power over the organization was he opened a few Home Depot hardware stores across the city. One on DeKalb, Hamilton, and U Avenues in Brooklyn. One in Manhattan on Bronx Terminal and others spread out throughout the city. These businesses didn't just serve as great investments to wash Genie's dirty money. They were also used to move his product and money. It was the perfect setup for a drug trafficking business. Imported wood and other building supplies coming in and out of the country over the water in cargo ships in which over 90% of them went either uninspected or under inspected like it's been for decades since the Italians controlled it. Now under the auspices and control of this new black gangster on the block, things ran with the same smoothness and efficiency.

Chapter 23
Let this be the last time you pull strap on me and don't use it.

After the last incident where the youngster Rico was kidnapped and robbed, Genie made sure from that day forward that all drop offs and pickups would be heavily monitored and guarded by soldiers far and near. For this shipment of 190 bricks, which was a pretty large order for a Eastern European crime syndicate who put down in Europe, Genie decided to employ the services of the organization's greatest rising star.

"Hey, youngster," Genie said to Supreme. "I have requested for someone to accompany you on that thing tonight."

"O.G., with all due respect, I can handle that on my own."

"Yeah, I already know you are more than capable. But this is a new account we have and so I have a lot riding on this one and wanna make sure shit goes off with no drama."

"Yeah okay. But haven't I made sure shit was straight on the previous ones?"

"No doubt. But this one is different. If this first one goes well, this will be our best customer. I mean, they are copping nearly 200 on this one. This is what we are transitioning to."

"Aight, O.G. Who teaming up with me?"

"Someone you haven't worked with before. Our best and brightest. Macky, come in," Genie yelled. Macky Boy walked into the room and sat down at the bar next to Genie with the same unpretentious air he's always had about him. "Macky, this is Supreme, Supreme, Macky." The two killers in their own right shook hands. "Macky, I know you guys hadn't really been properly acquainted before, but Supreme here is my young protégé and understudy," Genie said. "Keep him straight." Genie smiled. Macky nodded and looked at Supreme, not once taking his eyes off him, which was how he looked at everyone, as if to study and analyze them.

Sitting in the parking lot across the street from Home Depot, Macky, Supreme and two soldiers sat inside a four door black Jeep Wrangler with dark tints with their heads trained on the doors waiting for the dollies of crates to come out. At different points a short distance away from the store, there were white men sitting in various vehicles who had that unmistakable European look. They were obviously there to ensure the success of the transaction on their boss's end. Genie's fear was, if something went wrong, it could trigger an incident and lead to another war that no one needed. Having something go wrong with a new account with big timers was the least of his worries. And this is why he brought in Tony's young protégé and killer who was a sure lock to be the next boss of bosses.

"Hey, I need to go take a leak," an anxious Supreme said.

"No. You are going to have to hold it until after this exchange is made," Macky said sternly looking him in his eyes.

"Hey, kid. I'm a grown ass man and not some kid. I told you I have to take a leak and that is what I'm going to do." Before Supreme could open the door, he heard the unmistakable sound of a round being chambered. When he looked down there was a pistol equipped with a silencer pointed at his midsection. He then looked up to see Macky's eyes trained on him like a Cobra poised for a strike.

"Like I said, you wait 'til this is over and then you go take a piss. Do you understand me, Mr. Supreme?" Supreme knew this man meant business. Being a killer in his own right, he recognized that same unmistakable trait in others. And what he saw in Macky's eyes wasn't a bluff. Almost always, when he pulled strap someone died. And the only reason why he wasn't dead yet is because of the politics involved. He was Genie's understudy. A peon or someone who didn't matter would have been bodied.

"Okay. I see ya point, bruh," Supreme said with his hands in the air. "But let this be the last time you pull strap on me and don't use it." Macky grinned.

"If there's ever a next time you won't know anything about it," Macky replied with his dark eyes trained on him. Just as Supreme sat back in his seat like a kid who had been chastised by his parents, two vehicles with dark tints pulled into the parking lot momentarily. Macky's eyes rotated between the two vehicles and Supreme as if he was trying to make the connection, while the soldiers inside Macky's vehicle clutched their automatics with their eyes locked in on the vehicles ready to handle whatever was about to take place. When four of the hulking European goons stepped out of their ride to confront the two vehicles and donned the guns inside their suit jackets, the two SUVs pulled off just as fast as they had pulled in. Perhaps intimidated by the goons, they decided to take flight. Then again, maybe the person who set up the jack wasn't on cue and they became spooked. The entire time Macky had his eyes and his gun covertly trained on Supreme who was unaware of it. Unbeknownst to him, if he had made one wrong move, breathed the wrong way, or even acted like he was with those cats, he would have been the first to die.

"Friends of yours?" Macky asked.

"I don't have any friends," Supreme shot back.

When the vehicles disappeared out of sight, Macky pulled back his gun and placed it back into its holster while he and Supreme continued their stare down.

As the load was delivered and the new European account sealed, Macky motioned to his soldiers that it was done.

"Alright, driver. Let's go," he said with his eyes still locked on Supreme.

From that point on Macky didn't trust him. His instincts told him that those niggas who rode through that parking lot were commissioned by him to take the load, and if it had not been for him being there, it would have gone down, which is exactly why Genie wanted him there. For that reason, and having a gun pulled on him, Supreme automatically disliked Macky although he respected him to the utmost. But in this life they chose, respect was the goal and whether someone liked you or not didn't mean shit. People who are liked, and even loved, were betrayed all the time. But the type of respect born out of fear, people think twice about fucking with you or fucking you over. From this point on these two killers, who had much in common, were like oil and water.

CATO

Chapter 24
All Bets Are Off

Two weeks before Genie's wedding, he and Tracey went out to eat dinner and listen to some live jazz at her favorite spot, Dizzy's Jazz Club. Flanked by the soldiers, Genie and his bride to be strolled to a reserved table arm in arm in the back of the club. After taking their seats, the four soldiers all dispersed and posted up at their own tables facing the front door.

After getting their drink orders, the musicians came off intermission and resumed playing their smooth jazz tunes from the older sets of legends such as Thelonious Monk, Miles, Dizzy Gillespie, Coltrane, Mingus, Blakey, to the new school artists Bilal, Kenny G, Glasper, and Marcus Hill.

"Bae, you are really going to like this band here!" Tracey said excitedly. Tracey, whose father was a well known jazz musician and mother a back up singer, was a huge jazz fan and had pretty much converted Genie, who was still on 90s hip hop. "These cats here used to play with my father."

Just as the fourth set of music started and the bus boys raked the remaining plates, utensils, and food scraps off the table and into a bus pan, a redheaded white man, who had been sitting at a table on the other side of the club with a female and two other white men dressed in suits, wandered over to Genie, who had taken notice of his interest in him damn near from the time he and Tracey sat down at their table.

Standing there in front of Genie and his woman, the white man who was obviously drunk stared down at them.

"Excuse me," Genie said. "You are blocking our view."

"Mr. Smalls," the redheaded white man said smiling. "I didn't know a man like you was into jazz. I always thought cats like you was into gangsta rap."

"Who is this man?" Tracey whispered to Genie. By this time the soldiers got up, but were waved off by Genie who didn't want to make a scene, per Tracey's prior request. It took a second, but Genie recognized the white man as one of the DEA cat Moresco's field agents. Or more accurately, one of his dirty cop goons.

"He's nobody," Genie said condescendingly. "Hey, I'm only going to tell you one more time that you are blocking my view. Now please don't make me raise up from this chair. If I do, we ain't gone be rapping." The cop totally ignored Genie's warning.

"I'm Mr. Small's business partner, so to speak," he said to Tracey and totally disregarded Genie's warning. "Genie, why didn't you tell us about this lovely lady. Perhaps we could have included her in our deal," he said with a chuckle. Almost as soon as he said it, an incensed Genie shot up from his chair as if he was launched from a cannon. The first swing was like a blur as the pistol cut through the air and landed on the side of the agent's head that sent a spatter of blood and hair on Tracey's sequins white dress and on the face of the white lady sitting at the table over. Before the agent could get to his feet, another blow crashed down on his head. When the musicians realized the disturbance, they stopped the music after realizing what was going on just as a few screams began to replace the music. As the groggy agent tried once again to get to his feet, the soldiers rushed the table while Tracey frantically tried to stop Genie.

"Genie!" she yelled as the entire club of petrified onlookers stood with their backs to the wall as they let out a collective gasp at what they were witnessing. Totally ignoring his woman and standing the semi-unconscious white man up to his feet, Genie deliberately slapped him one more time with the pistol that sent more blood and red hair across the room, while the soldiers stood there as if they were afraid to intervene. The agent's three friends also stood there helpless as Genie's hulking soldiers warned them not to move.

"Genie! Genie!" Tracey kept screaming trying in vain to hold his arm. "You're going to kill him! Please, bae! Don't kill him!" Her pleas seemed to snap him back in reality.

"I'm not going to kill this muthafucka!" he replied. "Listen here, white boy! Don't you ever fucking disrespect me like that again in front of my woman. And tell your bitch ass dirty fed pig boss our little arrangement is over and he have your dumb ass to thank for it!" He then gritted his teeth and delivered a hard kick to the unconscious agent's ribs. "No muthafucka controls me!" he said angrily as he administered one last hard kick that moved the unconscious man's body and made a thudding sound. With every kick, the club's patrons let out gasped. Genie turned to a hysterical Tracey.

"Come on, baby. Let's go!" he said as he grabbed her by her arm. "Let's get the fuck outta here!"

As Tracey passed by the bloody white man she looked down at him with sympathetic eyes as she cried. The club's owner and his security stood frozen in one place and didn't say one word to Genie, as he Tracey and the soldiers all passed by them and exited the club, and they knew not to.

At this point it was safe to say that all bets were off between Genie and Moresco. For weeks Genie had been lamenting over having to make a deal with Moresco and had even considered reneging on it, followed by his untimely death a thousand times, but kept his eye on the bigger picture Tony often talked about. An ambush outside his home or his car exploding once he cranked it up, would have been easier to live with than being extorted like some low level chump on the corner. But again, he relented for the sake of the bigger picture. However, this incident in which one of Moresco's flunkies was of the mistaken belief that the arrangement between a crime boss and his boss somehow empowered him over a man who could on his orders have him and his whole family murdered was a deal breaker. This was the proverbial last straw for Genie. All bets were now off and like it or not, Tony would just have to accept it.

CATO

Chapter 25
A Bride for an O.G.

The day was November 23, and the venue was the Abyssinian Baptist Church in Harlem where Tracey and pretty much her entire family were baptized as shorties. The last few wedding guests braved the winter chill to scurry into the church, while the trench coat wearing soldiers, with walkie talkies in hand, lined the streets with their heads on swivels. The cars that spilled over from the church's parking lot, lined the street for nearly three city blocks, reminiscent of a celebrity funeral procession. The last time Harlem had seen this much fanfare was at Malcolm X's funeral.

A team of white Clydesdale horses, fastened to a white, silver, and gold carriage, that would transport the bride and groom to an awaiting plane that would take them to their honeymoon destination, stood restless. Their stagecoach driver, dressed in all white attire, including matching white gloves, sat high up trying to keep them calm and reassured with soft words and an occasional tug of the reigns. Inside the huge historic black church, filled with wall to wall patrons, Genie's day of reckoning, as Tony jokingly termed it, was finally underway. Standing there beside a clearly nervous Genie was his best man, Tony, steadily teasing him under his breath that his days of whoring and womanizing was now at an end. Not lost on Sugar, she gave them an occasional eye roll. The groomsmen consisted of Macky, Supreme, Horace, Sugar's bodyguard, Yancey, the late Cassadine's younger brother, Benzini, who had just been hired on. Other guests included a few friends and associates of Genie. Tracey's mother, an aunt and three sisters served as her bridesmaids, while her wheelchair bound father gave her away.

The pomp and spectacle of this occasion rivaled any celebrity or head of state wedding. Everyone in the church obeyed the dress code of white, royal blue, silver and gold. The small school age flower girls littered the isle with pink, red and white rose petals and carnations. And the clergyman dressed in all white robe with silver and gold trim and matching cufflinks, stood there stoically awaiting the arrival of the bride Queen. The various men sitting in the church pews were like the who's who of the gangster world. Perhaps the only time this many hoodlums came under the roof a church was to attend the funeral of one of their fallen comrades or associates.

"Ain't no sense in you sweating now, nigga," Tony smiled and whispered to Genie.

"Shut up, Stallworth," Genie shot back. "You think it would be proper for me to take a swig from my flask?"

"Ummm hell no! You brought your flask into the church with you, Genie?" Tony said with a chuckle. He could hardly contain his laughter.

"Yup. Sho' you right! Hell, Jesus made wine! I got my trusted silver bitch right here in my right pocket." Tony nearly burst out laughing. The guests, and even Sugar, noticed the sidebar conversation going on between the groom and the best man. Sugar gave Tony the side eye as she pretty much knew they were over there clowning.

"I ain't playing, Stallworth. I am real tempted to pull it out and take a shot to the head straight like that."

"Genie, don't do it! I know you are crazy enough to do it, but I'm telling you, bruh, don't do it," Tony said in a chuckle. "Think of Tracey."

"Hell, thinking of her is why I need a drink." Tony almost laughed out loud, but managed to place his hand over his mouth, hiding his laughter behind a fake cough. Again, Sugar gave him the side eye at their shenanigans. When he nodded and tilted his head towards Genie as if to say, *it's him*, he read Sugar's lips, "Would you two cut it out," she said shaking her head.

"It's him," Tony whispered. Again, Sugar shook her head and looked towards the entranceway to see the first bridesmaid and groomsmen, signaling the coming of the bride. Seconds later, Tracey, dressed in a beautiful white wedding dress accented with gold and silver awnings, slowly walked arm in arm with her father, as he maneuvered his electronic wheelchair, towards her husband as the instrumental version of *Forever* by Regina Belle and James "JT" Taylor, played by the band Genie hired. With both pairs of eyes locked on one another, and the guests' eyes locked on them, Genie took his place beside his bride and the long awaited wedding of the boss of bosses, Brooklyn's own black gangster, began.

After a few minutes and a few relevant words, that culminated with the mandatory kiss, and in keeping with Genie's request that this thing was short and sweet, the event was over and he and his bride walked arm in arm, followed by a cheering crowd, to the horse carriage to bring a fairytale ending to their day. Just as they climb on, a herd of unmarked vehicles rushed the scene and surrounded the carriage, followed by white men with guns who hopped from their cars and began pointing their guns at the carriage and its scared shitless driver who had his hands held high in the air. This was obviously more than he had bargained for. Then came the customary, age old introduction.

"Eugene Smalls, you are under arrest!" a voice said through the loud speaker as the shocked guests looked on with keen interest. Tony, Macky, Yancey, Sugar, Supreme and Horace also looked on. "Exit the carriage and come out with your hands up!" Smoking a cigar, Genie peeped his head out of the carriage and pulled off his shades to see pump shotguns, assault rifles and Glocks pointed at him. As he climbed down, the fed boys moved in with their guns steadily trained on him.

"What the fuck is this shit?" Genie asked scathingly. A smiling agent Moresco and the agent Genie brutalized, who still wore the scars, bandages and wires in his jaw from the night he nearly lost his life over a slight, emerged from the crowd of the gun wielding cops.

"Now Mr. Smalls. You know what this is. This is your day of reckoning," Moresco said as Tracey peeped her head out of the carriage and stared over at her newlywed husband with tears in her eyes. This is not how she wanted her special day to end. As Tony and Genie's organization looked on helplessly, a DEA agent placed the cuffs on Genie. Moresco then looked over at Tony and pointed his finger at him as Genie was being led away. Accompanied by four armed agents, Moresco then walked over to the crowd of shocked guests.

"Mr. Stallworth, surely you don't think your partner in crime is going down by himself, do you?" Tony stood there stone-faced and ready for whatever. "Wouldn't be quite right since you two are joined at the hip in criminality. You're under arrest too, Antonio Stallworth."

Cuff him," Moresco turned and said to the agents. Sugar stepped out and began her protests.

"What the fuck is this? Tony, you will be out by tomorrow," she said confidently.

"Nope. Only if he breaks out of jail. Or, he decides to cooperate," Moresco said with a chuckle.

"Well, that ain't happening, cracker!" Tony shot back. "Bae, just be cool and hit up Goldman." Aaron Goldman was Tony's Jewish lawyer he'd had on deck for a few years.

"Okay bae," Sugar yelled as the Feds led her man away. For her this felt like deja vu when Tony was arrested and led away by the Feds for Nathan Ward's murder at JLK coming off their honeymoon vacation. The only difference, this time was her stint as a boss Queen over the organization, she knew what to do and knew not to panic. She was now built for this shit and would possibly have to make her return.

Chapter 26
Hold Without Bond

Within the mandatory 48 hours of being brought before a federal magistrate, Sugar, Tony's lawyer and Genie's wife, Tracey, appeared at the arraignment in federal court. On the other side of the courtroom was agent Moresco sitting with a few of his field agents behind the federal prosecutor assigned to the case.

"All rise!" the marshal said as everyone in the courtroom rose to their feet when the magistrate who looked 100 years old, meandered in and took a seat behind his podium.

"Okay. Let's get right down to the business at hand," the magistrate said looking down at the paperwork over his glasses. He didn't waste anytime doing what he does, which was to deny black and brown defendant's bond.

"Your honor, the government simply asks that Mr. Eugene "Genie Boy" Smalls and Antonio "Tony" Stallworth be held without bond. They are a flight risk since they are looking at a life sentence if convicted, and not to mention an extreme danger to the community. We have a couple of wiretaps, surveillance footage and witnesses who will cooperate when that time comes." The judge looked down at Tony and Genie's lawyer who remained calm the entire time as if the case was bullshit.

"Mr. Goldman," the judge said.

"Your honor, first of all, this case is laughable. So much so, that I seriously doubt that any grand jury will indict, let alone a trial jury will convict. The only evidence, if you want to call it that, is that the government has is a couple of wiretap conversations that may not mean anything. And a few rule 35 snitches, who are more than likely trying to work off their charges wrought by their own criminality. My clients are both lifelong pillars of the community. They were both raised and schooled in Brooklyn. Mr. Smalls is a respected businessman who has employed many people within the community. My other client, Mr. Stallworth, is a highly decorated war vet who served this nation with distinction. He has no record other than a charge when he was a juvenile that was sealed after he agreed to go into the Marines. He is also a businessman who has business ties in the all five boroughs. His grocery stores employ hundreds of people within the communities. These men are not a danger to the community and neither are they a flight risk. Nothing in the records suggest otherwise." The judge looked down at the paperwork in front of him before taking a sip of coffee.

"Well, what about this manslaughter charge in Mr. Smalls' jacket?"

"Your honor that charge was later dropped after it was determined by a thorough investigation that Mr. Smalls acted in self defense."

"Yes, but he was nonetheless charged with it."

"Your honor, for God's sake, he was assaulted by two knife wielding men. He did what the law allowed him to do, which was to defend himself with deadly force."

"Yes, your honor," the federal prosecutor interjected. "But the law did not allow for Mr. Smalls, or any other civilian in New York, to possess or carry around a firearm. And in this present case a firearm was used on an off duty DEA agent who was brutally beaten by Mr. Smalls at a nightclub." The judge looked back through Genie's jacket.

"Well, I'm going to hold both of them without bond this time. The question of them being a danger to the community I'm not concerned about so much as I am that they are a flight risk. These charges of conspiracy carry enough time to motivate one to flee the country rather than face the music." Tony and Genie's lawyer shook his head in disgust while the prosecutor grinned. The judge's words were music to his ears. Chances are, there was no way he would let them out on pretrial release.

"This is the worse fucking hearing I've ever been involved in," the Goldman whispered to Tony and Genie. "This old fuck magistrate should have been retired 40 year ago. Or better yet, croaked." Tony and Genie chuckled. Even though they were going back to confinement at least until the next hearing in front of a district judge who would more than likely cut them loose, they still managed to find a little levity in the situation. Tony looked over at Sugar who remained calm. She had been this way before. Tracey, however, the look she had on her face spoke what her mouth did not. She was nearly devastated when the judge denied bond. A white collar, clean cut black woman from an upper middle class family in Rhode Island, of all places, she wasn't used to the gangsta shyt.

Genie looked at her and whispered, "I'll be okay." She gave a half smile and nodded her head.

As Tony and Genie were led out of the courtroom by two marshals, a smiling Moresco walked in close proximity to them so they could see his face. Neither of them even bothered to look his way to give him the satisfaction. To them, he was just another dirty, piece of shit cop.

CATO

Chapter 27
A Place of Captivity

The Metropolitan Detention Center in Brooklyn, New York is in essence a big county jail. Run by the Bureau of Prisons for the Feds, this nine floor, two-sided jail holds about 3,000 prisoners in various stages of the criminal justice system process. The buildings housed pretrial inmates, the newly arrested or indicted, those on federal writs, those just sentenced and awaiting designation to a federal prison, prisoners who are in transit transferring from one prison to another, work-cadre prisoners who were close to being released, INS detainees awaiting deportation, and snitches who were putting in work for the US Attorney's office and couldn't be placed safely anywhere else. Federal inmates called it a holdover facility.

When Sugar walked into the visitation booth she got a feeling of deja vu all over again from when Tony was in Rikers. Although the feel of the place was a little different, it was nonetheless a place of captivity where some people were awaiting the news that they weren't ever going home again.

After the guard escorted Tony to the glass window, he sat down in the booth and placed a kiss on the glass window.

"Hey, baby girl! What's good?"

"All is well," she smiled and replied placing her own kiss on the glass. "Where is Genie? Is he in the same unit with you?"

"No. Not yet, but I'm working on that. We got folks in here."

"Okay. Good. I made all the arrangements to make sure you are straight in here. I spoke with the lawyer and he told me that your hearing is set for next month in front of the district judge. He said the case is straight bullshit." Tony laughed.

"He didn't need to tell me that. I know it's bullshit. And so does that prosecutor and that DEA agent."

"Yeah, I know. But how can they just bring a case like this without any real evidence?"

"Baby girl, these are the Feds we're talking about. They are the most corrupt entity on earth. They can bring any case they want, even if it is pure bullshit. And they have the knack for making it stick because of all the resources and snitches at their disposal. They do this all the while they are in the drug trafficking business themselves. I know this for a fact, because while in the Marines I worked with DEA on their so-called drug interdiction missions. They are not a drug enforcement agency, but a drug regulating agency. In other words, they determine who can traffic dope and who can't. They have more field offices around the world than the CIA for that purpose. That DEA agent Moresco, is just one more piece of shit pig who wanted to get his palms greased. And this is what this whole thing is about."

"Really?"

"Yes."

"Well, why didn't Genie…"

Tony cut her off and put his finger to his lips for her to be quiet. The Feds were notorious for monitoring phone calls and visits in jail, which some niggas have found that out the hard way after being indicted over a one minute jailhouse phone conversation.

"Because he's a fucking hot head, not to mention an idiot at times," Tony said angrily. Sugar shook her head.

"Well, is there anything you need me to do, bae?"

"As of right now, no. But wait. There is one thing."

"And what's that?"

"Have the youngster look in on a few things. I wanna make sure that this situation is what it is with no surprises, you dig?"

"Sure, bae. I gotchu. But, bae, well, I'm not going to get into that."

"What's that, baby girl?"

"Horace and I had a conversation. But again it can wait." Tony monitored her as if he was trying to read her mind. He knew not to press on with it out of fear of them being recorded and have something used against him later.

"Okay, baby girl. Just holla at the lawyer about it and he will relay it to me."

"Okay, bae. Is there anything else I can do?"

"No, baby. At least not yet. But if and when that time comes, you will know it."

As Tony was being led away by the guard, Sugar's mind drifted back to his days at Rikers. To see her King being led away like some animal in a zoo was just as heartbreaking now as it was then. As the door closed behind Tony and the same feeling of anger and frustration returned, she renewed the same vow as the last time. Whatever needed to be done to ensure her man's life and his freedom, it was going to be done, no questions. Or she would die trying.

***

In another visitation booth on a separate floor, Supreme sat waiting for Genie. When Genie finally came out Supreme smiled and bumped the glass with his fist.

"What's up, O.G.?"

"Hell, you're looking at it, son," Genie said as he sat down on the metal stool.

"Yeah, I feel you, O.G. But what are they saying?"

"A whole bunch of bullshit. That's what they're saying. But listen. We ain't gone talk about that, because there's nothing to discuss, you dig? I wanna keep this short and sweet. You're in charge now, son.

"Huh?" Supreme asked with a bewildered look on his face.

"You're in charge. You are it now, son. At least until this shit blows over. I need you to run my businesses. Don't want them to go under in my absence. Are you up to the task, youngster?" Genie asked as he monitored him carefully.

"Sure, O.G. Whatever you need me to do. I'm here. But I have one question for you. More like a concern."

"Okay. And what's that, son?"

"You know there's going to be some blowback about your decision. I mean, there's going to be some beef being that I just showed up and all, you feel me? So perhaps someone else should be the one."

"Yeah. I feel ya. But you just let me handle that. My word is absolute. Even from in here. So you are the one." Supreme nodded his head and could barely contain his elation. This was the chance of a lifetime he had set out to secure for himself. All the hopes and dreams he held privately and at times expressed in a conversation with his mentor O.G. Bobby Rush about heading his own family when he jumped had just become a reality. This is what he had positioned himself for, and thus far everything worked out according to plan. The blowback that he was concerned about would be minimal. This was Genie's decision and it was final. His word since the day he was crowned boss, was in fact absolute.

Chapter 28
Make Way for the New Boss

Two days later in the back of one of Tony's grocery stores, which was still the organization's traditional meeting place under Genie's command, the same place where the Professor and other traitors in the family breathed their last breaths, the word was about to come down regarding the family's interim successor.

As the workers, block bosses, and lieutenants all filed in past the soldiers, who stood on high alert at the door, Supreme sat at the head of the round table where Tony and Sugar once sat. Macky and Horace sat on both sides of Supreme with the trademark stoic looks on their faces.

"Alright," Supreme said as he stood to his feet. As some of you know, the O.G. has a few legal issues that will be ironed out soon. I'm not big on speeches, so I'm going to get straight to the point. This meeting was called today to announce me as the new successor." Supreme peered around the room to see the reactions of the men. For those who know how to read body language, especially after an announcement of this magnitude, there were a couple people whose bodies said what their mouths did not. "Is there anyone here today who objects to the O.G.'s decision let ya nuts hang now or forever hold your peace." Again, Supreme paused to take a look around the conference room.

"Well, yeah. I have a question," one of Genie's lieutenants, Ramon said.

"Okay. I'm listening."

"I don't question the O.G.'s decision to make you the *boss*," Ramon said putting an emphasis on boss. Ramon wasn't known for his timidity. "But why are you bringing in all these gang niggas here?" Ramon said motioning his head to a few of the gang members in question sitting at the table. In a conference room full of real life gangsters and hustlers who ran their illicit businesses like fortune 500 companies, they looked totally out of place. "I mean, you are doing something that the O.G. never did, kid. What up with that?" Without showing any emotions, Macky and Horace casually cut their eyes over at Supreme as if they too wanted an answer.

"Good question. And I can appreciate it. The reason I brought these people in is because for one, they know the city inside out. Two, I know them. I've ran with them. I came up with them. I've banged alongside them. I trust them. I ain't doing anything around people I don't know, or more importantly, I don't trust."

"So what are you saying, kid?" Ramon interjected. "You don't trust us? I mean, if you don't trust us, you don't trust Mr. Small's judgment and leadership. And if you don't trust his leadership or us, why would you wanna keep us around in his absence?" The room, which was already silent, dropped a few more decibels, if that was even possible. The situation seemed to quickly escalate with this candid outburst from Ramon. As the old folks in the dirty south used to say, you could hear a mouse piss on cotton it was so quiet.

Supreme's indignation at being questioned wasn't lost on Ramon or Macky. As his eyes turned to narrow slits that you could slide a piece of paper through with ease, he put on his diplomatic face to hide his anger to the others. His gang buddies, who he hired on and gave corners to, weren't savvy enough to hide theirs. Ramon's questions and comments had struck more than one nerve. The mad dog looks they gave him would have intimidated the average cat, but not once did Ramon look away or break his gaze, which kept in line with his reputation as one of the realest niggas who ever walked the streets of the Bronx. Second to Macky, Ramon was probably the most lethal person in the room. An O.G. who came up at the end of Frank Lucas' and Nicky Barnes' reign, and who not only believed violence as a necessary tool, but something to embrace, he'd left bodies dating all the way back to the mid seventies. This cat killed more men than HIV.

"No, I'm not saying that at all. With any changing of the guard, there will also be changes to the organizational structure. The O.G. made me boss and to do that he had to trust my judgment. Now I am asking you cats to do the same by trusting my judgment and standing with me. Hopefully, my reign won't be long and the O.G. can come back and assume what is rightfully his. I didn't ask for this. It was thrust upon me. And I don't aim to disappoint my mentor. So again, are there any objections to me being boss? I don't think Ramon here actually objected, but I could be wrong. Well, Ramon. Are you with us?" Ramon paused momentarily to choose his words wisely. He knew that an objection could sign his death warrant, so he had to be careful with his words and his answer.

"No, I don't object. Mr. Smalls left you in charge and I totally trust his judgment on this since we go way back. But check this out! I want you and these gang niggas who fuck up the community to listen to me real good on this. If I catch *anybody* out of place, I'm going to waste them - no questions, no inquiries, no warnings, and no emergency meetings on the matter. My territory is my territory and I earned every inch of it. And from day one, it has always been off limits to niggas like y'all, and it's going to remain that way. My word on that is bond and I don't give a shit who's in charge, you dig?"

"Okay. Agreed. Y'all heard the O.G., right?" Supreme said, looking over at the gang banger cats. "You are not to go on his turf and that goes for your people too. This rule will be enforced like all others, you feel me? The one thing that you can expect under my leadership is this thing will run with the same efficiency and rule of law as it did under the O.G." Supreme turned to Ramon. "Is everything good now, O.G.?" Ramon looked at the gang bangers with contempt before cutting a suspicious eye over at Supreme.

"Yeah. No doubt," he said before walking over to Supreme's outstretched arms and gave him a lukewarm hug, signifying there was no beef. Ramon's two soldiers who stood at the door on high alert like two Rottweilers, not once took their eyes off Supreme or their boss.

"Glad that we have terms, O.G. Long health and wealth," Supreme said after Ramon walked out of the conference room with his soldiers flanking him. Supreme eyed him down until he left the room. The gaze was revealing. This somewhat contentious exchange between he and Ramon wasn't going to end with a hug.

"Well, okay. With that said, this meeting is adjourned." All of the men filed out of the conference room except Macky, Horace and Supreme's gang homies. As Macky was about to walk out, Supreme called out to him.

"Mack man. Are you with me?"

"Sure. I'm a team player. Death before dishonor," he said before walking out. Supreme then looked at Horace.

"I'm not going to even ask you, bruh," Supreme said smiling. "I'm making you my right hand, since we got back to a place that few understand." Horace smiled.

"Bruh, I am honored to be given a promotion next to ya, but I would be better served in the background. I'm just not the underboss type, you feel me?" Supreme smiled and nodded his head in agreement.

"Yeah, I feel ya. You always was low key, but the most dangerous man on the compound, truth be told. I knew the type of cat you were after you handled that business with that crash dummy jit I sent at ya. And don't act like you're surprised at that, because I'm sure you peeped game on it the moment it went down." Horace laughed.

"Yeah, I knew it off the rip, which is why I called your ass out. But that is all behind us now. We're on the same team this time. Congratulations kid," Horace said as they both embraced. "And best believe, I am behind you. I'm your eyes in the back of your head, you feel me?"

"Yeah, bruh. Respect!" With that said, Horace walked out of the conference room leaving Supreme, the gang cats and a couple of soldiers behind posted up at the door.

After Supreme plopped down in the boss's chair at the head of the round table and whirled around in it like a young executive who had just been given the keys to his office on Wall Street, his gang buddies all walked up to him and began kissing a diamond ring as a show of solidarity. This meeting and the kissing of the ring by his thugs was the icing on the cake. He had now arrived.

Chapter 29
Beware Of the Friendly Embrace

Robert "Bobby" Ramon Magwood spent a quarter of his life in prison. The first stint he did was for a knifing in an alley at the age of 11. He lured in a white pedophile politician out of Manhattan, robbed him and stuck him twice in the gut when he tried to grab and subdue him, leaving the white man to wear a shit bag for life. For that, he spent the next 7 years in the most notorious boys homes, also known as gladiator schools, inside and outside of the city. The next stint would be 15 years for manslaughter for the revenge killing of a gang member who murdered his sister's son in a drive-by. Thus began his career as a killer and his hatred for gang bangers. Since that time, he'd killed with ease and hated gangs with the same casualness. His penchant for violence subsided, as he got older as it does with most O.Gs.

He learned to use his street smarts and above average intelligence more as his role in the streets changed. He was now an upper mid-level hustler and up and coming player in one of the most notorious drug cartels in the nation. His people moved no less than 100 keys a month, which made him an important person within the organizational structure. Behind Macky, Ramon was a candidate for underboss and perhaps for the top leadership of the family. That was until Supreme showed up and was foolishly taken for a son by Genie. Ramon was obviously upset at Genie's decision, but he was more concerned about the bigger picture of some young upstart, gang-affiliated nigga controlling a multi-million dollar trade, in which he had a huge stake in.

Ramon, being a creature of habit, his daily routine was to visit his mother's grave, who'd passed while he was in the joint on that 15 year stretch. Since the time he touched down, he did not miss a day of taking fresh flowers to her grave with only one bodyguard with him and his chauffeur. Regardless of the dangers of an assassination, Ramon considered the moment too intimate to have a phalanx of bodyguards around him. His daily routine, after time with his old girl, was to grab breakfast and take a walk on the pier before going into his import/export business office, where he moved drum containers of goods around the world. All this was done before 9 am everyday. This morning, three days after the contentious organizational emergency meeting with Supreme, was no different.

After placing flowers on his mother's grave and saying a few endearing words to her, he climbed into his Bentley and headed to breakfast. Afterward, he walked the pier to clear his mind and walk off the chicken and waffles, before heading to work. Once inside his office, he didn't really pay much attention to the janitor he passed by in the hallway, as it was commonplace for them to be there early in the morning before the other office tenants arrived. Sitting down at his desk and looking over the weekly audit reports left there by the fine sister secretary, Clara, Ramon sipped on the coffee he got from the cafe earlier that had by now turned lukewarm. Turning the pages of the audit report, he went through each entry in the same fine tooth comb fashion he did in his illicit side drug business. When he opened the desk drawer to retrieve a marker to highlight something in the audit that caught his interest, an explosion and flash engulfed the entire office blowing out its windows. Ramon's body which had been cut in half by the bomb that was placed in his desk drawer, meant only for him, was blown way out in the hallway where it burned on.

The hug that Supreme gave him at the meeting was more like the kiss of death from an enemy rather than an embrace of peace and cooperation from an ally. Ramon's assassination would bring in an uncertain future for the organization as the finger pointing began. Although Ramon had many enemies, both declared and undeclared, who would benefit in his untimely departure from a life marked by money, power, gangsterism and violence, there were some like Macky who knew better than to point to anyone but the man whom Ramon questioned to become interim boss of bosses. This thing wasn't going to go over too well. It was going to be the catalyst for a renewed round of gangsta shyt and the reemergence of someone who was never expected to come back into the picture ever again.

The killing of Ramon started a brief mini civil war that was eventually put down by the organization lead by Horace who once again proved his worth. Although this shit was over as fast as it started, the blowback would be felt for months to come. Ramon's people felt betrayed by the family and wasn't going to forget about this anytime soon. It would take a diplomat like Tony to fix this situation and bring lasting peace if he were out on the streets, unlike Genie who would probably make matters worse because he would just have everyone who couldn't get past the beef and put aside all hostilities killed. Nevertheless, everything went back to normal, at least for a little while.

CATO

Chapter 30
The Bigger Picture

By now, Genie and Tony were in the same unit, but not yet in the same dorm. However, they would go out for rec at the same time every other day or when the asshole COs felt magnanimous enough to allow the inmates to get some sunshine on the basketball courts. This day, their dorms went out together and they were given the opportunity to talk.

"Mr. Smalls, what's good, my brother? You look like you are putting on weight in here," Tony said smiling as they embraced, while the soldiers hired to protect them, stood their distance looking around with a wary eye. Genie chuckled and clutched his stomach.

"Yeah, we gotta chef named Ray Ray who got a nigga hooked on those ramen noodle goulash." The two friends laughed out loud.

"Yeah, I can see the oodle noodle gut forming there," Tony said, poking his stomach. "Hey, but on a serious note, how is your wife holding up?"

"Crying every time she come visit me. Bruh, I'm to the point, I don't even want her coming here anymore to see me. I just can't deal with all the crying, you feel me? Hell, have a gangsta like me bout to cry with all that shit." Tony laughed and shook his head.

"Well, bruh, that's a woman for ya. You have lived long enough to know they are emotional creatures who feel their man's pain. You being locked up behind these bars and not spending your nights with her in your new marriage is a hard pill for anyone to have to swallow.

"Yeah, I can dig it man. I guess in reality, I am just as frustrated as she is, if not more. I know this is the life we chose, but this is the shit that a boss shouldn't be dealing with while his men are still out on the streets. I mean, that is some backwards shit, ain't it? I didn't become a boss to be rousted over bullshit like some petty, po hustling nigga on the corner." Tony chuckled and shook his head.

"Okay, Genie. Here comes the part I know you ain't trying to hear right about now, but you had to know it was coming whenever they let us out here together." Genie looked at Tony as they walked around the court amidst the inmates talking shit and living out their Kobe Bryant, LeBron James fantasies.

"Okay. I'm listening," Genie said as if he expected a scolding by his mentor and brother.

"You should have paid that pig, bruh. I mean, it's good business for people like you and me to pay our dues, man, to keep the heat off us. It ain't like we have a license to do the shit we do, you dig? To have a fed boy on the payroll is the ideal situation for dope niggas like us. That puts us on the same level with the mafia. We already had a few politicians in our pockets. But the Feds? And a higher up at that who could give us valuable info or better yet insulate us from making their shit list. Genie, you know you are my man, but you fucked up and royally. I told you many times before that these bigger picture situations must be adhered to in order to have life and longevity in this shit.

"You think I wanted to give those NYPD fucks my hard earned dope money? Fuck no! It would have been my pleasure to have their cars explode when they cranked them up. But that would have only been a short-lived, short-termed satisfaction. The bigger picture was to pay them off to keep them off me and my people. This is how things have been done before you and I were born into this shit."

For the first time in two years, Genie listened like a pupil listening to his teacher. There were no interruptions or disagreements on his part. He knew Tony was right. "Something else I must point out, Genie."

"What's that, T?"

"Very seldom have I distrusted your judgment, although I have called it into question at times as something I would or wouldn't do. Neither have I interfered out of respect that this thing was completely yours after I handed it to you. But this thing with that youngster Supreme. I don't think making him your temporary replacement was wise, nor was it good politically. I mean, I understand not choosing Macky since we both agreed to keep him in the shadows for a while. But this youngster you hardly know is troubling, bruh. I mean, why not choose someone like Ramon who has proven his lot in this thing?" Genie's face sunk in as they continued to walk. Stopping dead in his tracks he responded.

"Look, Stallworth! I have a good feel for people, just as you do. And that youngster is like the son I never had. I have vetted him in every way possible to prove himself and he passed each and every test with flying colors. Now the thing about Moresco, I admit, I totally fucked up on that one. But this thing with the youngster, I know in my heart I made the right decision. Give him time." Tony shook his head and held up his hand.

"And thinking with your heart to make decisions is exactly why you and I are in this detention center waiting to see what these fed fucks are going to do!" Tony shot back. "He's *not* your son and probably not even your friend. Did you know he and Sugar's brother did time together? And he tried to extort him?" Genie's face sunk in. "Of course you didn't. You didn't do your homework on this man before you put him all the way in your business. These are the type of things that the Genie I knew not long ago, wouldn't do. This delusion that he is the son you never had and this thinking and making decisions based on your emotions has clouded your judgment, bruh. And you are going to have to snap out of it or sink us all." Tony's candor touched a nerve. It seemed to incense Genie even more.

"Hey Stallworth! Listen here, man! I love you not like a brother but as my brother! I would die for you and take my own life or even take a fall before I put you in a situation, you feel me? But my decisions are *my* decisions. I have to live with them and so do you. You didn't hand me this thing we built to have me beholding to your every word or do shit how you did it. As far as that youngster is concerned he has handled himself pretty well out there."

"Yeah, by murking your friend and number one earner, who by the way, was the one person you could trust more than anyone other than me and Macky?"

"Hey! The youngster didn't do anything you and me wouldn't have done to tie up a loose end. By the way, how the fuck do you know he gave the order?" Tony shook his head and got in Genie's face.

"Genie, do you really believe everything you just said, bruh? You know damn well we wouldn't have had Ramon clipped. And you also know damn well that it was your protégé who gave the order. Ramon was rightly questioning the young nigga's decision to do something that you would not have dared done, and defending all that you put together. How was that a dying offense?"

Genie paused and looked off momentarily. Stallworth's words pierced his heart and jolted him. He was right. A high ranking O.G. like Ramon who paid his dues shouldn't have been touched.

"Again, your emotions are getting the best of you right now and placing everyone in jeopardy, including you and me. Time to wake the fuck up out of this fantasy that this little muthafucka is a long awaited son you never had." With that said, Genie punched Tony in the chin, dropping him to one knee. The soldiers stood there with a confused look on their faces. They didn't know what to make of the two men who they were commissioned by the organization to protect. The one C.O. present who was also on the take, was scared shitless, looked the other way as if he didn't see anything. The men on the court stopped their intense basketball game, that was more like a game of rugby, to become interested spectators. Tony stood to his feet, wiped the blood from his lip, looked at it, and smiled. Genie stood there in a combat stance waiting for whatever to take place, knowing full well he didn't have hands for Tony, but none of that mattered now. He was ready to take an ass whuppin.'

"Bruh, I'm going to give you that one. Maybe I deserved it. But one thing is for sure. You are going to have to come to terms with this new reality you created for us. And it is going to be up to you to fix it. If not, I will." Tony then walked away from his friend and brother, leaving him to ponder over the words spoken to him that he knew to be true.

Chapter 31
There is no way the rat is making it to trial

At the Law Office of Langston, Shepard and Goldman, Sugar went into the visit Tony's attorney.

"Mrs. Stallworth, come on in," the young female secretary smiled and said.

"Hello Mrs. Stallworth," the attorney said. The drain from his nose and the sniffling spoke to a 500 dollar a day coke habit he had. But nonetheless, he was a fed killer in the courtroom who never lost a drug trial. The rumor was, it was the coke he got from one of Genie's hustlers that gave him his edge. His rep was, as soon as a fed prosecutor found out that he or she would have to face off with him in court in a drug case, they would go straight into deal making mode. That was a testament to his reputation, since the federal prosecutor is perhaps the most arrogant individual in the criminal justice system, perhaps more so than most judges, being that they have the weight and resources of the federal government at their disposal.

"I'm good," Sugar replied, shaking his hand before she sat down.

"Well, I have some good news and some bad news. I will, of course, give you the bad news first. Tony and Genie were indicted by a federal grand jury. And that isn't hard to do since they can indict on hearsay, which is pretty much what this case against them consists of. It is a purely circumstantial case, but in this world of conspiracies, rule 35 snitches, and ghost dope, not to mention the threat of so much time for anyone who dared lose in trial, the Feds cases typically end in plea deals. Most become snitches themselves. But these people who I am referring to did not have me as their attorney," he said with a supremely confident smile. "The other bit of bad news is, the Feds have a few witnesses within the organization. As of now I am not sure who they are. I have a feeling that this person or persons will be left on the streets and not taken into protective custody to gather more evidence to help a seriously weak case. Now here is the good news. One of my attributes as an attorney who never lost a case to these fed fucks in a drug trial is, I have a knack for finding out who their rats are. Finding and ID-ing a

189

rat is, of course, the one thing that can stand between life on the streets and life in prison. And especially on a case like this one. Now I know what to do to a rat once I get them in trial. It can go either way as the outcome in a setting with a fed judge who is on the same team with the Feds, dumb jurors who believe everything the government and police say, and savvy snitches looking to save their own ass. Others, who have everything to lose, know how to deal with them before they get to trial. If you get what I'm saying."

Sugar nodded her head. She knew exactly what he was saying. This lawyer was cut from the same cloth as Bruce Cutler, the mob lawyer who represented John Gotti. He was very much fascinated with the gangsta shyt and got off on playing his very important part. He was no ordinary lawyer.

"When will you know who this person or persons is?"

"Well before trial. If I have to, I will file a couple of motions in the courts to postpone and stall until I find out. But you can rest assured I will find out."

Sugar again nodded her head and peered into space. There was no fucking way that snitch rat bastard, whoever he is, was going to make it into trial and take her man's freedom.

Chapter 32
Necessary Tools & Good Business Sense

After Ramon's assassination and the brief war that took place in the aftermath, Supreme took security measures to make even more changes to the organization. Everyone around him now serving as his security were gang members headed by Horace, who was now in charge of the soldiers and the muscle. Macky was promoted to an advisory role that pretty much sidelined him. It was obvious that Supreme hadn't forgotten about he and Macky's run in that night outside of Home Depot. Since that time, they were cordial, but that was until the paranoia had begun to set in following his decision to waste Ramon who was one of the most respected men within the organization. Now he didn't trust Macky enough to allow him access to him.

Within a couple of months in his absence, Genie's organization that he and Tony built would no longer be recognizable in terms of its members and its structure. Even the organizational policies had been changed by this new young upstart. The gang turf wars that Tony and Genie had pretty much erased in the cities five boroughs with their *no violence or no dope* policy, had begun to resurface with a vengeance. The state of the streets had begun its downward spiral back to a time that brought un-needed heat and crackdowns by the police. Under Tony's era, everybody ate. The hustlers were happy. The dope fiends were happy. The community leaders who got their cut were happy and even the police were happy. Violence was at an all time low and low priced, high quality coke was in abundance. It was considered the golden age of cocaine, much like the late eighties and early nineties. All that was beginning to be a fond memory now under Supreme's leadership.

With his own people around him and no longer burdened with the concern about being followed or seen by people within the organization, Supreme met up with someone who he wouldn't have been caught dead with a few months ago because of the G-code of no snitching. But his growing concerns over the prospect of being forced to give back the crown handed to him by Genie upon his release made him change that policy. Part of the game the O.G. Bobby Rush gave him while in the joint was that sometimes in street matters, using the cops was not only a necessary tool, but good business sense. The seat at the organizational round table was one he wasn't ready to give back any time soon.

"Mr. Supreme."

"Agent Moresco," Supreme replied with handshake.

"We have a lot to talk about. And perhaps after it's all said and done, that discussion will lead to a long and fruitful relationship." Supreme nodded his head as the two men sat down at the restaurant table to begin discussing their future.

Chapter 33
Cease and Desist

A couple of days later, Supreme received an unexpected visit from a most unlikely visitor. Sugar, Yancey and a couple of soldiers loyal to Tony all walked into his office located inside the bar he had recently opened. The soldiers went and posted up at the door as Sugar walked in with Yancey and sat down in front of Supreme in an aggressive manner. The no nonsense look on Sugar's face indicated to Supreme this wasn't a social call.

"Wow! What do I owe this royal visit by the Queen herself?" Supreme said with his hand extended. Sugar's eyes said what she didn't bother to verbalize. *Nigga, please!* Leaving his hand in the air she went right into her reason for the visit.

"Mr. Supreme, I didn't come here to socialize." Supreme's eyes dropped down towards the floor as he pulled his hand back before sitting down. By this time a couple of his soldiers entered into the room and posted up on each side of him behind where he sat.

"Okay. Well, what is the purpose of your visit then?"

"I came to tell you that from this day forward, you are not to hold any more organizational meetings on the properties owned by my husband. You are not to step foot in any of the Stallworth establishments. And more importantly you need to be finding a new plug. These things are no longer available to you or Mr. Smalls. Do I make myself clear?" she asked with a deadly serious look on her face, while Supreme's face displayed an unconfident grin.

"Yes. You are definitely clear on this," he replied. "I understand the part about not holding anymore meetings on your husband's premises. Hell, with all that went down with the Feds, I'm not even sure they haven't been bugged anyway. But the part about the plug I don't get. This is still Mr. Small's organization. Why would you wanna take the plug away? I mean, business is still good. Money is still good." Sugar smiled.

"My husband taught me long ago that not all money is good money. And your money is no longer worth the risk, sir. You have been warned and put on notice," she said as she stood up and headed for the door with Yancey in step behind her.

"Well, I have been warned. There is no doubt about that," Supreme yelled as he stood up. "But what I didn't hear is the or else part that normally comes with a veiled threat like that." Sugar turned around to face him.

"Another thing my husband taught me some time ago is to never broadcast my intentions. Again, you have been placed on notice. Find you another plug and stay the fuck off Stallworth property, you dig?" She then stormed out of the office with Yancey and the two soldiers in front and behind her. Even a young upstart like Supreme knew this was the proverbial parting of the ways and severance of all ties. Whatever action came behind that, if any, remained to be seen. Typically throughout history when one nation severed all ties with another, war ensued. In this situation however, war was highly unlikely since Stallworth was no longer in the business and therefore no existence of a conflict. However, the warning she issued was clear. She meant business and Supreme knew it.

Chapter 34
Somebody Gotta Die

Two weeks after the meeting he had with Sugar and a short drought in the streets, Supreme reached out to a Belize connect he met while in prison who was down on a manslaughter charge. Although his new plug didn't offer the same weight and price tag as Genie's old plug, Armando, the quality was still good and it was consistent, at least long enough to find others who could fill the void. So the show went on without much of a hitch. The only thing that had changed since the visit from Sugar was Supreme's growing distrust of Macky, who was the last person in the family that had real ties with Sugar and Tony. Although Horace was her brother, he didn't seem to have any objections or hostilities towards Supreme being the new boss like Macky appeared to have. The way Supreme had figured, if there was going to be any reprisals, Macky would be a threat since he more than likely still had loyalties to the old regime. This made him more and more paranoid each day, which was a boss's burden that most don't think about on the ambitious climb to the top.

"Hey," Supreme said into the cell phone. "That thing we discussed a couple of weeks ago, it's on. Go now. Make sure it's done proper." After hanging up the phone, he sat back in his office seat and began staring straight ahead with a menacing look on his face while the old school joint, *Somebody Gotta Die* by Notorious B.I.G played from the bar's speakers.

Once a month, Macky and his girlfriend spent a weekend on some island either in the Bahamas or Jamaica. This weekend however, they stayed home due to a stomach virus Macky's girlfriend came down with. His NYPD girlfriend, Nicola, never suspected him of murdering her aunt. She just concluded that one of her many enemies in Bogota and in the states was responsible for her death. After her funeral, it was discovered and released to the press by a pesky local Colombian investigative reporter that she was in fact, the niece of a notorious Colombian cartel leader Elvira "Perro Loco," crazy bitch, Rios, which had been a long held secret. This revelation eventually forced her off the force after being grilled by internal affairs and higher ups who wanted to know why she didn't divulge this type of information when she applied for the job. But with her aunt now dead, she no longer had a reason to remain on the force, which was only to tip her aunt off about investigations involving her organization and her associates in New York. Nicola was now pursuing a law degree like she had intended before being bribed by Elvira with money and a new BMW to remain a cop.

"Here sweetie," Macky said as he gave her some Gatorade to help with the dehydration caused by the vomiting and diarrhea.

"Thank you, bae," she said in a low exasperated voice. "Bae, again, I am so sorry that we couldn't go on our trip this weekend. I don't know where this virus came from. I hope it wasn't that Sushi I ate last night."

"Hey, baby, you don't have to apologize for being sick. These things happen. We have plenty of time coming up soon to go wherever we choose."

"Oh yeah? You're going to go on vacation or something?"

"Something like that," Macky smiled and said placing a kiss on her forehead. "And I don't think it was the Sushi that made you ill. Get some rest, baby."

"Okay boo. I love you."

"Love you too, beautiful," he said as he pulled the covers over her and turned out the light, leaving Nicola tucked away in her bed. After going into the kitchen to pour himself a glass of juice, Macky went into his study and began finishing up the book, *The Art of War*. After finishing the last chapter, he went and checked on Nicola, who was sound asleep. Feeling somewhat sleepy himself, he laid down beside her and dozed off.

Around midnight, the first of four shadows, dressed in all black, darted across the lawn like phantoms. The second, third and fourth followed suit before they all settled at the back of the two-story home. Huddled together, they went over their game plan.

After breaching the home using high tech burglar's tools, the hitters entered into the house and began methodically seeking out their quarry like super predators. In the darkness, the four shadows crept through the crib en sync. The only light in the home that revealed their presence was the intermittent blinking light from the microwave clock. Their meticulous movement and their measured footsteps was evidence that they had done this before. When the silent alarm vibration of Macky's wrist watch went off, he immediately went from being sound asleep to wide awake on high alert. Rising up in his bed with his eyes on the bedroom door and his hearing faculties on heightened alert to detect any movement inside the home, he slid his hands underneath the pillow and grasped the two Glocks with the 17 shot clips. Before placing his feet down on the floor, he looked over at Nicola who was all but comatose from the Nyquil she had taken earlier. After making the decision to wake her up, he placed his finger to his lips. Although still groggy from the effects of the medication, it registered in her brain what was going on when she saw her man clutching the two Glocks and looking at the door. Her own eyes then shifted to the door as her faculties had fully kicked in. Her NYPD training was now taking over any fear that one would normally experience with armed intruders inside his or her home. As Macky's foot touched the floor, Nicola reached into the holster atop the nightstand next to the bed. Taking out her Glock 40, she followed Macky's lead by climbing out of the bed and moving to the other side of the room on the wall across from the bed out of view. With her pistol held tightly with both hands and pointed down to the floor just as she had been trained in the academy, she pressed her body close to the wall waiting for further instructions, and kept her eyes on Macky who was on the other wall.

As the two waited for the next turn of events to transpire, the intruders who invaded the sanctity and sanctuary of their home, settled at their bedroom door with guns drawn poised to do what they came to do. While Macky stood there with his cold steely eyes focused and unblinking, he thought for this violation of an age old rule of transgressing a man's castle, all those involved must be made to pay for their decision with the ultimate price. And it was then and there he was resolute that the highest price would be paid in full as soon as they came through that door. His brain was now on kill mode, as were the people commissioned by some unknown actor to waste him.

When the first burst from the AK cut through the bedroom door like butter blowing it open, deafening machine gun fire quickly followed that literally turned the bed into shards of wood, metal fragments and shredded bed sheets. Amid the flying feathers from the pillows that looked like falling snowflakes in a winter blizzard, the killers inched forward to see if their quarry was under the sheets taking his last breath. Macky and his woman held their fire to await the moment these killers walked into the kill zone. When the lead gunman realized the bed was empty and the others trailing closely behind, finally came into full view, the deadly return fire began. They were caught in a two way cross fire that cut them down before they could respond and fire off one shot, other than the errant ones that went into the ceiling. Between Macky's Glock 18 machine gun pistols and Nicola's Glock 40, this shit was over within seconds. As they quickly reloaded, on the floor lay three dead assassins with the fourth, clinging to life, coughing up light colored blood, pieces of lung, and sputum. Macky went over and kicked away the mortally wounded assassin's gun to the other side of the room while Nicola tried to compose herself of the initial shock of the brief gunfight that was more like shooting fish in a barrel. Her wide stretched eyes was evidence that she had never been involved in any gangsta shyt before or any other situation in which she had to use deadly force. In fact, during her time as an NYPD cop she had never used her service gun at all.

After removing the mask of the dying assassin, to Macky's surprise the gunman, was a female.

"Who sent you?" he calmly asked. The female assassin who was out of Jamaica Queens, known as Buffy the Vampire, smiled and grimaced as the last of her blood flowed from her bullet riddled body with each pump of her weakening heart that was now struggling to do what nature designed it to do. While her chest moved up and down frantically and her breathing became labored, she managed to eke out an answer to his question as she involuntarily spat out a light spray of blood.

"Who you think, nigga?" she said in a Jamaican accent followed by one last deep breath before complete silence. Her suffering was now over. By this time, Nicola, was in near shock watching a fellow human being take her last breath. Her mind began to race as to why would anyone target her professional DJ and personal fitness trainer boyfriend. And at no time was this lost on Macky who told her from the beginning these were his two hustles he made his living on. Neither was the revelation from the dying female assassin lost on him, which was the more pressing matter on his mind. He knew exactly who gave her the contract on him. Who else would hire amateurs from the hood whose experience in death for hire didn't rise above the level of gang hits be sent to kill a professional killer like himself? A gang nigga. That's who would do this. The dilemma Macky faced from the beginning of the leadership change to remain a loyal team player under a man he didn't respect nor like, had just been put to rest for good, along with the assassins this man commissioned. The only question in his mind at this time was, when and where he was going to deal with this.

The news of the assassination attempt on Macky remained under wraps. His decision not to utter one word of the failed hit was intentional. His plan for all those involved was to let them sweat it out for a while before he decided to pay them a visit. The only people who knew about it now was Sugar and her bodyguard, Yancey, who was beginning to prove his worth.

"I really think Genie should know about this right away, Macky," Sugar said as she sat down at the kitchen table with a cup of coffee.

"I've thought about that and have decided against it."

"Well, why? Why not tell him?" she pleaded. "Genie has mad respect for you not to mention total trust in you and your judgment. I really think you should tell him about this."

"No. Right now, Genie is too emotionally involved in this. He sees Supreme as his son. Telling him while being behind bars right now won't serve any purpose. Besides, I don't want anyone to know about this but those responsible. The one thing your husband and my mentor taught me that I now live by is to never show my emotions, nor my hand, to an enemy. Genie will know about what happened after my enemies see my hand at the last possible moment, just before they take their last breath."

Sugar nodded her head and took a sip of her coffee. She knew Macky was right in not informing Genie about the man he called his son. To Sugar, she no longer recognized the man in Genie who was the closest thing to a brother to her husband.

Chapter 35
Unsealed Indictment

After receiving an urgent text from Tony and Genie's lawyer informing her of a very important development in her old man's case, Sugar didn't waste anytime going to his office. She got there before it opened.

"Mrs. Stallworth, Mr. Goldman will be with you momentarily," the female receptionist said. While Sugar waited for the lawyer, she looked at the pictures on the wall of his former gangster clients. Gotti, Gotti's hit man, Gravano, Paul Castellano, and even Whitey Bulger. The fanfare that came with being a mouthpiece for gangsters was something that the lawyer not only didn't shy away from, but embraced enthusiastically.

"Hello Constance!" Goldman said as he embraced Sugar. "Come into my office." Sugar followed the lawyer inside his office. "I was so fucking excited about this information I got from my fed prosecutor gold buddy that I almost took a trip to your house to tell you this personally. Here is the rat in your family," he said pushing a DOC profile picture to her across the table. "Do you know him?" Sugar was even surprised.

"Something like that. I've seen him before," she said nonchalantly.

"You don't seem surprised."

"That's because I'm not. He is not Tony's people. Tony don't make errors in judgment like this. If he did, he would take care of it."

"So whoever brought in this Supreme they are going to have to take him outta the equation soon," Goldman said before he took a sip of his hot tea. "The bright side of this is, he is a paid informant now which means he won't be in protective custody…which also means he can be persuaded or touched. The bad side to this is, the Feds didn't have a case on Genie and Tony, but with this asshole, who can recruit other rats, will make a weak case a strong one. This is how the Feds work. They now have a new almost fool proof system made possible by snitch testimony, which is why very few take them to trial. Okay, listen Sugar!" he said, looking her directly in her eyes. "You and I both know what I'm saying here. Supreme nor his gang members must not make it into court. Your husband's freedom depends on it."

Sugar looked at Supreme's picture as that old familiar coldness began to overtake her. The role she played in the last regime, she never wanted to assume ever again. But that was before the same set of similar circumstances that launched her into boss Queen mode before and inspired her to become something she never fathomed was now confronting her once again. But none of that shit mattered. The promises she made to herself to stay out of the gangsta shyt and the promise she made to her dear granny to be a good girl from here on out was now broken. And this was something she knew in the back of mind that was now apart of her. The words of her old man began to sound off once again like it did at her granny's crib in the moments before her legendary gun battle with the Russian mobster, Yuri Lavrov. *We are who we are. We are who we have become.* The only thing that mattered to her now was her old man, who no one was going to take away from her. If that meant everybody had to die, including the boss who brought this on the family, then so be it. This was no longer business, this was personal.

Chapter 36
Everybody Gotta Die On This One

The very same day, Sugar called an emergency meeting with Macky, Yancey and a couple of Tony's loyalists who didn't like the current situation with Genie's organization. The climate of the meeting can only be described as so thick one could cut it with a knife. Everyone there knew that this was one of those closed door meetings in which either war was going to be declared or someone within the organization was going to have a bad day.

"Okay. I'm going to make this short and sweet and to the point. As many of y'all know by now, Tony and Genie were indicted by the Feds. What you don't know is, there is a rat in the family who made that possible. Now, I don't have to tell you who this rat is, but I will. He is the same man who was allowed to become the boss of this thing my husband created and handed over to the man who made this monumental error in judgment that has placed us all in jeopardy. Under normal circumstances, this boss would have to correct his own mistakes. But this is not a normal situation. His judgment is in question and he is not in a position to deal with it so I will take care of it myself. No one is going to threaten my happiness and all that was built for us all.

"Now, I don't know how extensive Genie's mistake was, and I also don't know how wide Supreme's treachery is and who is on his team, but we are not going to take any chances. And we are certainly not going to leave any loose ends untied. Shit is far too serious to leave anyone living. So everybody gotta die on this one. Supreme. His associates. His workers. Everybody. We are going to implement a scorched earth policy here to save you, me and my old man."

"Sugar, I feel ya," one of Tony's former soldiers, Yanni, from the old regime, said. "And I am with you one hundred percent. But what about your brother, Horace? I mean, he and Supreme are super tight nowadays. In fact, I heard Supreme was going to make him underboss if Genie doesn't get out."

"You leave Horace to me. That's family. You just be ready to do what needs to be done when that time comes. Can I count on you?"

"You damn right you can count on me!" he said. "This bullshit has went on long enough. My people are suffering on the streets because of it." The others nodded their heads to give their approval. The decision had been made and nothing was going to stop this inevitable clash between the old guard and the new guard. The similarities of the war between Tony and the O.Gs. was striking. Now it was he and Genie who were the old guys in the way of the new ambitious youngsters who were not about to play by anybody's rules. This age old battle had come full circle and was about to get ugly out in the streets of Brooklyn and beyond. Sugar was about to revert back into what she was before, but on steroids this time. In order to overcome this situation with gangs that had consolidated for the sole purpose of taking over some shit her husband built, and the worst gang of all, the Feds, now in the equation, she was going to have to become a monster and one that was far more frightening than before. This was the end game.

Chapter 37
You are new to this shit

After getting dressed to put in a night's work in Newark, Horace placed the last of his articles in his overnight bag. The order came down that a Dominican named Cha Chi, had to be taught a valuable lesson in street matters to never bite the hand that feeds you. Cha Chi, a former boxer, was a wild man who lucked up on a loose, ragtag organization left by his uncle who got mandatory life in federal prison for running heroin. Unlike his uncle, Cha Chi was all over the place with his hustle due to his stated ambition of being a Dominican boss of bosses. In his shortsightedness and reckless disregard for the bigger picture, he didn't have the same respect for Supreme as he did for Genie, whom he actually feared. He knew that if he ever crossed Genie, who could very easily with one phone call put 500 men on the streets with automatics, Newark would bleed with Dominican blood. So he dared not cross him. But this new cat who was a former gang member like himself, he just didn't evoke the same type of fear in him. Supreme realized this and wanted to prove him wrong and give him a change of heart. Horace was going to deliver that message, which if he succeeded he was going to be promoted to underboss.

"Wow! I haven't seen you lately," Sugar said as she sat down on his bed.

"I know, sis. Been a l'il busy as of late. What's good?"

"I would like to have a word with you about something."

"Well, it's going to have to be quick. I have to go take care of some pressing business," he said before zipping up his overnight bag.

"Family business?" she asked.

"Yup. Always."

"And that's what I wanna talk with you about. Your boss is a rat. And just like all rats, he's gotta be exterminated."

"And why is that? Because Genie choose him to run things in his absence?" Sugar smiled and looked down at the floor shaking her head.

"No. Not at all. Genie's decision was his decision. And whatever consequences that came out of that was also his business. But in this life it doesn't work like that. His decision has placed us all in jeopardy."

"Is that all? A decision has been made to murk this dude because of his way of doing things? I mean, an occupational hazard of a gangster or dope nigga is prison or death, right? I don't see no one with a license to do what we do. Ain't none of this shit legal. So what? The man is doing things his own way and now that's a crime worthy of a death sentence. I don't buy it." This dismissive attitude from her brother, who was green as fuck on these matters to say the least, only seemed to incense Sugar.

"Hey! You are new to this shit, okay? You don't know shit about this life! And you obviously don't know shit about your new hero. But let me fill you in on some things real quick before you find yourself on the wrong side of what is about to go down," Sugar angrily threw the paper she was holding in her hand at Horace. It was the court documents of the sealed indictment with Supreme's name on it. "Read it!" she yelled. At first Horace hesitated. But eventually he picked up the paper and looked at it. "Yeah. He is a fucking rat!" Sugar yelled. "A rat that will sacrifice my man and his own mentor, Genie, who sees him as a son, just to have power! Hell, you may be the next sacrificial lamb. That mission you are going on tonight may be your last for all you know. He has to know by now that Macky has figured out that he was behind the failed hit on him a few nights ago. And he also knows where I stand on this and therefore questioning my little brother's loyalty to him." Horace's eyes showed both disappointment and denial. The man who he had some history with, although contentious and less than friendly, was being accused of being the most despised figure in the streets...a snitch.

"Okay. So if he is a snitch set to testify on Tony and Genie, why isn't he in protective custody?" Horace was now showing signs of denial.

"Because he is a paid informant. He is worth more out here on the streets than he is at some safe house. But fuck all that! And you see the indictment papers! But guess what? He won't ever make it in to testify against Tony. You can bet your ass on that, you dig? So little brother you have a choice to make right now! Either you are with us, or you are with him. There is no neutrality in this shit! I'm not going to keep on going with this to convince you of some nigga you don't even really know is a fucking snake. This is family versus some fuck nigga in the streets. The choice should be easy," she said looking at him with a deadly serious gaze. Horace knew his sister wasn't playing games. And he also knew what type of dude Supreme was from his dealings with him in prison. In addition to those indictment papers with Supreme's name on it, which he knew was real from being a law clerk in the law library at Martin Corrections, he found himself in a serious dilemma.

"Okay, sis, I feel what you are saying and won't allow anything to come between me and you, but I have to go take care of this thing tonight. We will chop it up when I get back," he said before grabbing his overnight bag and heading for the door.

"That's if you come back, little brother," she warned as Horace walked out of the room leaving her there on his bed. The emotions that she was experiencing watching her brother walk out of that door, was both anger and sadness over his lack of understanding on a situation this serious that could have some far reaching implications. Although the love she had for her brother was great, it was not enough to allow him and his new friend to take down her husband. How she had hoped that in this case, blood would be thicker than water.

CATO

Chapter 38
Beware of Those Routines

When Horace reached the Dominican neighborhood corner that served as Cha Chi's main hangout, where he often flossed among the peasants, there he was as big as day, sitting in the back of a tricked out maroon limo with a canary yellow top with three beautiful Dominican groupies. Thus far, the report that Horace got on him was 100% accurate. He was a man who dressed the part of a gangster and one who loved an entourage of women around him at all times. Even his bodyguards were women armed with automatics. Touching him would prove to be difficult, but as the professional hitter Old Man Red in the joint once told Horace, *ain't a man living, past or present, who can't be got. Most men are creatures of habit who have patterns born out of routines. Sooner or later a nigga like me will peep that pattern and collect his blood money.* Cha Chi was no different. Being the typical hood cat, everything he did was centered around the locale in which he was raised.

As Horace watched from a bed bug ridden whore trap hotel room across the street, he concluded what his game plan was going to be. The strategy was in and out. Two shots to the dome and one center mass to make sure the deed was done. While he sat there watching Cha Chi's movements like an eagle, he couldn't help but think about the exchange between he and Sugar. Other than the typical squabbles between siblings, this evening's contentious conversation was perhaps the most hostile they had ever been in. Like in past arguments, Sugar was always right and he would almost always have to go back and apologize. This time was no different. He knew in his heart, before he stormed out of the crib, that she was right.

Supreme was indeed a snake....a venomous snake who would be one until he lost his fangs. That part was always in the back of his mind. But him being a rat, he wouldn't have ever placed that label on him in a thousand years. Either way, there was no question where his loyalties lay. He put no one before his sister. Since they were shorties, it had always been them. Their relationship was one that was from the cradle to the grave, as far as he was concerned. But right now, this thing with

Cha Chi must be done and done right. However, the last thing Sugar said also began to weigh on Horace's mind.

That's if you come back, little brother. Perhaps Supreme's distrust and paranoia extended to him too and he had a surprise in store for him.

Why would he send me, a man he claimed he was going to make an underboss, all the way to Newark to do this thing? Horace thought to himself. Any apprehensions about this mission and suspicions about Supreme's alleged motives for commissioning him for the hit went away when Horace noticed Cha Chi emerging from the limo. Drunk and high as Giraffe pussy, Cha Chi stumbled behind one of the abandoned buildings in the alley to take a leak while his would be killer looked through the binoculars with a keen eye at his movements. Horace knew that this was not going to be the last piss Cha Chi would take, drinking all that beer that was brought to the limo by one of his flunkies.

Inside a span of twenty minutes, Cha Chi emerged from the limo for the third piss and went deeper into the alley this time after a police patrol passed by and stared him down. When Cha Chi got to a spot where no one could see him from the road, he pulled out his johnson and began pissing a long stream that only a beer drinker could muster up. While he continued to piss and talk to himself, a phantom dashed behind a huge city garbage container and disappeared out of sight. Cha Chi was too drunk and high to notice it. As he was about to zip up his pants, two of the girls who sat with him in the limo walked up to him laughing and talking loud.

"Papi, you cheating on us with another bitch back here or something?" one of the drunk women said.

"Bitch, I was taking a piss!"

"Well, let me see your dick then?" the other broad said with a chuckle.

"You wanna see Cha Chi's dick? Here it is. I'm not pulling it out for nothing either, bitch." he said as he pulled his dick back out. The red haired broad walked up to him, dropped down on her knees and began to inspect it as Cha Chi stood back with his head tilted down watching her play around with his shit like it was a slinky. "Now does it look like I been back here sticking that in some other pussy?" he asked.

"What you think?" The red haired broad said to the other.

"I don't know, bitch. It's kinda dark back here. Give it a taste test and see." Kneeling down on the pavement, she looked up at Cha Chi smiling.

"You want me to taste it, Papi?" she said in a sensual voice.

"Sure, bitch! You got it out. You may as well suck on it," he said in a slurred voice. The broad smiled and kissed the head of his dick then looked up at him with puppy dog eyes before she began twirling her tongue around it. Soon, Cha Chi was fully erect and she was fully engaged in rhythm, bringing his manhood in and out of her jaw and mouth while he stood there doing his best to remain on his feet. From the beer and Cognac he consumed, the black tar heroin he had been snorting, and the fire top head he was receiving, he could barely keep his balance.

"Hurry up, bitch! Don't hog up Papi's big dick! It's more than enough for both of us. I wanna taste it too!" the other chick said. While the two women took turns on the Dominican hood crime boss, his two female bodyguards who had enough of what they heard and saw, turned their backs and walked to the curb in front of the club hangout to give their boss all the privacy he wanted with the two hooker groupies. The third young girl was in the backseat of the limo nodded in and out of consciousness from the liquor and heroin.

While Cha Chi stood there reared back watching and moaning, the phantom that had seeped into the darkness behind the garbage container, reappeared but this time he was slowly approaching the three freaks in the alley. As it steadily moved closer with deliberate footsteps, one of the girls who had a mouth full of Cha Chi, seemed to catch a glimpse and pulled it out of the side of her mouth, causing it to make a popping sound. With saliva dripping from her mouth, she tried to focus her eyes on what was fastly approaching behind Cha Chi. She didn't know if it was the drugs, the booze, a homeless person or someone looking to do her Papi harm.

"Why did you stop, bitch?" Cha Chi said. Before she could get out a word, the other girl screamed just as Cha Chi's head exploded like a water balloon. One of the girl's ran while the other tried to grab the phantom, but was struck hard with the gun and knocked out. The two bodyguards heard the commotion from the screaming girl that dashed past them and ran to the alley. The first thing they saw was the young girl on the ground laying next to Cha Chi who was face down on the concrete twitching his last involuntary movements. When they caught a glimpse of the phantom who was held up behind the dumpster, the automatic gunfire started. The sparks off the wall from the bullets lit up the darkness of the alley as Cha Chi's people from inside the club all ran out strapped and began firing at the garbage can. The phantom returned fire as he looked for an escape route. The way he came into the alley was like no man's land with flying hot lead poison seeking out anything and everything that moved. After an approaching police siren sounded off, the brief gun battle stopped as the participant's anger over their fallen boss and benefactor had been replaced with self preservation. In New Jersey, a gun charge carried a mandatory five years, even if you don't use it. These gangsters were not trying to go do a nickel, not even for Cha Chi's dead ass. Fortunately for the phantom, this was his opportunity for a quick exit from the scene. Just as the first of four police squad car's tires came to a screeching halt in front of the club. Getting Cha Chi's people's immediate attention, one of the female bodyguard's caught the phantom's blur out of the corner of her eye. She stared at him as he disappeared into the night while she laid her AR 15 assault rifle down in the trunk of a car where everyone else had laid theirs before closing it. The police greeted her as they walked into the alley. Looking down at Cha Chi's body, they immediately began gloating and cracking jokes about his demise. To them he was just one more wild ghetto animal who got euthanized. This was the nature of the jungle streets in Newark and every other major city throughout a nation that celebrates violence and men of violence. As the pigs looked down at Cha Chi's corpse, everyone had the obvious looks of, good riddance on their faces. One less hood kingpin.

Horace, who was a high school track star just like Sugar, probably broke an Olympic record getting back to his ride that was parked 2 miles away. Damn near out breath and his heart racing with both adrenaline and fear of proving Sugar's admonition true that he may not come back, he sat there in the car to gather himself. After his heart rate finally decreased and the approaching sirens got closer, he put the vehicle in gear and drove away calmly while the song, *Casualties of War* by G-Unit blasted from the Black Range Rover's speakers.

CATO

Chapter 39
Dotting All the I's and Crossing All the T's

When Tony walked into the visitation booth, he recognized the troubled look on his woman's face. Sitting down in the chair he began monitoring her carefully.

"What's up, baby girl?"

"What ain't up, is the better question," she replied with a sigh.

"Ooookaaaay. Fill me in."

"Without going into details for obvious reasons," she said looking around at the glass and eluding to the fact their conversations were being recorded. "I told the lawyer I would speak to you on this. But old boy's son ain't right. And that is all I'm going to say on it. You fill in the blanks. I will handle it though. I'm going to dot all the I's and cross all the T's, you dig?" Tony's face sunk in. He knew very little about Supreme, but he knew his friend like he knew himself. He had lost control of the organization that he handed over to him by allowing a rat in his ranks.

"Okay. Then handle it. I won't say anything to him about it. But baby girl, be careful, okay? I know you are very capable, but still, be careful."

"Sho you right!" Sugar said smiling. "I was schooled by the best."

CATO

Chapter 40
Divided Loyalties

When Horace showed up at Supreme's club and base of operations, he immediately noticed that security had been beefed up. His army of gang members acting as his soldiers, they typically shot dice and told war stories of who was the greater thug. But on this night they were wary and on high alert. After Supreme could not get in touch with Macky, and he found out that the people whom he sent to murk him went missing, he knew something was coming, especially after Macky didn't return his calls. The invisible noose had begun to tighten around Supreme's neck and nothing had happened yet. He now realized what his mentor, the O.G. Bobby Rush once warned his ambitious pupil about. *Power is made to be grasped, but hard to hold on to.*

"Sup, bruh?" Horace said as he walked into Supreme's office. "You got some drama coming your way or sumpin?" Horace sat down in the chair in front of Supreme as Supreme's right hand gang homie stood next to him mad dogging Horace and Horace ignored him like he always did.

"Yeah. Something like that. But nothing we can't handle. So I take it that business got taken care of."

"I'm here, ain't I? Or did you expect me not to come back?" Horace said with a wrinkle in his forehead and a raised eyebrow. Supreme laughed it off.

"What kinda talk is that? I sent you to take care of that because I knew you were the most capable and realest nigga on the team. I knew you would come back unscathed."

"Yeah, okay. Well, what about the O.G.? Did you expect him to come back too after he handed over his organization to you?"

"What?" Supreme said laughing. "What's up with you, kid? Did one of those bitches bullets graze your head or sumpin?"

"No. Not at all," Horace said with a laugh that dripped with sarcasm. "My head is perfectly fine and my eyes are too. And you didn't answer my question?"

"Huh? You mean that was a serious question?"

"I'm a serious nigga, bruh," Horace said with a deadly no nonsense look on his face. Again, Supreme laughed it off as he got up from his chair and poured himself a drink.

"What do you think, kid? You think I would do some rat shit like that to a man who I look at like a father?"

"You mean a man who look at you like a son, don't you? I mean, all the times you and I hung out and chopped it up, you never expressed that, bruh."

"Hey man! Whatever it is you have on your chest, I suggest you go ahead and get it off. All this beating around the bush shit, I don't have the time or patience for."

"Okay. Since you won't keep it real and answer my question I'm going to go ahead and do it for you." Horace threw down the court document Sugar showed him earlier that had Supreme's name on it. With one foot in the chair, Supreme stood there with a drink in his hand and looking down at the paperwork on his desk.

"Hey, Buck, let me get some privacy here," Supreme said to his lieutenant. Buck gave Horace one last mad dog look before walking out of the office.

"Okay. What the fuck does this supposed to mean? So what? My name is on a piece of paper."

"No bruh!" Horace shot back angrily. "Not just a piece of paper. A sealed indictment. With your name on it. And you know I know this paperwork ain't no coincidence or some bullshit. I was a law clerk at Martin, remember?"

"Okay. My name is on a sealed indictment. That doesn't mean I'm a rat and it doesn't mean I'm going to bam the O.G. I'm just buying time and playing the cards I got dealt, kid. The O.G. is fucking stubborn and set in his ways. He should have paid the DEA cracker and he would still be on the streets."

"So now you're paying the cracker and helping him bury the O.G. to get him out of the way, huh?"

"You muthafucking right I'm paying him!" Supreme yelled. "That's good business! I mean, this is a Fed boy we're talking about! The O.G. should have paid him. Period!"

"Yeah. I agree. He should have paid him, so he wouldn't have a snake ass nigga like you with his fangs deep in his back." Supreme smiled and walked back over to the liter of Apple Ciroc. Pouring him another drink he responded.

"Okay! So I am playing for keeps. Where does that leave you? Are you going to ride this wave or what? The O.Gs. are finished. They had their time. Now it's my time. The last syndicate of O.Gs. that ran this city got closed down and closed out forever by these same niggas you seemed to have so much love for. The jungle creed suggests that sooner or later, the dominant Lion is run off by a younger counterpart, just like he did when his nuts hung low. Again, it's my time. Now you have a choice to make, kid. Ride with this wave and become a boss, or have that wave roll over you."

Horace's smile spoke deadly intentions. Underneath the table he clutched his 40 cal. Supreme seemed to purposely turn his back to him.

"Go ahead, kid. My back is wide open and my fire is in the drawer," Supreme said confidently. Horace's trigger finger started to perspire as he weighed the odds. Something, however, told him to look behind him, and when he did, Buck and two soldiers had their guns trained on him. "Again, are you with me or against me, kid?"

"Since day one, my loyalties have always been with one person in this world. And that's my sister, bruh. And whatever it is you plan on doing to me won't change that. So do what you gotta do." Supreme downed his drink with his eyes glued to Horace.

"Take him out and body him. And make sure he won't ever be found." Buck and the soldiers disarmed Horace. As they were leading him out of the door, Buck slapped him on the side of the head with his fire.

"I never liked your bitch ass from the jump!" Buck said with contempt. The soldiers held Horace's arms as he struggled to get back to his feet, while Buck laughed wickedly.

"Damn, kid, just look at you. What a waste," Supreme said shaking his head. "We could have ruled the world, homie."

"My grandfather told me to never be in the same tent with a snake," Horace said as he struggled to remain on his feet from the blow to the head.

"Well, you are about to go see him. Take that fuck nigga out of my sight!"

Chapter 41
The Final Resting Place for a Gangster

The Gowanus Canal is one of the top five most polluted sites in Brooklyn since its creation in the 19th century. During heavy storms, nearby residents' basements sometimes flooded with sewage. Other pollutants found in this shitty canal were mercury, typhus and a toxic sludge familiarly known as *black mayonnaise*. But that ain't all this canal is said to be polluted with. Street lore has it, that for decades it's been one of the popular dumping grounds for dead gangsters and other poor souls who probably made their last pleas for their lives on the canal's banks.

Buck chose this spot specifically for the man he didn't like from day one. He often dreamed of one day receiving the green light to body Horace, perhaps so he would be a lock for underboss. When they arrived there, the cinder blocks and chains that were to send Horace's body to its permanent resting place were already present.

"Well, nigga, is there anything you wanna say? Any last begging you wanna do?" Buck said with a sinister laugh. The two soldiers who found his words rather amusing chuckled and grinned like Cheshire cats.

"The last time I begged anyone for anything, my granddaddy slapped the shit out of me. I never begged again. And I ain't about to start now. Get it over with punk!" Horace said defiantly. He was resigned to his fate.

"Ohhhh okay! We got ourselves a nail here," Buck said to the two soldiers before he, again, slapped Horace with his fire. A handcuffed Horace fell over on his side, but immediately popped back up and began berating his would be killer.

"Is that the best you can do, fuck boy? I know dick suckers in the joint who hit harder than you, pussy boy!" Again, the 9 mm crashed into the side of Horace's head. This time he was slow to recover.

"How about that one?" Buck said. "Is it getting harder now, bitch? I got plenty more where that came from. We can do this all night before I end your insignificant life!"

When a groggy Horace stubbornly got back up on his knees to per-haps take more punishment, he caught a glimpse of two figures in all black creeping up on their position from a thick brush of bushes along the banks of the canal. Whoever it was, he knew they weren't there to cause him any more grief than he was already catching from Buck, who was doing his best Barry Bonds impression with his Glock.

"Like I said, you hit like a sissy!" Horace burst out laughing. The echo could be heard for miles around. He was resigned to his fate and wasn't going to give these dudes who he viewed as fuck niggas the satisfaction of seeing him in fear of his life, which he wasn't. This ob-viously incensed Buck who was trying to impress the two flunkies he had with him.

"Maaan, this nigga is crazy," one of the soldiers said. "Why don't you just go head on and murk him and get it over with, Buck? We got something to do. Besides, this shit is haunted out here." The two sol-diers looked around all wide-eyed at the surroundings. This was an-other myth about this place. It was said that the spirits of those who took a plunge in the shitty canal still roam the area.

"Look nigga! If you scared, kick rocks! This is real nigga gangster business here."

"Nah man. I'm just saying, this shit feel creepy out here. And that nigga ain't going to beg you for his life."

"Hey, young nigga! I'm in charge over you! You're a fucking peon to me, kid. I don't do what you say, you do what the fuck I tell ya! You feel me?" Buck said as he got in his face.

"Yeah. You got that," the youngster said as he stepped back to cre-ate space between them. As Buck continued to check the young thug, Horace peered in the direction he saw the two figures. No longer seeing them, he concluded they were probably two people who stumbled up on some shit they didn't wanna be involved in and tore out. Or then again perhaps it was just a case of him imagining shit from the blows to the head.

"Now, nigga, where were we?" Buck said to Horace.

"We were on the part where you are a career bitch ass nigga," Hor-ace said as he again saw the two dark figures reappear to give him hand signals. Now he knew that they were not a figment of his imagination.

Realizing what was going on, he let out a laugh that was ten times louder than the last as he realized who these mystery figures were.

"You're going with me tonight, Buck. You do know that, right? Are you ready to die with me?" he said mockingly. A bewildered Buck looked at him with a confused look on his face. *How can a man who is about to die be joking?* he thought.

"Nah, nigga. The only person who's going to die tonight is your bitch ass! You ready boy?" Buck asked as he pointed the gun sideways at Horace's head. On cue with the shadowy figures hand signals, Horace flung himself to the ground, just as a total of three shots rang out that hit Buck in the back of the head. He fell down face first on the ground like a fallen California Redwood tree. Before the two young thugs realized what was going on, the two figures in all black quickly walked up and hit them off with several shots that put an end to their short-lived stint as Supreme's soldiers. The deadly whispers of the silencers spooked an owl who must have watched the entire event from a nearby tree. He flew away so fast, a few of his feathers dislodged from his flapping wings and floated to the ground like snowflakes. The hooting sound he made sounded haunting.

"You alright, sir?" one of the figures said from behind his ski mask. Horace stood to his feet.

"Yeah, I'm alright. Just a little dizzy. Who are you?" The figure pulled off his mask and revealed himself. It was Macky Boy smiling like a young school kid. The other figure followed suit by pulling off his mask. It was Yancey. Sugar's main bodyguard. Horace smiled.

"We saw you being led out of the club and we figured they wasn't taking you on a camping trip," Macky said.

"Picture that," Horace said, looking down at the bodies of the dead men. "I hate the outdoors." Yancey and Macky chuckled.

"Let's get you back home to your sister," Macky said before the three men ghost the macabre scene, leaving behind the three corpses on the banks of the canal to further pollute the area.

CATO

Chapter 42
The End Game

After Supreme's Belize supplier and his young mistress walked out of the penthouse, they climbed into his rose colored 2017 AMG C63 convertible Benz. Laughing and kissing after a night of creeping, the Belize Kingpin turned the ignition key. When the car misfired his curses could be heard loud and clear up and down the city streets that this shit shouldn't be happening to a ride he paid so much money for. The mistress smiled, curled up close to him and clutched hold to his arm. Again he turned the ignition key and once again the car misfired.

Seeing her man's frustrations, she laughed and asked, "Voy a tratar de que amor." Let me try it, sweetheart.

The supplier's initial frown at the question was soon replaced with a smile. "Adelante. Tal vez su suerte es mejor que la mi," he said. Sure. Maybe your luck is better than mine.

When the mistress turned the ignition, sure enough, her luck was better than his. The Benz cranked up with ease on the first attempt. As he leaned over and kissed her on her lips, the car exploded sending their charred body parts scattered all over the streets of Belmopan, Belize's capital. His fatal mistake was to refuse Sugar's request to cut off Supreme's coke supply. In responding to that request, he called her a cunt whore bitch who should stay in a woman's place. The obvious message in this brutal offensive on Supreme and his interests, this thing was going to end tonight.

When the first explosion rocked Supreme's club, followed by automatic gunfire and gut wrenching screams, Supreme knew his day of reckoning was at hand. Little did he know at the time, all over the city, every dope spot and territory he owned was hit simultaneously with the same viciousness, which was Sugar's way of doing things. There were car bombings and fire bombings of clubs and brownstones all over the city that lit up the Brooklyn skyline. For the city, the fireworks came early this year. Supreme's lieutenants were killed wherever they were found. For this end game Sugar put 200 soldiers with automatics on the streets to seal the deal. This thing was going to end tonight.

Supreme's soldiers, who were used to ambushing people in drive-bys or creep-ups, now found themselves being hunted down like wild animals. Caught totally off guard, they ran inside the club with their guns in their hands. Behind them came a barrage of bullets that dotted the walls and shattered windows. Supreme yelled at them.

"What the fuck are y'all running in here for? Y'all supposed to be gangsters! Get the fuck back out there and do what I brought y'all on to do!" he said as he himself took cover with a pistol in his hand. The doubts and second thoughts obviously started to enter his mind as he looked at his frightened soldiers in disgust.

"Maaaaaan, they crept on us! Shit is spraying from everywhere. They even got grenades!" one of the gang members yelled frantically. This only seemed to incense Supreme even more.

"Bitch made muthafucka!" he yelled before kicking him out into the open where he was immediately cut down by a hail of bullets. He lay right where he once stood. Thinking that could have been him, Supreme ran farther back in the club along with his soldiers. As they again took cover behind anything they could find. One of the gang members yelled out for someone to call the police.

"Shiish! Shut the fuck up!" Supreme said under his breath. "I think they're gone. Did y'all see who it was?"

"Bruh, how the fuck we see who it was with all that lead coming at us?" one of the thugs said.

After about five minutes of silence, Supreme and what was left of his crew peeped out of the windows to see the bodies of six of his men. From the looks of it, they never had a chance. The shock and terror on their faces told the story of men who were not ready to face death. While their boss remained held up inside with what was left of the detail of soldiers responsible for guarding the headquarters, his mind raced with paranoid thoughts of who could be outside waiting to waste him. With the amount of enemies he'd made as of late it could have been anybody, including Cha Chi's people, seeking revenge for his death. Then again, it could be Horace since Buck and the two soldiers ordered to body him, never returned. Or it could even be Macky or even the boss Queen Sugar herself who levied a veiled threat against him not long ago. Or then too it could be the O.G. who gave the order from behind bars after finding out he's on his paperwork. Whoever it was, their message was loud and clear. They were there to play for keeps.

When the power shut off leaving them in pitch darkness, the real panic started to set in. Outside, the tapping shoes of rushing men, whose footsteps spoke resolve and urgency, could be heard along with faint voices giving commands. One of Supreme's soldiers again repeated someone else's call that they should call the police to come rescue them.

"I already tried," one of the thugs said. "But I believe they jammed the phones. My phone won't work," he said looking at his phone.

"Jam the phones? How the fuck can they do that?" another voice yelled out. Supreme quickly admonished them, trying to save what little reputation he had left.

"We ain't calling no fucking police! Your bitch ass going to get up there and fight if they come in this club! That's what I paid you for! Now get the fuck up there before I body you myself!" Supreme said, pointing his AK at the frightened thug's head. Realizing he was serious, the 4 gangsters ran up front to face the music. An eerie silence and an open front door met them as they crouched down behind whatever they could find just in case they had to escape the flying lead once it commenced. When the infrared beams began seeking out targets inside the darkness of the shot up club, a new panic set in as they all ran to the back where Supreme was to find him gone. He had ghost the scene and left them there to fend for themselves. This shocking display by a man they all looked up to as the ultimate gangster, totally took out any fight they had in them. Broken, they decided to surrender and throw themselves on the mercy of the very men who were commissioned to kill them. As they were about to walk outside, they were met by several fully armed men in black paramilitary suits and masks. Leaving their guns on the club's floor, they all held up their hands and inched forward to an uncertain fate.

"Where is your boss man?" one of the gunman asked in a muffled voice behind the ski mask.

"He tore out and left us. He's gone," one of them said. The gunmen looked at them then looked at one another. Then suddenly a hail of automatic gunfire rained down on them cutting them all into. Their lifeless bodies lay cluttered on top of one another right where they once stood. Sugar's orders were crystal clear and non-negotiable. Everybody had to die on this one. No prisoners. No witnesses. No survivors. This was her scorched earth approach to the end game that was playing out on the streets of Brooklyn, and Tony and Genie's lives depended on it.

When the word got back to Sugar that Supreme had left the city, she put out an APB on him in the tri-states and beyond. Every place he was known to frequent, from the strip clubs, to the high end, high priced restaurants to the gang hangouts, there were well dressed professional killers looking high and low for him to collect the million dollar bounty that was placed on his head. When Horace mentioned to Sugar about his family ties in Florida, to her surprise, he had folks in Panama City where she and Horace's people lived. The Feds were also interested in his whereabouts. After missing Tony and Genie's preliminary bond hearing, where he was supposed to make a statement against them for the purpose of denying them pretrial release, they sent out their people to find him as well. The judge, who was nothing but a rubber stamp for the government, granted the prosecution a postponement against the stern objections Tony and Genie's lawyer. This meant they would have to sit a little bit longer. Perhaps this was a good thing with all that was going on in the streets.

After Macky was given a solid tip on Supreme's whereabouts, he, Sugar, Horace, Yancey and a couple more soldiers all set out for Panama City, Florida. Word was Supreme was held up in a notorious apartment complex called the SAP and being guarded by his cousins and some of their gang member homies.

Soon after arriving in the Bay County city limits, Sugar and her people didn't waste any time pinpointing the building where Supreme was hiding. The plan was to find him and take him in alive, if possible. If not, they'd kill him and anyone else who got in their way. Little did they know, however, Supreme had a mini army of young nails around him looking to impress the legendary founder of their gang, which bore his nickname, *Supreme Beings*. Even some 1,200 miles away, Supreme still carried clout with young gang members.

Sitting inside a black Yukon with dark tints across from the Macedonia housing projects in Panama City, also known as the SAP, Sugar and her crew sat with their eyes peeled on the building Supreme was said to be held up in. The two young men posted up outside and a few people coming in and out, was a dead giveaway that this was the place he had taken up refuge.

Out of bounds and out of their territory where they had hundreds of soldiers at their disposal to impose war on anyone and any group, this thing could get messy. Since this was a Monday night the cops weren't rolling hard like they normally do on the weekends when the block is jumping. So that was one element that they didn't have to deal with. However, it wouldn't take long for the cops to respond to this area, which was by far the most notorious side of town. By far, most of the black homicides, took place right there in the SAP. So the plan was shock and awe. Go in brutal and come out brutal.

When Sugar walked across the street into the projects, not long after darkness had fallen, she immediately commanded attention from some of the young thugs who had never seen anyone that fine and dressed as she was. Some of them made cat calls while a couple of the bold ones approached her to put down their best player/pimp game. As she stood there, entertaining their lame ass game that was intended to woo her, Macky, Horace, and Yancey all snuck through the back way to the building where Supreme was held up while the soldiers remained behind inside the ride to keep a wary eye on Sugar, to make sure nothing happened to her.

"Hey, shorty, where you from?" one of the youngsters asked her.

"I'm from where I just came from," she said smiling.

"You sho' ain't from 'round here. You look like you from up north. You ain't them folks, are you?" The young jit stood back to take a look at her with a suspicious eye.

"Yeah, I'm them folks alright," she said with her hand on her pistol inside her jacket's pocket unbeknown to them. One of the youngsters laughed and looked at his homie.

"Nah. You too fine to be po po. I swear I seen you somewhere before though. I seen you out at the LaVela this weekend, didn't I, shorty?"

"Oh that was you I saw?" Sugar said as she began to put on her act, walking up on him flirtatiously. She was nowhere near the club he mentioned and didn't even know a thing about it. "You was the one standing by the bar who I wanted to holla at, but when I came off the dance floor you was gone."

"Yeah okay, shorty. That's what's up. So what you tryna say is you came here to see me then?"

"No, I actually didn't know you stayed over here."

"I don't stay here," he said as if he was offended. "I stay on the beach, baby, in a condo."

"So what you doing over here then?" Sugar asked as she moved closer to him smiling. The youngster laughed and looked at his partner who was either shy or leery of Sugar.

"I'm over here gettin' money, baby girl."

"Oh yeah? Like what you got? You got some loud?" The youngster laughed nervously as he again began to inspect her. He had heard from the streets that a black female undercover was going around getting cats sale charges.

"What? You think I'm them folks, huh?" she said, walking back up to him.

"Deke, man, be careful of that broad," his partner said. "Sumpin' ain't right about her, bruh." Sugar turned and looked at him before taking a couple of steps towards him.

"Young nigga. Why you standing all off to the side? You scared or sumpin'? I'm all by myself. Why you looking all paranoid? I need to be smoking what you been smoking."

"Yeah, okay. I don't sell dope, baby," the youngster replied before walking off. Between he and his partner, he was obviously the smarter of the two.

"So what you want, shorty? I got some fire ass purp. I got some tabs too. What's up? We can go back to my condo and chill." Sugar laughed.

"Oh yeah? I bet you tell all the females that," she said looking past him to see that her people had made it inside the building.

When Macky walked up the stairs with his knit hat pulled down over his head, one of the cats who had been guarding the entrance way stepped to him.

"Hey, bruh. What's up?" he said, walking towards Macky.

"Nothing much. Just looking for someone."

"Looking for who?" When he moved closer to Macky, a sharp burning sensation went across his neck as a black-gloved hand simultaneously suppressed his screams. Then came the calm and resignation in his eyes followed by blackout. Yancey pulled his body down to the next door out of sight and left it there. Now joined by Horace and Yancey, Macky peered in through the window to see Supreme and some more people playing cards with music blasting in the background. One of the men who had been standing guard was about to make his way back outside to join his partner, whom he had no idea had just died a horrific death. And when he walked outside, the same thing happened to him. Just like his homie, his death was messy, but quick. After pulling his body over along side his partner's, out of sight in the dark building, the apartment was now wide open and Supreme's life was in extreme danger. As he sat at the card table with two Puerto Rican broads standing on each side of him like felines affectionately brushing up against their master, he had no idea what was coming his way all the way from Brooklyn.

When Horace and Macky walked in, at first Supreme didn't see him, but one of his gangsters did.

"Who is these niggas, man?" Supreme's head tilted up with the Black and Mild in the corner of his mouth. He looked as if he saw two ghosts. Before he could reach for his gun that was in arms reach on the table, Macky pointed his Glock in his face.

"Go ahead, Mr. Supreme," Macky said with a blank look on his face. "You can make it to it." The two wide-eyed females took a couple of steps back to put distance between them and this big money cat they had just met. Although they wanted to get into his pockets, and believed that dream he sold them that he would rescue them from the project life and take them back up to the city with him to be stars, they weren't about to catch a bullet for him.

"'Sup, homie?" Horace said smiling. "You think you're looking at a ghost, huh?" Supreme smiled.

"No, homie. I knew you weren't dead. I only wanted them to scare you." Horace laughed mockingly and shook his head.

"Well, they didn't do a good job of that either. Now we're gonna need you to stand up real slow." Before he followed Horace's orders, Supreme looked around to weigh his odds. As far as he could see, he had two guns trained on him with one at the door standing guard for any surprises. However, what he didn't see is what was waiting on him downstairs.

"Now you cats know that I have folks all through this housing project, right? I mean, they are bound to hear the drama in this building and they will put up a fight."

"You don't think we factored that in coming all the way here to pay you a visit?" Macky asked. "Now walk towards me with your hands extended out."

As Supreme walked towards Macky, one of the girls turned off the lights and the room went dark. Afterwards mayhem ensued. The gunshots began ringing inside the apartment amidst screams. When Horace turned on the lights, Supreme's soldier lay face down with his eyes wide open. One of the Rican girls lay on her back holding the bullet wound to the side of her neck as her friend screamed in Spanish for someone to call EMS. Making their way downstairs, Macky and Horace relentlessly pursued Supreme. Just as they were about to corner him, they were met with deafening gunfire that seemed to be coming from every direction. Supreme laughed as he fled the scene.

"I told you. These my niggas in here," he yelled. Now trapped inside the building, Horace and Macky were forced to run back upstairs and into the back room of the apartment. Looking out of the window for an escape route, they caught a sign of Yancey who the gangsters ran passed and posted up outside the apartment door. He was crouched down in some bushes as if he was waiting to receive orders for the next move. Macky and Horace knew that the eerie silence was a sign that the thugs were about to rush inside with murder, murder, murder on their minds. With time running out, Macky managed to get Yancey's attention who gave him a hand signal to leap from the apartment's window. As Yancey positioned himself to give cover fire, Macky and Horace both leaped from the window as the young SAP gangsters rushed the room they were in with guns blazing. Yancey returned fire unleashing a deadly hail of lead poison hitting two of the gangsters. One of them fell from the window and made a thudding sound when he hit the ground. Yancey hit him off with two more shots that ended his night and his life. The other fell back on the bed with two chest wounds that bled like geysers. His screams that he didn't wanna die could be heard all over the apartment complex. The cover fire from Yancey was just enough for Macky and Horace to make a run from the building. As the three men made a mad dash away from the scene, gunshots rang out like the 4th of July and the grass and dirt behind them plowed up with each bullet that landed.

After Macky and crew arrived near the entranceway that led across the street to the truck, and heard the approaching sirens in the distance, they knew that this was their cue to flip the script.

Immediately, after Supreme ran to a waiting car and got in, the familiar feel of cold steel pressed up against the side of his head. He knew what this was, as it was something that he'd felt too many times before in his gangster life not to recognize it. Placing his hands in the air almost instinctively, he looked up and it was Sugar with a look of both resolve and death in her eyes.

"Tell your man there with those beady eyes not to move. Tell him don't even look over here at me or you will get the first bullet to the brain before I blow his head off," she warned.

"Stand down, bruh," Supreme said to the driver as his heart raced. The driver was a crack head named Joe who was the project flunky who would do just about anything for a hit.

"Now get your snitching ass out real slow," Sugar said as she moved back with her gun pointed. We've got plans tonight," Sugar said leading him away from the car at gunpoint.

***

Suspended in the air with chains, when Supreme woke up, he found himself in pitch darkness and smelled an odor that was so awful it actually stung the inside of his nostrils. In the background, he could hear faint sounds of people talking and country music playing. It was after the creaking sound of a door opening and a blinding light that came on, that Supreme realized he was in a barn. He also realized that the man standing below a few feet away looking up at him smiling was a hillbilly looking white man. Standing next to him was Sugar, Horace, Yancey, Macky and the two soldiers. They too looked up, but they weren't smiling. Their faces had a no-nonsense look and finality. He knew this was not going to end well for him.

"Hey Mister, how's your night going so far, partner?" the redneck said in a hillbilly drawl before he spat a brown substance from his mouth onto the ground. Supreme didn't say anything as he was trying to recover from the blow to the head from Horace's Glock and the bumpy fifty mile ride to Cottondale, Florida, inside the trunk of one of the vehicles.

"Where the fuck am I?" Supreme asked.

"You wouldn't know if I told ya," the redneck said. "But since you must know, you are all the way out in the boondocks where no one can find you. And where no one can hear you scream."

Sugar, Horace, Yancey and Macky continued to stand there.

"Who the fuck are you, white boy?"

"Who the fuck am I, you ask? Just call me *dirty white boy*. That's all."

"Okay, Supreme. Enough of the small talk. You know what this is," Sugar said looking up at him. "You crossed the line when you tired to fade my husband and the man who loved you like a son and gifted you his organization. But that wasn't enough for you. You had to do what this generation is used to doing. You bit the hand that fed you. You snitched on the man who was willing to leave it all to you. You are the product of an era where snitching is apart of the hustle. My era, we do people like you." Supreme laughed out loud.

"Are you fucking kidding me? There were snitches in your era too and in the previous ones. Who you think schooled me? I was taught by O.Gs. to use everything I had as a hustler to have longevity and success out there in them streets. The police are apart of that hustle, contrary to some bullshit street philosophy you were taught. Yeah, I utilized the Fed boy, Moresco. And too bad the O.G. didn't. He would be here running his own shit. I'm a young nigga and I knew that this was the smart thing to do."

"So you saw the opportunity to stay in power and you took it at Genie's, and more importantly, my husband's expense?"

"Fuck yeah! I did what you and anyone else would do. I played my cards like they should have been played. But I wasn't going to show up and testify on them though. I ain't no fucking rat. I kept a card in the deck that the Fed boy don't know shit about. I filmed all of our transactions as the O.G. instructed me to. Just a little insurance, just in case."

Sugar smiled and shook her head as she looked down at the ground and paced under Supreme who hung from the rafter of the barn like one of those pieces of meat inside a smokehouse.

"So you had all this figured out, aye? And you think that tape is your way out of this situation you find yourself in, huh?" Supreme looked down at her with a puzzled look on his face.

"I won't lie. That video is the key to all our troubles. You stall me out here, I will give you a copy of it and you can use it to free your old man and the O.G."

"Okay. So let me get this straight. If I spare your life tonight, you will give me the video of the dirty cop taking your dirty money everything goes away?" Supreme smiled and nodded his head.

"Yeah. I will give you the video, you give it to your lawyer and that will free your people."

"Hmmm. Sounds like a very good deal. I must admit. But what if I told you that we already have a video of you both cavorting with each other?" The confusion on Supreme's face was priceless. His anxiety had just increased threefold. The redneck chuckled and spat his brown dip on the ground. "Yes, Mr. Supreme. We have the tape," Sugar said. "Did you think me going out of my way to come see you, having a gun battle with those crazy ass SAP boys, and bringing you all the way out here in God knows where, was to negotiate or strike a deal with you? This isn't some shit you're going to barter yourself out of. Besides that, you tried to touch my family and Macky. So, no sir. This is your day of reckoning. This is the end game."

Supreme's heart rate ticked up with those words. The increased fear caused his adrenaline to rush through his veins like a flash flood. Something about her words seemed final. He knew that his only whole card was the video, but little did he know, Macky Boy had trailed Moresco, per Tony's order, and also filmed every transaction between the agent and Genie. Once Supreme took over, Macky kept filming. There was enough on those videos to not only free Genie and Tony, but to bury Moresco and his gang of dirty DEA agents.

"Well, Mr. Supreme, hope you enjoy the rest of your evening with what's coming," Sugar said as she turned and began walking out with Macky and Yancey behind her. Horace, who had done time with the dirty white boy at Martin, a pig farmer who often used his swine to dispose of unwanted human evidence, gave each other dap before Horace gave Supreme one last look and shook his head.

"Homie. You gone let this go down like this? You can vouch for me."

"Yup. The same way you were gonna let that go down with me," Horace said as he walked out.

***

When the first 600 pound monster hog entered into the barn, followed by the rest of the pack which numbered over a dozen, they began instinctively snorting and sniffing the air as if they were identifying their meal. Perhaps smelling the perspiration and fear that emanated from Supreme's pores, they began salivating like dogs. At first Supreme didn't know what to make of it, being a city boy. But when the first hog bit down into his calf, slicing through cartilage, muscle and piercing his fibula, he knew exactly what was about to take place. Between his high-pitched screams, pleas for mercy and the blood that squirted from his badly mangled leg, the swine went into a feeding frenzy, totally ignoring the cries and kicking from their meal while the country music blared in the background. They started from Supreme's lower extremities and worked their way up, but not before he endured the type of suffering no man nor beast should have to endure. When they had their fill there would be nothing left of him as they have been known to consume hair, nails and bone, which made them the very best solution for human disposal issues that many a gangster ran into.

As Sugar, Macky, Yancey and Horace made their trek back to the city, Sugar couldn't help but think of the irony of this last street matter she had ever planned to be involved in. When she met Tony, he and his organization were locked in a struggle with the old guard black syndicate that had been in power since the time of Frank Lucas and Nicky Barnes. Now it was Tony and Genie being challenged for jungle supremacy by the younger guard. The O.G. Cat Eye Jones once told the story of the old lion, young lion to his syndicate partners to convince them that Stallworth had to go. This time Stallworth and Genie were the old lions whom the young lions, Supreme and his young gang bangers were looking to fade into oblivion and take everything they had built. In this story, however, this time old lions prevailed because the young lions didn't consider the power and resolve of the lioness. This was their *end game*.

***

Sitting out in the pearl white Maybach waiting for her King to emerge from the dungeon that held him in captivity for the past couple of months with an air of uncertainty constantly hovering overhead, a sense of deja vu filled the air. Sugar sat there in deep reflection. The sunglasses hid her eyes, but not her thoughts. This time wasn't like the aftermath of Rikers Island where there was a question mark at the end of that chapter. There was a real finality this time. The flight that was to take them away to a far away land and cradle of all civilization in which they decided on the moment they stepped foot on its soil for the very first time a little while ago, awaited them at JFK airport. They were about to take Ike up on his promise of living out their fantastic life free from drama and not a worry in the world, if that is what they so desired.

Tony didn't have any inhibitions or reservations about leaving everything behind in the capable hands of Macky Boy, as agreed upon by Genie, and rightfully so. He deserved it, and more importantly, he had earned it. He was to be the boss of bosses and Genie, who had to do a year for the gun he used to beat one of Moresco's men with, was to be retired upstairs like Tony and every other Fortune 500 company executive. After the videotape of the Moresco payoffs were given to Tony and Genie's lawyer, Aaron Goldman, a couple of copies of the tape found their way to the media, the Chief Federal Judge for the Eastern District, and the US Attorney's office. It didn't take long for Moresco and his men to be indicted on racketeering, bribery, and police corruption. Choosing to opt out of a life behind the very bars he had put many a hustler, Moresco sent a bullet through his brain one day from his service Glock beside his swimming pool. His days of shaking down dope dealers had come to an end.

As Sugar held her stomach that housed the new life that grew inside her with each passing day, a new life that represented change, a new focus and a new direction, she knew that now more than ever, it was time to bring closure to a world that gave them both drama as well as power, wealth and affluence beyond imagination and measure. This new life, which one of the two person's responsible for its existence knew nothing about, not only sealed the deal and closed the old chapter in this story, perhaps forever, it started a whole new book in an entirely different genre.

When Tony emerged from the federal holding facility's basement, donning the smile he had worn ever since he found out that his legal troubles were over and he was free to leave and resume his life, his Queen met that smile with her own. As he continued on towards his woman and the life she carried that embodied his future, not once did their eyes deviate from one another.

And so it goes. Once again, in less than four years Sugar was summoned to do something that was instinctual for any ride or die woman who loved her man more than she loved life itself. For the second, and perhaps final, time she transformed into something that she thought to be long suppressed and never to see the light of day again. But she did it all for her man, Antonio Stallworth.

THE END

Stay Connected with Us!

Text **LOCKDOWN** to 22828 to stay up-to-date with new releases, sneak peaks, contests and more…

Thank you!

Submission Guideline.

Submit the first three chapters of your completed manuscript to ldpsubmissions@gmail.com, subject line: Your book's title. The manuscript must be in a .doc file and sent as an attachment. Document should be in Times New Roman, double spaced and in size 12 font. Also, provide your synopsis and full contact information. If sending multiple submissions, they must each be in a separate email.

Have a story but no way to send it electronically? You can still submit to LDP/Ca$h Presents. Send in the first three chapters, written or typed, of your completed manuscript to:

LDP: Submissions Dept
Po Box 870494
Mesquite, Tx 75187

DO NOT send original manuscript. Must be a duplicate.

Provide your synopsis and a cover letter containing your full contact information.

Thanks for considering LDP and Ca$h Presents.

Coming Soon from Lock Down Publications/Ca$h Presents

BOW DOWN TO MY GANGSTA

By **Ca$h**

TORN BETWEEN TWO

By **Coffee**

BLOOD STAINS OF A SHOTTA **II**

By **Jamaica**

WHEN THE STREETS CLAP BACK **II**

By **Jibril Williams**

STEADY MOBBIN

By **Marcellus Allen**

BLOOD OF A BOSS **V**

By **Askari**

BRIDE OF A HUSTLA **III**

By **Destiny Skai**

WHEN A GOOD GIRL GOES BAD **II**

By **Adrienne**

LOVE & CHASIN' PAPER **II**

By **Qay Crockett**

THE HEART OF A GANGSTA **III**

By **Jerry Jackson**

LOYAL TO THE GAME **IV**

By **T.J. & Jelissa**

A DOPEBOY'S PRAYER **II**

CATO

By **Eddie "Wolf" Lee**

IF LOVING YOU IS WRONG... **III**

By **Jelissa**

BLOODY COMMAS **III**

SKI MASK CARTEL II

By **T.J. Edwards**

BLAST FOR ME **II**

RAISED AS A GOON V

BRED BY THE SLUMS

By **Ghost**

A DISTINGUISHED THUG STOLE MY HEART **III**

By **Meesha**

ADDICTIED TO THE DRAMA **II**

By **Jamila Mathis**

LIPSTICK KILLAH II

By **Mimi**

THE BOSSMAN'S DAUGHTERS 4

By **Aryanna**

Available Now

RESTRAINING ORDER **I & II**

By **CA$H & Coffee**

LOVE KNOWS NO BOUNDARIES **I II & III**

By **Coffee**

RAISED AS A GOON I, II, III & IV

Gangsta Shyt

By **Ghost**

LAY IT DOWN **I & II**

LAST OF A DYING BREED

BLOOD STAINS OF A SHOTTA

By **Jamaica**

LOYAL TO THE GAME

LOYAL TO THE GAME II

LOYAL TO THE GAME III

By **TJ & Jelissa**

BLOODY COMMAS I & II

SKI MASK CARTEL

By **T.J. Edwards**

IF LOVING HIM IS WRONG...I & II

By **Jelissa**

WHEN THE STREETS CLAP BACK

By **Jibril Williams**

A DISTINGUISHED THUG STOLE MY HEART I & II

By **Meesha**

PUSH IT TO THE LIMIT

By **Bre' Hayes**

BLOOD OF A BOSS **I, II, III & IV**

By **Askari**

THE STREETS BLEED MURDER **I, II & III**

THE HEART OF A GANGSTA I & II

By **Jerry Jackson**

CUM FOR ME

CUM FOR ME 2

CUM FOR ME 3

An **LDP Erotica Collaboration**

BRIDE OF A HUSTLA **I & II**

THE FETTI GIRLS **I, II& III**

By **Destiny Skai**

WHEN A GOOD GIRL GOES BAD

By **Adrienne**

A GANGSTER'S REVENGE **I II III & IV**

THE BOSS MAN'S DAUGHTERS

THE BOSS MAN'S DAUGHTERS II

THE BOSSMAN'S DAUGHTERS III

A SAVAGE LOVE **I & II**

BAE BELONGS TO ME

A HUSTLER'S DECEIT I, II

By **Aryanna**

A KINGPIN'S AMBITON

A KINGPIN'S AMBITION **II**

I MURDER FOR THE DOUGH

By **Ambitious**

TRUE SAVAGE

TRUE SAVAGE II

TRUE SAVAGE **III**

By **Chris Green**

Gangsta Shyt

A DOPEBOY'S PRAYER

By **Eddie "Wolf" Lee**

THE KING CARTEL **I, II & III**

By **Frank Gresham**

THESE NIGGAS AIN'T LOYAL **I, II & III**

By **Nikki Tee**

GANGSTA SHYT **I II &III**

By **CATO**

THE ULTIMATE BETRAYAL

By **Phoenix**

BOSS'N UP **I , II & III**

By **Royal Nicole**

I LOVE YOU TO DEATH

By Destiny J

I RIDE FOR MY HITTA

I STILL RIDE FOR MY HITTA

By **Misty Holt**

LOVE & CHASIN' PAPER

By **Qay Crockett**

TO DIE IN VAIN

By **ASAD**

BROOKLYN HUSTLAZ

By **Boogsy Morina**

BROOKLYN ON LOCK I & II

By **Sonovia**

CATO

BOOKS BY LDP'S CEO, CA$H

TRUST IN NO MAN

TRUST IN NO MAN 2

TRUST IN NO MAN 3

BONDED BY BLOOD

SHORTY GOT A THUG

THUGS CRY

THUGS CRY 2

THUGS CRY 3

TRUST NO BITCH

TRUST NO BITCH 2

TRUST NO BITCH 3

TIL MY CASKET DROPS

RESTRAINING ORDER

RESTRAINING ORDER 2

IN LOVE WITH A CONVICT

Coming Soon

BONDED BY BLOOD 2

BOW DOWN TO MY GANGSTA

CATO

www.ingramcontent.com/pod-product-compliance
Lightning Source LLC
Chambersburg PA
CBHW071301250626
47159CB00004B/1267